THE WITCHES

TRILOGY:

CHIMERA

Cathleen Dunn

www.CathleenDunn.com

The Witches Trilogy: Chimera/ Cathleen Dunn -- 1st ed.
ISBN 978-0-9899310-1-4

My sincere thanks to The Circle: Ann, Julie, Tami, David, Lee, Ken, Stephen, Carol and Karla... because, you know.

Olivia touched the petals of the iris in the outdoor market. So fragile – and beautiful. Their plum color faded to violet, then pale lavender at the very tips. These would be wonderful in the dining room on the old table, the only thing she had taken from the plantation house when it had burned over a century ago. She'd even posed her own death in the fire and had left the house to herself under another name...but she had never rebuilt. The charred bits were still there, overgrown and anonymous. She stuffed the thought, pushing away the feelings that came with it. She lived in Seattle now, not Louisiana.

She was paying for the flowers when she felt a tightness on the back of her legs, a tingling feeling that moved up her spine and made her scalp prickle with a rush of adrenaline. Another witch was close by and could be a strong one, but the feeling was not at all disciplined – usually a dangerous sign.

She looked around, careful not to focus any-where. *Don't think about it, just feel.* There was a pair of Northwesters in fleece, several well-groomed couples in jeans and button-down shirts, a well-dressed young professional... Olivia didn't sense anything from them. *Who is it? Why can't I tell?* An older couple browsed in the kiosk next to her. Ah! The gooseflesh still – could this be them? No... then a ratty group passed her, probably runaways, and she felt the tightness even more strongly down her thighs. It was one of them – a girl with dark brown hair and green eyes. The girl stepped around Olivia trailing a haze of magic, but nothing definite, no structure, no training. As a test, Olivia looked hard at the girl and directed a thought toward her: *Turn around – look at me.* No change. *She doesn't know; she has no idea.* The brunette was now on the sidewalk with her group, who were laughing. The girl smiled languidly, not interacting. Classic born to the caul witch, Olivia thought. Always feeling a lit-tle separate from everyone else. She was positive; ei-ther this girl had no idea about her abilities, or she was unaware how to use them and of the hazards that came with the power.

She browsed her way down the street, following unnoticed as the girl and her friends went into Ruby's Diner, a well-worn place that served strong coffee and large platters of greasy, old-fashioned breakfast. The food was so cheap and voluminous it was a favorite hangout in the Broadway district, especially for runaways.

There were so many runaways here on Capitol Hill, finding awkward acceptance amongst the residents. Some in the neighborhood had even pulled together to create the Home Alive program after punk singer Mia Zapata had been murdered there in 1993. Mia hadn't been homeless, but like the street kids she had been out at two a.m. one morning and had ended up dead only minutes after her last contact with anyone. Olivia gave thousands to Home Alive even now. Still, that was just money, easy enough to donate. It was a whole different level of intimacy to take on an apprentice... Goddammit. The *last* thing she wanted was an apprentice, but she didn't want this uncontrolled element in her neighborhood, either. She didn't know anything about this girl and realized she would need to and very soon – before someone or something else got to her.

A few nights later Olivia sat atop the stone wall that edged the community pool and listened to its waterfall as she watched Taylor with her companions. She leaned back to look at the moonlight on her burgundy leather pants. Clouds intermittently trapped the glow in shadow, then released it again to paint a sheen on everything. The bluish haze and the dark sapped vibrancy from colors and made it the perfect setting to be invisible. Olivia loved being invisible and did it often. She could observe in solitude while people around acted without presumption. Being invisible also meant that people could pass through her, which was always revealing: for a moment they blended and Olivia could feel their memories, hopes, emotions, loneliness... A passing couple walked through her legs and gave Olivia a rush of their anticipation and sexual energy. Feeling their emotions was deeply personal, and she mentally looked away as they passed through but smiled at experiencing their mutual crush on each other.

Now she watched Taylor and her friends at the end of the Ave while they in turn watched a pair of feral cats hunting in the alley behind a restaurant. Occasionally the scruffy malkins stood immobile to bluff something living that came their way—other times quickly gulping down anything vile they found. Scraps or wildlife, either was fine when not much was around. They came out to where Taylor and company were standing, and one tried to lure the cats with kissing sounds and calls of "kitty, kitty, kitty." Olivia laughed at that – why would an alley cat know the word "kitty"? The brown cat left immediately, crouching backward under a hedge and could be heard brushing its way off through the leaves. The other stood his ground and hissed, baring very long, sharp teeth. Then he turned glowering and strode into the bushes, tail straight up except for a kink at the very tip. After a minute more of talking Taylor and her friends turned and made off down the sidewalk. As Olivia crossed the street after them she saw both cats come out of hiding. Apparently one of them had snagged a treasure in the hedge – a pliable, drooping mouse was tucked into kinktail's furry mouth. They trotted down the alley together, the brown cat trying to get her face close for a bite of the mouse and the other turning his face away right and then left, keeping it just out of reach. She smiled, watching as the duo zigzagged down the alley, then followed Taylor's group receding down the sidewalk.

Several blocks later, Taylor split off from her friends onto a side street. It was thickly dark here, away from the streetlights on the Ave. Olivia was surprised to see the girl leave her group. Typically runaways sought the security of friends in the darkness when they were most vulnerable – helpless and sleeping. As they continued further Olivia alerted to a feeling of maliciousness. She saw a man in a hoodie, his hands in his sagging front pocket and his headpiece pulled down with his face in shadow, watching Taylor from a side street. The girl couldn't see him standing next to a narrow juniper until she was a few yards away. He stepped out onto the sidewalk and walked toward her, passing innocuously as if uninterested, then turned once Taylor's back was to him. As he moved toward her she turned and stared at him, her face expressionless except for baleful eyes. Stone cold still she stood and the man stopped, apparently unsure now of his intended prey. Taylor's expression didn't change as the hooded stranger took another step toward her and

Olivia heard the distinct message emanating from her: "Don't." She watched the standoff, feeling intensity and anticipation. Both stood frozen, Taylor's emotionless gaze fixed on him the whole time, and after three or four seconds the would-be assailant turned away. Olivia could tell the girl was not at all intimidated as she stared after the retreating figure before pivoting and continuing on her way. She never looked back. Good, Olivia thought, she'll need to be tough. But which blood-tint did she have?

After another block Taylor stopped at an old craftsman-style house with a raised wraparound porch. In an earlier life it had been beautiful, built probably in the mid-1930's. The porch was wide with thick stone columns at each corner and extended rafter beams that supported a broad, low-slung roof. Now, though, the porch was starting to sag and weeds filled the flowerbeds. Taylor stopped beside the corner column and looked through the window before slipping in the back door. Olivia crouched down and watched. The kinktail cat joined her as she observed, apparently winning the war for the mouse since he still had possession of it. He settled in next to Olivia to eat it, starting with the tender little mouse feet.

Olivia patted the cat on the head and sent her attention back to the porch. Narrowing her eyes and concentrating, she looked past the walls into the house and then relaxed to let the magic flow through her and give her what she desired. The wood seemed to disappear and the sight inside was visible to her as if in brilliant sunlight. Taylor paused alone in the kitchen, listening. In the living room Olivia could see a couple on the couch watching one of those cheap reality tv shows. The woman had overly processed blond hair and he had his filthy sock feet on a coffee table that was littered with junk, including long, brightly-colored fingernails the woman was gluing on. The man heard Taylor come in and yelled into the kitchen.

"Get in here – where the hell have you been?"

Taylor came just inside the living room. "With some friends."

"Horseshit. You don't have friends except those stupid street kids. Why do you do that anyway?"

Taylor stayed silent and he answered himself.

"Probably all you can get, you're so goddamned dumb. Couldn't even graduate high school."

And whose fault is that? Taylor clenched her jaw to prevent a retort.

"Why don't you go get a job? Oh, yeah...who's going to hire a sorry stupid ass like you? You couldn't keep the last one. Be more like your sister. She gets good grades and got into college – and as soon as she leaves next month your ass is out of here, too. Get out and find your mother, wherever the hell she is."

Taylor stared at him. "As if you didn't know – I'm sure you do."

"I'd advise you not to go around saying that, you little bitch!" His threat was low, dark. Then he muttered: "I don't know where she is." He looked back at the television.

"Do you mind? I can't hear my program." Ms. Straw-for-Hair was now fanning her fingers to dry the glue.

He snarled at her. "Shut up." While she looked mildly surprised he shouted toward the hallway opposite where Taylor stood.

"Karen! Get in here and clean the kitchen with your sister!" Apparently she didn't appear fast enough because he got up and left the room, returning with a petite girl whom he held tightly by a handful of hair. She looked terrified and whimpered as he jerked her across the room.

Taylor was immediately between them grabbing his wrist, digging in her nails to try to make him let go. He did, but only to use that hand to slap her, the momentum bouncing her against the wall. She narrowed her eyes against the stinging tears, refusing to give him the satisfaction and pulled Karen into the kitchen away from him. He returned to the couch where the blonde sat in overt silence, still fanning her nails but with a little less gusto.

Olivia shook her head. *What a piece of work he is...* She watched Taylor comfort her sister then start to clean as they had been told. *...and now there's a sister to deal with, too.*

In the kitchen Taylor smoldered. "I hate him. I hate him so much." The sister tried to look at Taylor's cheek, but she turned away.

"It's okay."

Karen hugged her. "Come with me to school."

"How? You have to live in the dorm the first two years; I can't afford anything on my own."

"We'll find something for you."

"And what about Mom? I can't leave here yet."

Karen was silent a moment. "Come on, let's finish the kitchen." She started picking up dishes.

Meanwhile, kinktail finished his mouse, putting the head under a bush for later, and came over to Olivia purring. She scritched him under the chin while she watched Taylor and Karen finish their cleaning and quietly pass back through the living room, careful not to wake the man now sleeping on the couch. When they were both in bed she let the picture in front of her fade until it was only the wraparound porch again. Then standing up, she willed herself home and was instantly there, leaving nothing behind her but a shimmer in the night air.

The Jaguar was a particular joy of Olivia's – it was so finely tuned and tight that Olivia heard only a harmonic, throaty murmur inside the cockpit, even when she shifted gears. Just a change in engine pitch and the car tucked in closer to the road. She loved this car. It felt a faultless match for her from the first time she had gotten inside, the deep leather cushions nuzzling her thighs, everything wrapping around her within perfect reach, the instruments glowing in this high-tech pet of hers. The 2005 XK coupe was a powerful toy, but right now she was going a slow 35 miles per hour up 3rd Avenue in the early summer evening – the perfect transition road leading to the nondescript entrance of the Highlands.

3rd Avenue was a rustic north-south route, not as frenetic and crowded as the freeway or Aurora. Huge old trees canopied the street, dappling sunlight onto the road below. It used to be the old view road overlooking Richmond Beach until new money built huge houses that blocked the view. Now the modest, older bungalows sat across the road from the newer monstrosities that had taken their place.

She signed in at the Highlands guard gate and continued down an even more primitive road; no sidewalks or curbs edged the path yet it meandered through some of the most exclusive homes in Seattle, camouflaged in a mature wooded setting. There were mid-century moderns with flat roofs and walls of glass, French baroque chateaus in pale stone with mansard roofs and oval windows, other mansions in exotic stone and wood. Most Seattle inhabitants had heard of the Highlands, but few people knew where it actually was. There were no house numbers, no addresses displayed here. Either you knew where you were going or you lived here, or the guard directed you after a thorough vetting of your invitation.

Turning up a winding drive she entered a wide brick plateau where cars were unloading occupants under the *porte cochere*. The house was huge – around

9,000 square feet of living space with great rooms to hold a hundred guests – an elegant arena for fundraising events like this one for Seattle Opera, or for the Art Museum, or for PAWS and Pasado's Safe Haven for Animals. It nestled into the dark green woods on the hillside, almost disappearing except for the glass ceiling rising two stories over the pool. Over that a clutch of northwest pines camouflaged the structure. On the rare clear Seattle day the blue expanse of Puget Sound could be seen from the windows that lined the west side. Olivia left her car with the valet, crossing to the beveled glass doors that reflected the setting sun and threw rainbows onto the walkway.

Pausing for a moment at the entry, she checked her reflection in the glass. She usually avoided black but tonight her cocktail dress was worthy of the sixties. Her shoulders and arms showed elegantly through sheer sleeves. Below that a black crepe-de-chine sheath fitted her curves closely. Plain nude pumps were nearly invisible and large diamond chandeliers clipped to her ears proffered the perfect amount of flash. Simplicity, drama, and a restricted amount of bling. Satisfied, she walked into the entryway.

The living room was easily thirty by forty feet rising to a vaulted ceiling; the architecture set off a vibrant mix of classic and modern art on the taupe walls. Guests stood by the pool under the glass roof where Olivia found her friend JaneAnn.

"This turned out really well." Olivia complimented her; it was JaneAnn's house they were in.

They looked around at the well-polished people being served drinks and appetizers by efficient staff, here to give money to the Opera and listen to the night's entertainment.

"Thank you. At two thousand dollars a seat I made sure of it." JaneAnn paused to exchange greetings with a guest and then turned back to Olivia. "So, tell me about this girl you found."

Olivia took a drink from a passing waiter. "Let me throw a privacy spell." She put up her hand, a small gesture only, before she spoke. "Her name is Taylor. She feels strong, but I don't think she knows a thing about her power. I thought she was a runaway at first, but she lives in a crummy house on Capitol Hill with her sister and a real jerk who I think is their dad, or maybe stepdad. The guy is really nasty; he hit Taylor when she tried to stick up for her sister."

"Could the sister be witch as well?"

"I don't know – I didn't get close enough. I'll scry them and find out. Unless you want to..."

Just then someone came up to thank JaneAnn for hosting and they spent a few minutes in pleasantries before going back to their discussion.

JaneAnn looked at the guests around. "What did you put in the privacy spell? What do they think we're talking about?"

"Oh, tonight's entertainment and then the Alaskan Way tunnel if they come by a second time."

JaneAnn smiled at that. The second one was sure to keep people away. "So the stepdad or whatever is abusive…"

"…and he's booting them out of the house next month."

"Lovely. Just in time to meet you."

"You were supposed to be there with me. You know, she might be yours instead of mine."

"But I wasn't there; it was your path she crossed. Maybe it'll be good for you – you spend too much time alone now anyway."

"I don't want another apprentice." Olivia's voice was flat. "Ever."

"You know how this works. Your path, your re-sponsibility. There's always a reason or a payback."

Olivia didn't answer and JaneAnn pressed her.

"What happened to the woman who said life is made up of memories and relationships? You hardly see anyone now except Alejo and me."

"What are you talking about? I'm involved in all kinds of things around town."

"You're living on the surface – are you going to let these fundraisers and events be your life now instead of how you used to be? You used to be amaz-ing." She paused a moment. "Maybe this is for Celeste."

Olivia stared hard at JaneAnn, then relented. She wasn't trying to be mean, she knew, just honest. "Damn it." She looked at the floor. "*Damn it*. I am not going to get any more involved than I have to. At all. And that's the end of it."

"Okay, fine...Do you even know whether she's Blue/Black or Silver-Tint?"

"I think she's probably Silver-Tint the way she stuck up for her sister, and some guy almost jumped her on the street and she glared him off without hurting him. But she's powerful enough to – I could feel it."

"You'll have to get her blood and find out. I'll charm it with you and we'll find out together." Jane-Ann knew her friend well; this would be her first apprentice since Celeste had died and Olivia blamed herself. She'd be there for her any way she could.

"Thanks."

"Sure. Hey, let's cruise the room and visit until the recital starts. Sit with me during the singing?"

The singing was tonight's entertainment. Olivia was passionate about raising money for Seattle Opera's conservatory for aspiring singers. The program was intense – a year long – and donations for living expenses, vocal coaches, performance spaces, and other fees were critical to keep it going. But what incredible voices came out of there! Young men with rich, smooth tone and women whose voices were silvery waves of sound. Both learned a control and freedom of voice that could sing Mozart's stunning *Der Holle Roche* by the Queen of the Night, or string together a *Don Giovanni* legato phrase with precision and emotion. Always when

Olivia listened it was bliss for her and she could let her thoughts settle.

This time though, an irritating thought rooted in reality poked at her. Taylor. Grrr. How bothersome. She knew she couldn't leave gracefully until the arias were done but as soon as they were she said her good-byes to several guests, promised to call JaneAnn the next day, and asked for her car.

As she waited for the valet to bring her car around she considered where to go. She had several places she liked to clear her head and think. She loved the view from atop the *Arc-de-Triomphe* in Paris – looking east she could see down the *Avenue des Champs-Élysées* to the *Place de la Concorde* where the city spread out below her in all its sparkling glory. However, transporting herself around the world just to think atop Napoleon's victory monument was a huge waste of energy and magic. A perfect place closer to home would be Four Columns Park right here in Seattle. As she passed by the little guardhouse on her way out of the Highlands and back onto 3rd Avenue toward downtown, she pictured a change of clothes in her mind and then brushed her hand over her dress in a downward arc. The black dress disappeared as if phosphorescent and became jeans, a sleeveless cashmere sweater, and a fawn-colored trench. She settled into the ride, turning the Jag onto Aurora Avenue where the lanes were better maintained so she could increase her speed. With little traffic this late at night she made an easy trek into Seattle, crossing the Aurora

Bridge high above the ship canal. Just before the Battery Street Tunnel, which crossed under the city, she turned off and took surface streets to Boren Avenue.

She parked halfway up the hill, looking left as she crossed Pike Street toward Elliot Bay. The huge glass portico arching over Pike Street at the Convention Center stood mammoth and beautiful, all shining glass and steel curves reflected in the lights underneath. At one hundred fifty feet high, the glass roof was a breathtaking sight, covering the entire city block. Up the street in the other direction the huge silvery dome of the First Covenant Church arose behind an old brownstone, looking like a giant lustrous moon peeking half above the horizon.

As Olivia crossed Pike and stepped onto the wide curved steps of Four Columns Park she faded into nothing, reappearing atop one of the columns. She stood there a few moments, looking at the lights of Seattle, the Space Needle in the distance, then the ground below as she moved to the edge and cantilevered her toes over it. She let her thoughts slip where they wanted, allowing memories to take over. She realized she was avoiding the Taylor decision, but it wouldn't hurt to procrastinate just a little longer. Olivia loved this place. These limestone columns were easily 35 feet tall and used to adorn the Plymouth Congregational church downtown. Martin Luther King Jr. had visited there in 1961 and Olivia could still feel his energy faintly captured in the columns. *For him to leave a mark this long after such a brief visit...* When the church was to be demolished a few years later to make way for a freeway through downtown a local builder named Hauberg had saved the columns and donated them to the city for this tiny quarter-acre park. Three concrete steps and a plaza had been poured decades later, a simple wide swath leading from the intersection to where the columns still stood. It was a diminutive but charming urban rest, comforting and solitary, and she lay on her back atop the column to enjoy the stars.

As she mused a haziness emerged across the plaza below. It coalesced into a grayish-plum miasma at the bottom of the column, ragged and undulating. Then wrapping around the column it ascended, oozing partially into it and creeping up to Olivia as she mused. It flowed up her legs, barely touching her skin. As Olivia lifted her head suddenly, sensing a presence, the mist closed tightly around her. Gasping a squeak, her eyes widened and then she laughed with delight.

"Eidolon!" she was thrilled to see this mist and ran her fingers through the smoky plum shadow. Seeing her long-time familiar, her link to the magical world, was always a delight. Although a genderless spirit, she used the male pronoun for him and he had agreed to it, especially after learning about the marvels of sexuality which didn't exist in his dimension of mist and magic. He was curious, wanting to understand the mortal world, and sometimes blended with Olivia to experience touch and taste and hunger and all the other wonderful things that made up the Seven Deadly

Sins. In return he supported and protected Olivia in the magical world.

"I almost surprised you." he said. "What consumes you so much that you didn't sense me sooner?" He had a formal way of speaking and never had picked up popular vernacular in all the years she had known him. Not all familiars were the same; she knew some that mimicked mortal habits out of curiosity or amusement.

"Nothing – just memories and looking at stars."

"Are you going to take Taylor on as apprentice?" He was direct, as usual.

Olivia hedged. "I don't know – Taylor is new and untrained and it's powerful here in Seattle. Lots of dark in the winter, lots of suicides. Those emotions release energy that concentrates power here like a vortex. I'm a creature of it, used to it, but Taylor... "

"Olivia, that's an excuse and you know it. This is your responsibility."

He was right and she did know it. Of course he was right; he lived in the logos – the dimension of magic – and could read the threads out there. Cause and effect, use and payback. Olivia didn't answer him because she didn't like to be pushed. His ability to read her was either comforting or irritating depending on her mood.

"What did you see when you scryed her? Be honest." Eidolon knew she hadn't done it yet – looked into Taylor's past, her personal life. Olivia decided he was irritating tonight – especially because he was right.

"Fine. We'll do it now. You go ahead." She waited to see where he would place the vision and kneeled when the shimmer began at her feet. A swirling image sharpened and she could see Taylor with someone else; the other girl in the house with the same green eyes. The sister. The house they were in was the one she had seen, lower middle class, worn and unkempt. Olivia touched the image of the sister to see if she had magical abilities, but there was only a mortal aura. She touched Taylor to make sure and the same electric charge as in the market went down her back. Absolutely, Taylor was the one. But why was she friends with the runaways?

"What else?" She asked Eidolon.

More people appeared, images and feelings flitting by: their mother when the girls were small, trying to care for them both and working two jobs until a man came into sharp relief. *The one from the house.* Fear and hatred accompanied his visage. He belittled them, slapped them and hit them, just like she saw the other night – Taylor usually putting herself in between them, even when she was small. She couldn't tell when the mother stopped showing up in the visions. Recently, it seemed, but it didn't show why. Then the man came in the dark to Taylor's room. She couldn't have been older than thirteen. Olivia was sickened at watching but didn't stop; she needed to know what it was showing her. She could feel what Taylor felt: years of this man sometimes forcing himself on her and it made her gag. Olivia swallowed it away...Then the man turned his attention to the sister. *No!* She could feel Taylor as she offered herself instead to prevent it. The sister never knew. What else...Taylor had done well in school at first, then worse as the abuse continued. Visions of her unable to block out the memories and concentrate: hiding in the closet with her sister while shouting was heard in the living room, then failing a test the next day. Putting herself between her mother and stepfather and then missing school, too embarrassed to show the bruises, the swollen eye, or cheek, or jaw. By protecting the others she ended up with nothing. The image faded.

"Jesus."

Olivia was disgusted with herself; what a superficial dilettante she was! Her with her little cocoon of pretty things and philanthropy that she didn't want disturbed while Taylor hung with runaways who wouldn't judge her miserable situation. But she couldn't risk another apprentice – not with Dantin and his sociopathic familiar out there.

She knew both Eidolon and JaneAnn were right; this was Olivia's payback for her extravagant lifestyle through magic and maybe even for what had happened with her last apprentice. She had to rebalance the scales and had little choice but to accept it.

"I have to know for sure what blood she is. Can you tell?" Sometimes Eidolon knew, if a witch was powerful enough to read out in the logos, or if they'd been active before, but he didn't this time.

"Well, no sense putting it off. Let's do it to-night. The next question is, how to tell Taylor?" One of the oddest things Olivia ever had to do was approach someone to tell them they were magic and she would be their teacher, and she knew for a fact the easiest way was directly. But there was very little chance she and Taylor would be in the same situation or fall into a conversation together.

"I'll use magic to bring her to me. I can charm her when I get her blood tonight...so we may as well get to it." She stood up, stepped off the column and was on the ground without breaking her stride as if it were three inches instead of thirty feet. Since it was after one in the morning no one noticed. And no one noticed Eidolon swirling imperceptibly about her as she walked to her car, or her Jag disappearing on its own, or that she disappeared right off the curb, reappearing with her ethereal companion in Taylor's bedroom.

Only the glowing numbers of the bedside clock lit the room, but it was enough for Olivia to see. She approached Taylor's bed and paused to listen to the house around her. No other sounds. She relaxed and began what she had come for. A small vial appeared between her fingers and Olivia bent over the sleeping girl to place it in the crook of her arm, bringing her forearm up until the glass was surrounded by skin. Taylor stirred restlessly and Liv held perfectly still, pausing the charm filling the vial with blood until the girl was still again. Only a few more seconds and she had what she needed. Holding the vial to the light she made sure it was full, but that pulled her attention away from the open door until Eidolon suddenly alerted her that someone was entering the room.

Olivia backed up three strides, tucking herself behind the door as it swung open further. She placed her palm against the wood to feel who was there. The stepdad. He stood a few moments and looked around. *Why?* Olivia thought. *He can't possibly know I'm here...* He came into the room but she could tell he didn't know she was there. Olivia readied to leave until she remembered she had to charm Taylor so the girl would follow her the next time they crossed paths. She would need to touch her or touch something she was sure to be wearing next time they met.

She held still, waiting for the stepfather to leave, until she saw he was staring at Taylor in the bed, fingering the button on his pants. *Oh, are you kidding me? Not while I am right here.* She suspended him and immediately he was motionless and unaware by her command.

Stepping up to him, she took a really close look. The unwashed hair, little bumps and pockmarks on his neck and cheeks, and oh, he smelled! Like old sweat and salt. She stood in front of him and looked into his face, wondering what made someone the way he was. She'd known far worse in her life, but it didn't make him any less disgusting. She didn't want to touch him to send him back to his own bed in forgetfulness, so she concentrated the charm in her mouth and blew on him. As expected, he inhaled and began to move. With unseeing eyes he turned around, moving out into the hall, back to his own room with the reality-show skank.

"You really need to get out of here." She whispered to Taylor and murmured the charm, touching her brunette hair. Then she steeled herself, feeling foolish. This was business. She wouldn't let her guard down again.

"Okay, let's do it." JaneAnn motioned with her coffee cup to the granite counter where a small white saucer waited for them. Olivia uncapped the vial in her hand, Taylor's blood from the night before, and poured it onto the glass. They both leaned over the dome of blood, intensely interested. Olivia tipped her head to look at it from an angle.

"Silver-Tint. Just as you thought." JaneAnn was satisfied with the faint silver sheen she could see on the surface of the pool.

"I want to make sure." Olivia touched it with a tiny golden pick tipped with red powder. Immediately the blood flared into a silver flame about four inches high where it remained until the pick was removed. The relief in her face was undeniable. A Blue/Black would have been trainable but naturally inclined to cruelty and a hunger for power. It was good there weren't many of them; so far the Silver-Tints were the majority.

"She'll need protectors. Something Dantin can't get around."

"Another chimera or Will-O-Wisp or some sort of demon? I think it's smarter to have different layers." JaneAnn had definite ideas but this was Olivia's apprentice.

"Yeah, I agree. I think Eidolon, and Daphne and Chloe, and maybe another chimera like Eidolon and I want him to pick. Someone who can test her when the time comes but is irreproachable."

"Need anything from me?"

"Not that I can think of, but that may change if she turns out to be a brat. Then I will give her to you, bad karma and all."

JaneAnn laughed and then turned serious. "I'll be honest with you; I'm afraid of what Dantin could do. I can take care of myself, but if something happens with Taylor and you need me, let me know."

"I will." Olivia touched her friend's hand. "Thanks."

Taylor wished for the millionth time she could afford dinner in one of the places on Broadway. The restaurant she was currently swooning over had replaced the exterior wall with six French doors that were now open to the summer twilight. Diners hung in happy limbo between inside and outside and long cream-colored curtains billowed softly in the air. Inside the restaurant, rustic terra-cotta walls and rough-hewn furniture counterpointed sparkling golden and crystal chandeliers in this elegant yet shabbily chic place. She loved Broadway Avenue, loved the restaurants that had been teased out of broken down buildings and vintage storefronts right next to urban specialty stores and the neighborhood grocery across from where she stood.

Taylor noticed a black limousine parked at the grocery, awkwardly trying to fit into the lot as the driver rolled its long profile back and forth to give way to other cars. *That's not too bright,* she thought. Capitol Hill streets were so tight cars could hardly pass each other and there was no parking unless your timing was brilliant, yet here was twenty feet of automobile taking up precious room. As she watched a woman approached and the driver opened her door for her, but before entering she stopped to stare directly at Taylor. The woman from Broadway Market, Taylor realized, less than thirty feet away and making a pointed issue of noticing her. She was in her thirties, perhaps, with dark russet hair and finely sculpted features. Her eyes were large and doe-like but not turned up like Taylor's. They were round and the long lashes swept down at the outside corners, the color warm like liquid chocolate. Full lips balanced high rounded cheekbones. Taylor found herself staring back for a long time until the woman got into the car and the limo poked its nose into the tight street. Taylor turned to walk away, then turned back for another look. *That was really strange. Who is she?* Dismissing her curiosity wasn't easy for some reason and in an unusual move, Taylor decided to follow the limo.

The limo couldn't move quickly in traffic and she kept up easily. It turned left where Broadway Ave passed the little Harvard Exit theatre and went creeping down a narrow neighborhood street. Noise from the Avenue faded away and became chirping birds and a faint whoosh from the breeze through the huge old trees. At the end of the block the limo turned left again and stopped halfway down the street. Taylor hid behind a hedge and watched the woman get out, thank the driver, and enter a hidden door to an underground garage. Taylor looked up to see a huge brick edifice, a massive triad of Tudor mansions. Rows of pointed gables on steeply peaked roofs topped the tall walls and beautiful oriel windows bowed out from the brick façade. As the limo whispered away down the hill she came closer, slipping into the courtyard and looking around. The landscape was beautiful: lots of lawn inside a circular drive that served the trio of mansions, deep flowerbeds, and a cluster of huge evergreens with a teak bench underneath. Taylor craved exploring this beautiful place and dusk was deepening over the manicured garden; perhaps no one would notice her.

Gingerly, she took a few steps along the path and stopped but couldn't detect any activity. All was quiet as she walked along. Each entryway was different, she saw: here an artistic wooden lattice created a private area where clematis climbed up the woodwork sprinkled with hundreds of delicate purple blossoms. The mass of flowers scented the air like expensive tropical perfume. The front door was painted aubergine and the curved brass door handle and key plate stood out in sparkling relief.

Another had a small brick courtyard like the Tudor façade; there was even a gargoyle atop the corner column protecting the home from evil. She could hear a trickling waterfall nearby and through the large window next to it she saw an eclectic library. Rows of books carpeted the walls on long shelves, their repetition giving way occasionally to small icons from other cultures. A few looked very old: a primitive woven basket, a slim urn with vertical handles, a crystal vase backlit and adorned with a figure in frosted relief. She'd seen one in the window of an antique shop; what did they call it? Lalique? Vintage books with matching gold designs on their spines reposed on the shelves with newer books and magazines.

Taylor had been there nearly an hour and by now glowing, milky moonlight flowed through the courtyard, reflecting off the calla lilies and painting the sidewalks. This place was so perfect and elegant. Karen was spending the night with friends and Taylor loathed being home alone with her stepfather and his useless girlfriend. She quashed that – she wouldn't ruin this with ugly thoughts. Sitting on the bench under the firs she looked at the beauty around her but the ugly thoughts intruded. Kicked out next month. How would she live? The only job she'd ever had was at a burger place and had gotten fired because she had been late or missed work when her stepfather had kept her from going. She bet he had done it on purpose. No job she could get could support her; she knew no one except the runaways. Nowhere to go...no options at all. Hopelessness washed over her so strongly her stomach knotted and she doubled up to cry. *God, I want to die...*but couldn't bring herself to take that step. Her head ached from the pressure of stifling her pain and her palms seared where her nails dug into her clenching fists. She was mortified someone might come out and find her, this worthless girl intruding on their carefully cultivated existence. Taylor slipped off the bench, tucked herself under it against the trunk of the fir and cried herself out until only dry sobs came. Then she lay still, looking at the lush expanse of lawn bathed in moonlight, letting it calm her until finally she fell asleep.

A robin announcing his territorial rights woke her up. She could hear him going from perch to perch in his domain, singing and alerting other robins to stay away. He landed on the bench and looked at her through the wood slats. Taylor smiled as she looked at him through hazy morning eyes, waking up slowly in the sunlight. She heard more birds; a car drove slowly by on the street outside the courtyard. The courtyard! She knew she needed to get up and go before someone saw her but she was so warm. She thought she must be lying in sunlight but then realized the tree was shading her. She looked down to see a tan blanket covering her. *What the hell...?* Scooting from under the bench, she brushed herself off as she looked around but saw no one. Grabbing the blanket, she balled it up quickly and took it with her as she walked quickly across the lawn and out to the street, taking one last look into the courtyard. Strange morning. And she'd had strange dreams last night...floating, indistinct figures around her, and her skin crawling, a kind of tingling up her back.

A block away she stopped to inspect the blanket, snapping it into the morning air. It was new, a nice one, too ... with a note pinned to it. Her heart sank. But the note was just a phone number and the name "Olivia" in a flowing, artistic script. Mixed embarrassment and suspicion washed through Taylor. In her experience people didn't offer anything without wanting something in return. She fingered the paper and put it in her pocket, miserable and confused as she walked toward the Ave. She had to go home; Karen would be back from Angela's soon and she had to be there but knew she would be in all kinds of trouble for being out all night. It was so stupid. Her stepdad didn't want them around but was mad if they weren't home when he suddenly had some urge to torment them. She'd stopped trying to make sense of it. Everything was an excuse for a beating. Or worse.

She walked slowly, looking at her feet and making herself take each step. The last thing she wanted was to go home. When she looked up finally she was at tiny Cornish College for the Arts. She needed to think up her story for being out all night. Picking a piece of curb under a tree, she sat and watched the shadows of leaves on the sidewalk. The morning light felt soft on her arms as she sat there, and she drew up her knees and rested her chin on her arms.

The leafy patterns had moved a full foot when her reverie was interrupted by a tight feeling down her legs, like in the dream the night before. She heard someone approach and looked up to see the woman with the auburn hair and doe eyes from the limousine. Taylor was taken aback by the presence this woman had; a definitive walk and a polished look gave her an aura that moved with her. Long, lean legs gave shape to crisp khakis, and under a cream snakeskin jacket she could see a narrow athletic frame in a top of forest green. The woman stopped abruptly next to her and waited, looking at the girl on the curb and seeming for all the world like she expected Taylor to speak first.

After a few moments Taylor asked, "What?"

"Are you all right?"

Taylor was wary. "What do you mean?"

The woman looked at her squarely. "I know you slept in our courtyard last night. I gave you the blanket."

Taylor felt her face go numb. She cast for something smart to say but got nothing. She finally managed, "Why?"

Olivia dropped to her haunches, looking into Taylor's face. "What if you didn't have to live with your stepdad?"

Taylor was shocked. How did she know? And then deep suspicion washed over her. She'd heard stories from the runaways – someone giving an offer out of the blue, an easy way off the street, but it never turned out well. Never. Usually it was a lie. Something demeaning always was required in return, or people just...disappeared. Offers were not to be trusted. She drew in her legs to get up and leave when a question stopped her.

"Did I say it would be an easy way off the street?"

Taylor snapped around to look at the woman. *Did I say that aloud? No. I know I didn't!*

The woman ignored Taylor's expression. "Look, I'm going to show you something, and you'll either believe it or you won't. You decide." Olivia hated to waste words, preferring to cut right to the chase.

Moving so her back was to the houses across the street, Olivia opened her palm to Taylor and a tiny flame emerged from the center. Olivia turned her hand, facing the palm downward and little spears of fire crept up over the sides of her hand as she turned it, engulfing the skin. Taylor could smell smoke, as if from a campfire.

"Touch it." Olivia said.

Reaching out, Taylor could feel the heat licking off the hand. She burned her fingertips, gasping and jerking her hand back involuntarily from the sharp pain. She looked closely through the translucent flames, but there was just delicate skin on the slim hands. No burns or fireproof gel or anything that would explain. She studied Olivia's face but there was no pain, no emotion at all as she met Taylor's gaze.

After a moment Olivia closed her hand and the flame disappeared. It didn't dissipate; it was simply gone and the hand was pristine, no blisters or burns. Not even a smoky odor lingered in the air. Taylor felt a body buzz creep over her.

Olivia broke the uneasy silence. "I'll show you how to do that, and other magic, too, but we can't stay out here. If you want to know more you need to follow me." She stood up again on the sidewalk, looking down at the wordless Taylor who was now viewing her own hands as if imagining them covered in flame. Olivia wasn't sure her last comments registered and she tried a different tack. "Taylor, are you listening or not?"

Taylor didn't like hearing her name from a stranger and couldn't fathom where this was leading but had no sort of reply. None at all.

Olivia looked slightly impatient. "Look, I know about you. I know about Karen and about your stepfather. I don't think you have any options. If you want one, come back to my house with me."

She didn't wait for an answer but turned and walked away without looking back at Taylor, who felt a tsunami of curiosity wash through her. Then she realized that if she didn't follow, the truth was her options would remain exactly zero. She stood and made long strides to catch up.

"I have to get back soon, before Karen comes home from Angela's."

"I know. You'll get there in time." Then silence again as they walked further until Taylor couldn't stand the awkwardness.

"That limo has got to be hard to find parking for." Taylor could tell the redhead was surprised by the way her eyes widened and she stopped and turned to her.

"Well I didn't really think about that because it was rented. I imagine the driver took it back to the garage after he dropped me at home." She smiled coolly at Taylor. "I'm Olivia."

"I know. I read the note."

"So we're all caught up then."

They continued in silence and Taylor let her thoughts flow freely but no scenario she dreamed up made sense. *Had she said magic?* They walked back the way she had come, through the courtyard and across the lawn and she crept a guilty look at the bench as they passed by. Olivia's corner entrance was set back and more private. An old wisteria vine created a dense wall of foliage around a simple and elegant entry. Deep blue salvias and hostas ringed the flagstones. Olivia inserted her key in the lock and they stepped into the dark entryway. For a few moments Taylor couldn't see anything as her eyes adjusted. Then she followed Olivia left, down a hall and through a dining room where she was surprised by a midnight sky filling the ceiling. It was painted in hues of cobalt and navy blue sprinkled with tiny copper stars. Pale grey walls soothed the striking effect and under the table and chairs dark grey carpeting flowed into the next room where Olivia was headed. Taylor paused and stared; she had never seen such a beautiful home.

"Come on." She gestured to Taylor. I'll make us some coffee." They entered the nook adjoining the kitchen. Although it could be a breakfast alcove, there was no table. Instead two well-used and comfortable looking velvet slipper chairs sat next to a curved bay of floor to ceiling windows. Morning light flooded the nook and a granite counter delineated the kitchen on the opposite side. Olivia moved into the kitchen and started coffee, telling Taylor, "Here come visitors to see who you are."

She could hear the clicking of toenails on the kitchen floor before she saw the two greyhounds come padding in. They looked shy, with heads down and long drooping tails, and on outrageously long legs they floated quietly to Taylor. Art deco dogs, all sleek and lean like an Icart etching. One put his nose in Taylor's slightly curled hand; the other stopped and leaned against her leg, asking for pets. She ran her hands down their necks and was amazed at how soft their fur was, like holding a bunny. So sweet and quiet, not like other dogs that wagged wildly and got excited, jumping up. So gentle. She thought they would be hyper and asked Olivia. No, quite the opposite, was the reply. Their names were Doobie and Bailey. Taylor scratched and stroked the two for a while longer, closing her eyes and soaking up the calm they emanated while she listened to the coffeepot gurgle. Then apparently they tired of the attention and turned away, lying down on puffy floor cushions next to the lounge chairs. Taylor sat in the chair next to Bailey, watching Olivia pour coffee and taking it from her when she came over. Olivia stood looking at Taylor for a moment before speaking.

"So, why are you here? Why am I talking to you?" She sat across from her. "Taylor, what would you want right now if you could have anything?"

Taylor took only a second to answer. "To get away from my stepfather. Put my sister through college. Money. A job."

Olivia gestured. "Put your hand out, palm up." Taylor did.

"Watch." The faintest shimmer appeared for a millisecond. When it was gone, a crisp stack of hundred dollar bills lay in Taylor's hand. "Money. One of your wishes."

Taylor hardly heard. The money was tangible; she fingered it but she couldn't tell how it had happened.

"How do you do that? Like a card trick?"

"Not really."

"Can you do it again? I want to see how it works."

Olivia did it again, Taylor watching her sleeves closely to see if there was something hidden in the cuffs. But she couldn't see anything there. "Okay, how do you do that?"

"Magic." I sound ridiculous, Olivia thought. Momentarily, she wished for centuries past when belief in magic was instant after seeing it, though ignorant fear had come with it. Nowadays, convincing someone was so awkward.

"Right. Sure." But for Taylor there was another, maybe more important thing: "So I can keep this money. It's real?"

"Yes, it's real... And it's not a trick, it's true magic." She watched the disbelief sweep across Taylor's face.

"Okay then, do something else. Something that can't be faked." She looked around. "Make Bailey float."

"No, I'm not going to do that. It would scare him. What if I lifted you? Would you be convinced?" And she focused on Taylor, who lofted to the ceiling and stayed pasted there as she gasped and squirmed, scraping at the smooth ceiling for purchase. Olivia let her stay up there long enough to stop being frantic, then let her down slowly.

"Relax, Taylor. I won't let you fall," she said as Taylor came off the ceiling.

Taylor was furious when she landed, shoving Olivia as she bit off the words. "What – Why did you think *that* was okay? You wouldn't do it to Bailey because you said it would scare him, But it's okay to throw me up there?"

Olivia was unflappably calm. "Levitation was your idea, not mine. And you sound like you believe what just happened."

"That's impossible!" Taylor's reality was spinning around her. "How did you do that?"

"It's not a trick. You can see it's a plain kitchen, nothing special." She looked around the kitchen and unable to help herself, Taylor did the same. Still, she tightened.

"I'm not stupid. I've seen shows on television. They look real but there's always a trick."

Olivia folded her arms. "All right Taylor, what would not be a trick? You choose. That way you know I haven't set it up already."

Taylor's eyes circled the room for something to ... what? Light on fire? Make appear? Make disappear? Stupidly, an elephant sprang to mind and she discarded it. This was so foreign to her. Meanwhile, her host was quietly waiting.

"I don't know. Something – something really big." She wanted something she could experience not connected to this room and not something small. "Send me somewhere far away."

Olivia was amused. "Well, where do you want to go?"

With Taylor's sharp "Oh!" Olivia could see her opening the tiniest crack of belief. She pushed a little more. "Well?"

Taylor picked the most remote place she could think of. "Nepal."

"Fine. You'll need a jacket." She swept her hand over the two of them and they were suddenly bundled in long down-filled coats. "Come on." She took Taylor's arm firmly and the room disappeared around them accompanied by a rush and a head buzz. She couldn't see anything for a second, then the black haze lifted from her eyes and they were standing in a dirt road that hairpinned down a brown rocky mountainside. But then she was sick to her stomach. Holding back a retch, she closed her eyes.

"Here, sit down." Olivia steered Taylor to a small boulder. "It'll pass. You get used to it." She eased Taylor onto the rock.

Taylor folded her arms across her knees and placed her forehead there, looking at the ground between her feet until she was right again. "Okay," she said finally and lifted her head.

She suddenly understood the word "breathtaking" as she drank in the vista around her. She had no idea the sky could hold this much volume. A cloudless bowl of sheer blue above was matched by a brown barren valley below. Miles away, straight across the valley, Himalayan peaks ringed them, sharp and craggy with frozen tips. In the valley she could see several clay and stone buildings, some small, one large. Brightly colored flags there flapped off some sort of line. They looked like the flags that adorned car lots, she thought, then instantly withdrew such a common description for this stunning place.

"What is that?" She pointed below.

"That's the Rongpuk monastery with its prayer flags and bell," replied Olivia. Distant people and animals moved slowly in the pale sunlight. They could hear the faintest sound of a cowbell in the thin, still air. She pointed across the valley. "Mount Everest – locals call it Sagarmatha – and Lhotse mountain right next to it. And over there, that lone spire? That's Ama Dablam."

Taylor said nothing. For several minutes they looked at the peaks together. They were brutally beautiful, so high in the atmosphere the dark edge of space crept along the points.

"Let's go down." Olivia took Taylor's hand and immediately they were at the monastery. The exterior wall was an austere grey clay and a row of rough-hewn wooden posts supported the roof. There cylinders with carved figures adorned the posts, strangely decorative on the primitive structure.

"What are those?" Taylor asked Olivia, who stepped over to one of the cylinders and touched it. It spun slowly under her hand, the carved face changing features as it turned.

"They are prayer wheels. Inside are copies of a mantra that is supposed to spread blessings as you turn it." She encouraged Taylor. "Go ahead. The correct way is to turn it clockwise. And remember to have respect for the belief, whether or not you believe it yourself."

Taylor reached out and touched the wheel. It spun easily, as if on a cushion of air. It looked so old, she had expected it to creak and catch. There was a row of them, seven in all, and they walked under the eave to turn each one. She looked back at them. So beautiful...

Just then a figure appeared around the corner, a monk dressed in traditional garb, the mustard yellow and red of his robes warm against the grey wall. He was surprised when he saw them, then relaxed and placed his palms together in front of his chest, fingers upward. Olivia did the same, palms flat together in front of her, elbows out to the side. She touched her fingers to her lips and bowed slightly.

"*Namaste.*"

The monk bowed in return. "*Kun kasto?*" he asked Olivia.

"*Madhyam path.*"

He then looked at Taylor next to Olivia. "*Yo ke ho?*"

"*Bahini,*" returned Olivia.

"*Ahh...*" He smiled and nodded, turning to Taylor with the same greeting. "*Namaste.*"

Taylor smiled awkwardly and nodded in return. He patted her on the arm as he passed and disappeared into the monastery. He seemed unconcerned about the two strangers in city clothing and Taylor stared at the empty doorway after him, completely unsure what to think.

"What was that all about?" She was impressed at Olivia's command of the language and customs.

"Namaste is a greeting. Then he asked about you and what path I take."

"What path?"

Olivia explained. "In Buddhism the *Madhyam path* means to be neither too self-indulgent or menially living. There's a similar way of living as witch. I'll teach you about it."

Taylor was feeling unreality and smoldering excitement. Could this really be real? She had a falling feeling. Then she started to shiver in spite of her coat and she pulled it more closely. Olivia grabbed her arm.

"Time to go."

They were back in the kitchen in moments, Taylor still shivering and dizzy from the trip. She sat in one of the velvet chairs as she recovered, while Olivia brought her a cup of weak tea.

"Here. Small sips will feel good on your stomach and warm you faster."

Taylor had to ask the obvious. "You're really a witch?"

"Yes."

"I'm a witch as well?" Realizing the ridiculous-sounding question was coming from her own lips.

"Yes."

Taylor looked down at Bailey lying on his cushion and he looked up at her with soft brown eyes, unconcerned at the two of them disappearing and reappearing as they had. He was welcome comfort in her confusion. "What happens next?"

Olivia saw acceptance at last in her new pro-
tégé. "You stay with me while you learn, but in my
house. My neighbors might not understand if you keep
sleeping under our bench." She smiled.

Oh. The bench! Taylor was relieved to find she
wasn't embarrassed about it now. Ah, but that was
trivial compared to what had happened. Then she remembered.

"Karen! Is she a witch, too?" She was picturing
everything they would do together.

"No, I'm sorry. Just you."

"But we're sisters!" Taylor's disappointment
was immense.

"That doesn't make any difference. One can be
and the other not, just like being a blond or a redhead
or an athlete or a genius. Everyone has their own abilities."

"I can't leave her there, with him. I'm scared of
what he's capable of. Our mom..." She trailed. "Look, I
just *have* to take care of Karen. I am not leaving her
with him even one night." She was emphatic, insistent.

"All right, Taylor. She's going to school in a
few weeks, right? We'll make sure she gets there today
instead. I promise she won't be alone with him. But
Taylor, you can't tell her about this. If she doesn't
have your abilities it's dangerous for her to know."

"Why?"

"Can you imagine if your stepfather knew?
What would he do to take advantage of that? You
don't know enough yet to protect her. Besides, how

would she feel if she knew you could do magic but she couldn't? We can decide later whether to tell her."

Taylor paused at that. She wouldn't put anything at all past her stepfather.

"Let me take care of everything. Karen will be well off, I promise. She'll have everything and then some."

"But how do we keep him out of it? If Karen can suddenly go to school like this, he'll be suspicious. He'll smell money and try and get in on it. I know him." Her lips tightened.

"Oh, I can take care of that, too. Trust me."

Taylor hesitated, about to ask how, but then nodded abruptly. "Okay. And... I don't want to remember *him* – ever."

"If you don't want to remember him, what about Karen? You'll have different memories."

"No. We always imagined what it would have been like without him – with just us and Mom. It's hardly been two years since she disappeared. Can you do that? Just erase him and fill in the memories with our mother?"

"Are you *sure* that's what Karen would want?"

"Yes. We talked about it all the time. Olivia, can you make that real? Then she can go to school and I'll be here with you." Taylor looked almost pleading.

Olivia was relieved. That would solve a wealth of problems. "All right. I'll take care of her school; I'll give her a trust fund. She won't even have to do work-study as long as she makes grades. But listen, you tell her nothing. Got it?" Her look left no doubt she meant it.

"I promise."

"Good. Let's go get your things and take care of Karen."

"There isn't much here that I want." Taylor was looking around her room. They'd already taken Karen to school, getting a summer dorm with early classes and setting her up nicely. Taylor gaped as Olivia paid all four years at once and created a half-million dollar trust for Karen just to go to school. She hadn't realized how wealthy she was in addition to her magical abilities. But it made sense; why be poor when you could have anything you wanted? Taylor and Karen had said their goodbyes while Olivia kept out of sight as the unknown benefactor. Now they were back at Taylor's house following Olivia's instructions.

"Look around and make sure everything of Karen's is gone too. We don't want him with proof of either of you." Olivia wanted as little complication as possible. Taylor's memory would be changed when they got to Olivia's.

Taylor was gathering the last of what she wanted, pictures and things with special memories, when the front door banged shut. Three, four footfalls came in and stopped in the living room, then walking slowly, crossed to Karen's room.

Taylor shot a terrified look at Olivia. "All her stuff is gone! He'll know something's up!" She whispered it but Olivia was unconcerned.

"Let him." She turned toward the door and pushed Taylor behind her.

"Taylor! What the hell is going on here? Where is all of Karen's–" He stopped and stared at them from the doorway.

"Who are you?" His scowl was especially nasty.

Olivia spoke over her shoulder to Taylor. "Do you have everything?"

The man looked at the two, comprehending, and threatened Taylor. "You're not going anywhere." He pointed at Olivia. "You, get the fuck out of my house."

Olivia kept her eyes on him and repeated her question to Taylor. A small "yes" came from behind her and without a gesture, Olivia transported her new apprentice and her few belongings back to the Tudor manor, appreciating the shock on the stepfather's face.

In seconds, though, his focus was back on her and he advanced, full of bluster. "You don't come into a man's house and take what's his! You're about to be one sorry bitch." He reached toward her and Olivia caught his forearm easily, holding it immobile while he struggled to get away. Then he swore in pain as she brought his wrist down and him with it until he was on the floor. Olivia looked down at him without emotion.

"You're breaking my arm!" He tried to fight, but surprise was adding to his weakness.

Olivia's tone was measured. "You will leave Taylor alone. You will leave Karen alone. Understand?"

The man's words choked out through the pain in his wrist. "Oh, you think because you have some fancy-ass jujitsu move that I'm just going to obey you? You can't hold onto my wrist forever and then I'll make you sorry."

"Really. Okay then, go ahead." Olivia dropped his wrist. He stood, glaring and rubbing his arm while he assessed her.

"Oh, yeah. Lucky grab on the wrist I sprained last week," he lied. Then seeing he was taller and heavier, he started to smile, a disgusting leer that spread across his face.

"I've got something for you." He clenched his fists. "Just you and me here, alone in the house." Olivia remembered what Taylor had said:

"I'm scared of what he's capable of. Our mom..."

Olivia stepped aside into invisibility. She avoided him easily as he recovered from his astonishment and reached about for her. *Could he have...?* She swept her arm through him to read his thoughts. Yes, he had killed their mother – beaten her to death in the kitchen one night while the girls hid in Karen's closet crying. He only realized later he'd done it when he had come back to finish berating her and she had been limp, dead and blue and bruised on the floor. He'd taken her into the hills somewhere that very night, dumping her into a wooded ravine. He actually thought he was clever for not having gotten caught in almost two years.

Olivia was disgusted. She'd love to make him call the police and turn himself in, lead them to her body, go to jail forever. She was on the verge of doing so but remembered she'd promised Taylor to wipe his memory from her – hard to maintain if there were stories about it in the paper and reporters.

She reappeared behind him, whispering. "You piece of shit. You leave those girls alone or I'll make you tell the police how you killed her and where you buried her."

He spun, forgetting all about Olivia's invisibility. "You can't fucking make me do jack. And you'll never get the chance." He narrowed his eyes and advanced on her.

"I can make you do anything I want." She flicked her fingers and he backed away from her, although he struggled not to. When he was tucked in the corner unable to move, he snarled more invectives at her. She shook her head.

"That mouth you have on you. You really are unpleasant and sarcastic. Let's give you a reason to shut up."

The next string of profanity came out of him in a voice so high-pitched it actually made Olivia laugh.

"That's lovely. Very nice. Yes, threaten people with that."

She let him titter on, squeaking threats and curses until he finally petered out and glared at her. The hate and the threat in his eyes were very real. A squeaky voice wouldn't remove him as a danger; she knew it.

"Let's make sure you don't hurt anyone else. Ever." She stared hard at him until his expression changed to confusion, then alarm. He reached down and scrabbled at his pants, frantically pulling them away from his skin.

"Go ahead, take a look."

He ripped open his pants to find his groin covered in blisters and pustules, the oozing sores spreading down his thighs, certain items suddenly misshapen.

"What the fuck!" he squealed.

"Flesh-eating bacteria. I don't need to tell you any more than that, do I?"

A primitive wail burst from him followed by sobbing. "Please...please, God..."

"You leave those girls alone, and no more abusing anyone, in any way, for any reason."

"Yes! Yes!" He was staring at his decomposing genitalia, hyperventilating.

"The first time you do, it will come back."

"I promise! Just..."

"Don't think about testing me, either, to see if it really will happen. Oh, never mind... if you do and it comes back, I really don't care." With a flick of her fingers it started to dissipate, returning him to normal. She stopped it when faint scars still showed on his groin and he looked at her, fearful.

"That's a reminder so you can't fool yourself into thinking this wasn't real."

She turned and walked out the front door, leaving him to stare at his damaged goods.

It took her a moment to remember where she was. Through sleepy eyes Taylor looked at the bronze silk comforter and complementary mounds of pillows around her. Overhead a gauzy canopy draped over corner bedposts, spilling down the carved wood to pool at the floor. Antique furniture, sleek lucite lighting, and an eclectic mix of items appointed this lush bedroom. Everything glowed from the sun backlighting the silk drapes. Never in her life had she been in a place like this. Now she lay on the soft bed, looking up at the translucent canopy, amazed that this was her room.

The rich smell of coffee came to her from downstairs and she got up to follow it, finding Olivia sitting at the kitchen counter with company. The woman under the soft brown curls smiled at Taylor.

"Good morning. I'm JaneAnne."

Taylor looked at Olivia. "Is..." She trailed off.

"Yes – she's a witch, too. You can talk in front of her. Here, have some coffee and a scone and we'll get started." She pushed an artisan bag across the counter along with a cup.

JaneAnne was more measured. "Olivia, give the girl a minute; she just woke up."

"I let her sleep until ten-thirty. Why wait?" Then she shrugged. "Okay."

JaneAnn turned to Taylor to talk but she was already answering Olivia. "I don't mind getting started right away. I want to."

"See? She's ready."

"Fine." JaneAnn sighed. "Well, obviously you can tell Liv and I have been friends a while."

Olivia continued, "Eidolon should be here soon, too."

"Who's Eidolon?"

"He's Olivia's familiar."

Taylor looked down at the greys lying on their beds. "Another greyhound? Or a cat?"

Olivia answered. "No, those are just old stories. A familiar is a spirit, a chimera. They live in the logos, where all magic exists. They can look like an animal or possess one, but they usually don't."

"And they do a witch's bidding?"

JaneAnn shook her head. "That old story's wrong, too. They're more a partner or a friend, but they have their own lives. Speaking of..." She pointed beside Taylor, where a plume of plum smoke was taking form. It slipped around Taylor where she sat on the kitchen stool and she gasped her shock, then gingerly touched the haze and was astounded.

"I can feel it! I can tell he's there!" The mist was soothing, friendly and she could hear him saying hellos inside her head. He was warm, masculine.

"Eidolon likes this form. It's closer to his natural state." Olivia explained.

Taylor was delighted. "He's wonderful."

"Well, not all of them are so friendly."

"What do you mean?"

"Some will try and possess a witch, take them against their will."

Taylor was wide eyed. "Why?"

"We have mortal bodies that can feel, taste, touch, hear, see colors. And we have emotions, too. Sensations like ours are a huge experience for chimeras. They want to know how it feels, so some try and take it."

"What do I do if that happens?" She had a draining feeling.

"I'll teach you protection spells and you've got to learn discipline. Always be on guard."

JaneAnn stepped in. "Liv, you're going to scare her."

"She should be scared. Well, reasonably scared."

JaneAnn tried to soothe the discussion. "Taylor, it's like driving on the freeway; just be scared enough to make you pay attention and be careful. That's all." She watched Taylor relax a little.

Olivia went on. "So you'll need protectors while you're learning. Daphne and Chloe will be your guardians until you can take care of yourself. Ladies, we're ready for you now." She put a hand on Taylor's arm to move her back. "Don't be surprised."

"At what?" But then Taylor jumped as two columns of flame burst into the breakfast nook, then instantly disappeared. Slowly they returned, undulating, and Taylor realized they had human form. Luminous, beautifully sculpted, female form. They were Aphrodites made of white-hot embers.

"Who are they?" Taylor's eyes were wide. The two figures calmly regarded her through glowing eyes.

"They're Will-O-Wisps. Have you heard of those?" asked Olivia.

"The flickering lights people would see in marshes at night – people used to think they were spirits. Sometimes they would follow the lights and get lost or drown."

"Very good." The closest one answered Taylor, a velvety smooth voice with a hint of the flame that waved across the lips. "In fact, the Sea Sirens are our cousins. Plenty of sailors followed them beneath the water."

"But the Japanese understand us better. They call us *kitsune kami,* or fox-spirit." The other picked up the thread in the same velvety voice. "Guardians."

"I'm Daphne," the first one said.

"Chloe. Nice to meet you, Taylor." She wafted just above the floor, and Taylor saw that her thighs tailed down into softly curving flame.

Olivia regarded them, pleased. "Just like a chimera, they live out in the logos and are entirely magic. And they're practically undetectable until they flare. Then they disappear instantly so they're hard to track. Perfect guardians against chimera – and most other things."

"You might not see us..."

"...but we'll always be around at first..." Chloe stepped in.

"...until you can handle yourself," Daphne finished.

Olivia was all business. "So the sooner we do this, the sooner you can start learning." She leaned forward and put her hand on Taylor's cheekbone, looking into her eyes. Immediately Taylor's world collapsed into blackness, followed a millisecond later by an explosion of sensation. The room around her became intense and prismatic – colors were extent, appearing to have far more depth than she'd ever seen before. Inanimate objects looked as if alive and had a sort of extra dimensionality to them, and every noise was pinpoint clear. Taylor gaped at the room. It was as if she had lived all her life without really seeing what was there. The room became translucent and an amazing pastiche was superimposed on it. She heard layers of voices. Shadowy figures moved around her, outlined in a kind of glowing energy. A few looked at her curiously as they went about their business, but most didn't notice, as if she didn't exist in their world. Most surprising was the radiance everything had, glimmering and flowing through everything, including her, and it crackled around her with a rosy glow. She could feel it course through her, vibrating her like a string on a violin.

"I had no idea. It's so beautiful, and the colors are so intense!" She was enthralled. "And Olivia...I can feel it."

JaneAnn nodded. "It is something, isn't it? That's the logos flowing through you, what you'll tap into for magic." She loved this part.

Olivia took her hand away. "You'll get used to it, but you really need to work on self-discipline so it doesn't distract you." Taylor was still staring around her, a neonate discovering the world anew.

"Taylor! Did you hear me?"

JaneAnn threw back her head and laughed, a warm throaty sound that descended like musical notes and Taylor could tell it was genuine. A tinkling symphony of sound in Taylor's newly enhanced perception.

"Oh, Olivia, leave her alone for a while and let her enjoy it. She's got Eidolon and Daphne and Chloe with her."

Shaking her head, Olivia joined her friend in another cup of coffee and waited while Taylor went from room to room experiencing everything. Finally her new student sat down with them.

"Wow – just wow. I didn't know all that was out there."

"I know; we'd better start your lessons so you can handle it."

At that, JaneAnn got up to go. "I have a lot to do this afternoon, too. Taylor, it was a pleasure. I'm sure I'll see you often. Olivia, I'll talk to you later." She disappeared.

Olivia spent that afternoon schooling her novice in keeping her mind on one track and not being distracted, and a few simple things like levitation and manipulating items. Every day there were lessons and hours of practice. Over the next month Taylor improved immensely.

She practiced fire as Olivia had instructed: "Look at your palm and visualize the flame there – not too big at first! Believe it will be there..." and it was. When she was afraid she would burn herself Olivia bolstered her: "It's just a vision of flame for you, but it's real for everyone else. Don't think of yourself as mortal." When the flame flicked on and off at her command she increased the size until it reached several feet. Daphne and Chloe were always around for this exercise, cooing and murmuring over the diminutive flickers like they were new puppies.

"Ohhh, look at that...so cute!" Chloe reached out a slender hand to pet it.

"Can I hold it?" Taylor was amused to find Daphne could lift the fire off her palm to stroke it and then put it back. She couldn't help herself; she was so enamored with Taylor's little flames. Taylor realized she was practicing more often and improving her talents just to come up with new amusements for the two Will-O-Wisps, like skittering a flame puppy across the floor while it played with a toy, just like a real one would. Successes sometimes came with mistakes, however. Forgetting to specify how much flame she wanted one day was an error she didn't care to repeat, and it had taken both Daphne and Chloe to absorb the inferno before it did any real damage. But Olivia simply made her repair the house where she'd burned it and she learned some new skills doing it. Mistakes were to be expected she was told, but only a few of them. "Think it through first," Olivia had said, "*before* conjuring."

One morning Taylor was practicing levitation, trying to focus. She had started with small objects with Olivia teaching her: "In your mind, reach out your hand, pick it up, and hold it there. Then remove your hand but leave the object." Over and over she pictured it, but nothing happened until Olivia coached her: "Let the energy flow through you and wrap what you want with it. Then command it to obey." Taylor could tell when she succeeded; the feeling rushed through her, electric and thrilling with a sharp intake of breath in response to the jolt. Then her object was there, floating in front of her. She marveled at its supernatural behavior. The thing was suspended and she had done it herself!

Her mark today was larger, an old Kennedy fifty-cent piece she worked to levitate. It wasn't as easy as she had thought it would be. If her concentration slipped so did the coin and she dropped it several times, or it flew off to the side and she didn't know where it would go. Sometimes it tinkled to the floor where Bailey and Doobie ran to it, thinking it was a treat. She did need more discipline, she thought, just as Olivia was always pushing into her head. Still, the thrill and wonder of doing it at all wasn't lost on her.

Over lunch one day Olivia told her about spells. "There are such things as magic words. They help you focus power or make things happen for you."

Of course, Taylor was curious. "How do they work?"

"It's something called True Name. Each sound has its place in the magical logos, and that sound can make something happen. A spell is sounds creating a path to more complex magic. That's why most magic words and spells don't make sense."

"What about amulets and potions? What are those?"

"You infuse an object with whatever magic you want and send it off to work later."

"Like a love potion?"

"You're not supposed to do that. It's against free will." Olivia looked serious. "It's very difficult to do, anyway."

"Why are there so many stories about it?"

"What a powerful notion – to be able to choose anyone you want and make them love you? Probably everyone has wished for that. But the blowback for forcing someone against their will is harsh."

"Like what?"

"If you abuse magic, or are mean or selfish with it, it will turn back on you. Or eventually it drains you. It can sap you dry. You can be rich and have fun, but you need to give back. Be nice to people. Protect people or help them – give money to charity, even. But do good with it or it can all come back on you."

"Like karma."

"Like karma." Olivia nodded.

"Will we make potions or practice spells?"

Olivia shook her head. "Not till later. I don't want you to become dependent on them and right now it's more important for you to build your strength." She didn't need Taylor playing with magic. She wanted Taylor to protect herself.

"Come on. Time for afternoon lessons."

After weeks of so much input, Taylor felt burned out. Work, work, work. Practice, Practice, Practice. It was like drinking from a firehose. She had learned to hate the phrase, "Do it again." And she missed her sister.

Now she sat on the couch, sapped of any interest in magic and wishing for leisure time. She looked at the greys lying on their sides, flat on the carpet, eyes closed and mouths slightly open, as if closing their jaws were too much effort. *I would love to be them... not a care in the world.* She decided to tell Olivia, and this time she wouldn't back down.

"Olivia, I'm exhausted – I just can't do it this afternoon. We've been at this every day for weeks. It's beautiful outside."

Olivia looked at her apprentice and saw she was serious. "Okay. Take the day for yourself and we'll do lessons outside tonight. We'll go downtown and I'll show you how to be invisible."

Taylor went upstairs to her room and called her sister. She answered after six rings.

"Hi, Tay!" There were voices in the background.

"Hi, Karen. How's it going?"

"Fine. We're getting ready to go to a party. The women's crew team won their regatta today and Smith House is throwing a bash for them."

"Oh! What time is it there?" She'd forgotten Karen was on the East Coast.

"Six o'clock, but we're going to prefunction at Robin's and then go over around eight."

"Sounds like fun."

"I love it here! The classes are hard but that's okay. I have two papers due on Monday and a load of Political Science to study tomorrow."

Taylor wanted to tell her she was studying, too, but knew she couldn't. She realized she hadn't thought of a cover story for staying at Olivia's.

"Did you find a job yet?" Karen's voice was loud in her ear; she was trying to talk above the other voices in the room with her.

"No. I'm trying to decide what I want to do." A slew of stories popped into her head, but she knew whatever she told her sister had to be carefully constructed.

"Well, I'm sure you'll get something. Or maybe you could start at community college and then transfer to a university." She took the phone away from her mouth to shout "Okay!" to someone on her end. "Hey, we're leaving now. I'm sorry I couldn't talk longer, but I didn't know you would be calling."

"That's okay. Have fun. Be careful."

"I will. I love you, Taylor."

"I love you, too, Karen."

"Bye." Dead air signaled she had hung up. Well, that was unsatisfying, but she was glad she'd called and Karen was enjoying herself. This was all harder than she had thought it was going to be.

When evening finally came and they left Olivia's the sky was a pale violet with scarlet and golden streaks over the Olympics. They decided to take advantage of the late summer warmth and walked downtown while Olivia explained invisibility and Taylor practiced. She was startled when someone suddenly walked through her and she could read their feelings. After that she stepped aside if at all possible but easily mastered the art of being transparent.

They walked to Seattle Center, passing the Space Needle in all its glorious kitschiness, golden elevators traveling up and down its thin stem. One place Olivia truly liked was the Pacific Science Center with its light and airy quintet of gothic arches rising a hundred and ten feet over reflecting pools. No walls marred the beautiful skeleton of renaissance-inspired architecture. It was open and lacy, exactly what the original architects had been trying to achieve. They stopped to enjoy it and Olivia turned to her witchling.

"See that black building over there? The tallest building in downtown?" She pointed to the Columbia Tower. Taylor nodded.

"Meet me there, on top of it." Then she was gone.

Taylor looked at the Columbia Tower. It seemed a long way away. *Really, Olivia? Seriously?* She focused on the building and tried to be there, imagining herself joining Olivia but failed, leaving her standing on the sidewalk. She concentrated again, taking in the three curvilinear edifices of the building. It was a beautiful thing, all dark and powerful looking. Smoked glass windows made it a massive obelisk of black onyx, standing upright and supporting the sky. It was a mile away at least. Clenching her teeth, Taylor set her mind to appearing there and joining Olivia ... and nothing happened. Repeatedly. *What am I doing wrong? She said if I want something just picture it and let the magic make it happen.* She focused hard on the towers and then loosened, waiting for the energy to wash through her. Nothing.

Then she realized she was envisioning like a mortal, from where she stood instead of where she wanted to be. *Think as a witch, believing you're already there.* Of course! If she pictured it in the distance she would remain right here. The moment she thought it she was next to Olivia, who actually looked surprised.

"You didn't think I would make it, did you?" Taylor said. Then a wave of exhaustion lapped over her and her knees wobbled. Stepping back from the edge she sat down abruptly on a metal rail behind her. Olivia sat beside her and shook her head, smiling.

"I'll be damned."

They sat in silence a few moments, Taylor waiting for her unreliable legs to settle. Big magic for a newbie; Olivia wasn't surprised Taylor was spent. She sat down next to her, waiting for her to recover while they both looked around, appreciating the view. From this perspective, the crown of the closest building was a mammoth structure and the effect was breathtaking. City lights reflected off the vertical walls of glass below, the last remnants of it sparkling up into the night air. The city spread out below them and across town the gothic arches at the Science Center were only inches high.

Looking around, Taylor saw the rail she was sitting on edged the roof, attached to a scaffold for window washers. She leaned forward to peek over the precipice. Sleek black windows stretched straight down a thousand feet and for a millisecond she had a sense of falling, but it passed, replaced with the thrill of so unnatural a sight. That surprised her: liking the black glistening span and the danger of being so close to the drop. It was breezy up here as well. Taylor could hear ribbons of wind curving around the buildings and she stood up, placing her feet wide to let it tug at her clothes and hair. She lost herself in the feeling, making small adjustments in posture to counterbalance the ebb and flow of the mistral. It was scintillating.

They could easily see Lake Washington with both its bridges, now glittering with strings of head-lights. They moved to the east side where they were protected from the breeze and looked across the water. The minitropolis of Bellevue was nestled there, the tiny clutch of skyscrapers glowing, lit from within. Taylor had a question she'd been burning to ask.

"Olivia, why all the bad press for witches? If we have to use it for good, then...."

Olivia thought a moment. She didn't want to tell Taylor about Dantin or about the blood tint yet.

"Way back, there were two kinds of witches – real witches, and people who just knew about medi-cine, or poisons and potions. People came to them for healing but also asked for evil favors, too. Revenge on a neighbor and things like that. Even if a real witch wouldn't use magic to hurt, people were afraid because they thought we would. Then organized religion trying to wipe us out didn't help any, either. They portrayed us horribly."

Her lips tightened. "What they didn't know is that most witches protect innocents from the malicious chimera out there. Usually it was them doing the things people were blaming us for."

It took Taylor a moment to absorb this. She thought of Daphne and Chloe and Eidolon and all the things she'd seen so far. None of it seemed evil.

They moved to the west side, where greenish-black water stretched between Seattle and Bremerton. Brightly lit ferries crossed it, at the moment looking lonely and small as their lights passed each other in the dark. The Olympics were invisible in the night blackness; only a few dots of light showed there was anything out there.

Directly below them was Pioneer Square and its canopy of trees. The light was yellowish there, like Victorian gas lanterns. There was a darkness and dullness about it that Taylor could read. It felt... guilty, like trouble or some lurking bad intent was down there. It made no sense – she had been there both during the day and at night and it was a lively area. She asked Olivia.

"Why does it feel like that?"

"That part of Seattle is very old. Magical energy builds up over time and a lot has happened there. You feel shadows of happiness but violence and sadness, too. Fear, grief, and anger release stronger energy than anything else and that adds to the logos. Remember we talked about the logos, the essence permeating everything? You pull on it for magic?"

"Yes."

"It's saturated with essence down there. On its own it's just sortilege, part of all the sorcery that exists. Whether it's bad depends on what it's used for and how it's paid back."

Taylor nodded. The place was vibrating with magic. It pulled at her and she wondered if her powers would be stronger down there. She looked at her chaperone who was gazing intently down at the darkened square, the breeze lifting strands of russet hair across her face and luffing the collar of her jacket.

"Olivia, why are we here?"

Olivia turned her head slightly but kept her eyes on the neighborhood below. "Why are we on this building or why are we over Pioneer Square?"

"Why do we exist? Witches."

Now Olivia did look at Taylor. "Honestly? I don't know. No one has ever told any of us some all-encompassing reason we're here. Are we supposed to do something special here? Sorry, Taylor, I just don't know that one."

"Could it be that we're supposed to take what was evil and reuse it for good? Maybe we're supposed to rebalance the logos everywhere so it's positive. Or protect humans and weaker witches?"

"It does seem like it should work that way doesn't it, giving back and all..." Olivia mused.

They both returned to the murky square below. Patrons could be seen moving under the trees between bars and restaurants and art galleries. It was Tuesday night and a flight of patrons came out every week in good weather for the Art Walk to support local artists.

Olivia gestured. "It is full of power, though, and you can use it. Reach out to it – feel it and pull it to you. Inhale it, Taylor." There was intensity in her voice.

Taylor concentrated on connecting. She breathed in deeply to draw it toward her and immediately felt it come, a freight train thundering toward her. Her fingers warmed, then stiffened, followed by an impact through her chest that knocked her back on her heels. The voltage of power raced through her, expanding her lungs until she was bent back, her face to the sky and her arms wide. She shook with the feeling.

Too quickly it passed and left her permeated with a glowing, buzzing feeling. She lowered her head and looked at Olivia.

"I never knew anything like that could exist."

Olivia smiled. "Taylor, there's so much out there. Just you wait and see." She stood, adjusting her jacket and cuffs and tipped her head toward Capitol Hill. "Why don't you take the two of us home?"

"Do you think I can do that?" Taylor was astonished, remembering how hard it had been to get here.

"You just had a flood of magic fill you. If there's a problem I'll help, but I'm sure you can take us both."

Taylor easily pictured them standing in the breakfast nook with its two slipper chairs; it was her favorite place in the house aside from her own room. She didn't want any distraction, so taking a deep breath she turned her face to the sky and brought her hands to her chest, fists clenched to concentrate her power in one spot. She felt the rush, the electricity, and it made her dizzy for a moment. Then the stars disappeared and she knew without doubt she had been successful. When her vision cleared both she and Olivia were home, exactly where she had pictured. Yes! They were home, and she had done it herself! Trying to settle down, Taylor focused on slowing her breathing, leaning forward to rest her palms on the curved countertop and enjoying her success while Olivia stood watching in her usual quiet way.

But Olivia was worried. Now that Taylor had rocked the logos, everything would know she was here.

"I think we're ready. Can you show me, Eidolon?" Olivia opened herself and waited for her chimera to take her into the logos. Today they were testing Taylor. Olivia had taught her protection spells and discipline, and how to keep herself closed to prevent a chimera from possessing her against her will, but there

CATHLEEN DUNN

was nothing like practice with the real thing. She and JaneAnn had argued heatedly about it the day before.

"Olivia, you need to tell her what you're doing. You can't just set one on her and watch. She'll be terrified."

"You don't always get any warning. I want her to learn to keep her guard up. Daphne and Chloe tell me they've had to deal with more of them lately, so they're becoming attracted to her."

"But at least explain what's going on."

"I will. After."

JaneAnn's tight lips told her she didn't agree, but she said nothing else. They'd been having this disagreement for the past week with no different outcome.

Now Olivia was out in the logos, looking at it from Eidolon's point of view. They could see Taylor in her room, the scene spread out like a movie beneath them. Approaching them was another chimera, the one Eidolon had suggested for testing Taylor.

"And you're sure we can trust this one?"

"Absolutely." She could hear him in her head. Olivia got right to the point with the other chimera.

"Don't go easy on her, but if you get in you have to give her up right away."

"I have no interest in staying. I've been in mortals before, but I'm not a sensation junkie like some of us."

Olivia was quelled but only slightly. "There are two Will-O-Wisps watching her just in case."

She could feel the other become wary. Daphne and Chloe could snatch a spirit or anything else and be gone with it before it could react. Olivia had seen them do it before – a flare, a grab, and in an instant the thing was gone. And they liked Taylor; they'd be all over this one if it tried anything at all. Still, Olivia had a knot in her stomach.

"Let's get it done."

Taylor was in her room, practicing as Olivia had told her to, stretching her powers by reaching further out to pull in more energy, then using it to conjure or explore the logos. She was relaxed now, used to compassing the netherworld that Olivia had opened up for her that first day. She barely glimpsed the dark thing, an amorphous shadow that rushed her so quickly it was barely an instant before it engulfed her. The feeling was overwhelming: a body rush, adrenaline, then tingling everywhere and an explosion of hotness in her chest. She felt … hunger? Hungry. Yes, definitely. Ravenous, in fact. For food and for dancing and sex and bright colors and excitement. She felt joyous and filthy at the same time: emotions, sensations, anger and rage, lust and embarrassment, hysteria and laughter stretched her to breaking. She was feeling everything possible, and all at once.

Then terror began…extreme terror. She was suffocating in a tube of her own sensations, being sucked down. She tried to call Olivia but was being muffled and heard herself scream as if far away. It was like swimming in molasses and she couldn't get out.

Then came Olivia's voice, tiny and faint. *Taylor!* But she couldn't move and crawled slowly toward the voice without progress until suddenly whatever bound her released her and she found herself back in the workroom with her hands on Olivia's forearms, gripping tightly.

"Taylor!"

She looked around, astonished, and then burst into tears. Wide eyed and frightened, she clung to Olivia.

"What the hell was that? What *was* that?" The feeling of carnage was still sharp and she melted back into sobs.

"That was what I told you to be careful of – a chimera."

"Like Eidolon?" Taylor couldn't imagine Olivia's familiar doing such things.

"No – that was a stranger. It tried to take you."

"Why?"

"Because you let it."

"What?" Taylor was shocked.

"Keep your guard up all the time. Don't just trust whatever happens to come by."

"I didn't! It came at me so fast I didn't have a chance to defend myself."

"Then you'd better defend yourself all the time, whether you think something's around or not. Where those things come from there's no color, no taste, no fragrance, no sensations like the sun on your skin, or music or sex. They want to experience that and will do anything to get it from you."

"I..." Taylor didn't know what to say. Olivia was relentless.

"Look, your mortal body with all its delights and emotions is an irresistible toy. Don't let one take you or your life will be hell, so you'd better learn to stay sharp."

Taylor's hurt and confusion burst out of her. "You don't even seem to care what I just went through! It's as if you don't have feelings!"

"Taylor, I'm sorry if I seem tough sometimes, but I'm responsible for making sure you stay safe."

"Can't you do that and be a little nicer? Why do you always have to be so cold, so businesslike?"

"Taylor, how could I possibly have prepared you for that? You would have been terrified before we even started. Now you've been through it and it's done and you know all about it."

Taylor was still expressionless, absorbing the words. Right now she hated Olivia. "Just leave me alone."

Olivia stood up and left Taylor's room, going down the hall to her own room where she closed the door, leaning back against it. She could still see her novice, her big green eyes, the tears making her lashes stick together in little points. What an innocent. Olivia thought she was going to be sick.

A few days later Olivia stopped by Taylor's room. There was an uneasy, silent truce between them. Taylor had been trying to convince herself that Olivia made a sort of twisted sense but they'd hardly spoken. Hard to believe only two weeks earlier they'd celebrated Taylor's success on the Columbia Tower. Now Olivia stood uncomfortably in her open doorway.

"Hey, Taylor, I need to go out to my horse property tomorrow. I'm hosting a polo match to raise money and I'd like it if you came along."

"Horse property?"

"I own a home by Lake Sammamish that has horses and stables."

"And we're going for a polo match?" Taylor looked like Liv had asked her to examine a squashed bug. "Isn't that for stuffy rich people?"

Liv shrugged. "Come and see for yourself. At the very least, the place is beautiful. If you've never ridden a horse I'll show you how."

That sounded all right. "Do I have to get dressed up?"

"No, polo's like the Kentucky Derby; some people dress up, some don't. Most people your age will be in jeans so wear yours and maybe that plain white shirt you have. You can wear that riding, too."

In the morning Olivia came down in something similar, dark blue jeans and a button-down shirt with soft stripes and a feminine curved hem. She wore black riding boots with low heels and had a garment bag over her arm. "I'm bringing dressy clothes because I'm hosting the event, but you don't have to change. I'll introduce you as a relative from Minnesota or somewhere."

"Oh, thanks. Minnesota. Do they even play polo there?"

"Oh, sure. They have an all-women college team, too. More colleges play than you would think. Wazzu in Pullman has a team. Look, if you don't like Minnesota you choose where you're from."

The ride was quiet except for a few polite sentences between them. Neither was sure how to make up for what had happened. They rode the 520 bridge over Lake Washington, past Kirkland, past Marymoor until the scenery turned pastoral. There they took an exit onto a two-lane road where brilliant green meadows stretched between the few homes there. Barns and houses matched and even the farm equipment was perfectly accessorized on manicured acres. Like pictures of Kentucky horse farms, Taylor thought. Laying her head out the window she gazed up at the canopy of trees overarching the road. In the August sun the dark green leaves made a broad living tunnel over them and Taylor breathed in the summer air that whooshed past her face. It was nice to be somewhere new.

Olivia turned onto the circular drive of a house painted white with black trim and nestled in huge clusters of purple pansies. The broad picture windows were cupped by black shutters and a curving sidewalk approached the front door. They parked and got out, Taylor standing a moment to look around. Matching outbuildings seemed to spring up out of flower beds and lawns and a running horse weather vane adorned the roof to complete the storybook design. Olivia walked them over to the stables where people and horses were a crowd of activity.

"Let's go for a ride. I'll show you the property so you know your way around. Later I'll be so busy you might end up on your own."

Riding horses turned out to be easy. Taylor was intimidated by their size, but they were sweet, putting their noses in her ear and snuffling her. They rode around until she had a general idea of the layout while Liv explained the agenda for the day. When the polo players arrived, looking lean and tan as they disappeared into the stable, Liv checked her watch.

"Guests are starting to arrive, too, and I need to greet them. You can keep riding if you want. The teams will come out in about an hour." She heeled her horse in the ribs and trotted back to the stables.

Left on her own, Taylor stayed on horseback; it gave her the feeling she belonged. She loved the beauty of the place. Sun lit up the long blades of meadow grass, making them look greenish-gold, and the sky was a robin's-egg blue with white puffy clouds in the distance. She rode to the large white tent where caterers had filled tables with food in silver chafing dishes and added mounds of fresh flowers to make the whole thing more opulent. She was amazed how a plain piece of lawn could become a lavish and elegant restaurant, but she could also see people tailgating in the parking area, setting up impromptu picnics at their cars just like at football games. Certainly not what she had expected. She headed back to the stables, riding as close as she dared to the polo team. She could see a sliver of view into one of the stalls where a pony was being prepared. There was a smooth curvy saddle, then long strips of soft fabric was wound around each of the horse's legs, and after that shin guards went on over the wraps. Another person braided the tail, neatly tucking the long strands of hair into a little loop at the end and securing it. When they finished the pony looked light and swift but sturdy and well-protected. Taylor realized she was looking forward to this game of polo.

She gave her horse to a stable hand and walked back to the tent. Olivia had been correct; there were people in casual clothes and dressed up. She could see Olivia talking to some people by the buffet, her attire elegant, as usual. She wore her riding boots, a white shirt with a ruffled neckline, and a beautiful coat in brown velvet with a stiff collar and large buttons, like the ones colonial soldiers had worn. In the tent, people milled about, drinking champagne and laughing together as they waited for the match to start. Some of them held little cards in their hands. Taking one off a table Taylor saw it was basic rules of the game. Thank goodness, she thought as she read it; at least she would know what a chukker was.

The players came out and warmed up by cantering around the field, swinging their long handled mallets in pendulum-like arcs or sometimes complete circles. They all wore stiff leather shin guards from ankle to knee just like the horses, otherwise, the uniform was simple, white jeans and a shirt with a huge number on it and a leather hardhat. Without exception the riders were all lithe and good-looking in a polished athletic way, both the men and the women on these mixed teams. She turned her card over to read about the players and saw the ponies listed, too. They seemed to be as popular as the players. People were discussing them like athletes or celebrities, using terms like "handicap" and "made pony," "good confirmation," "skid boots," and "coronet boots."

JaneAnn saw her and came over. "Having a good time so far?"

"Yeah, but I need to Wiki this stuff. I have no idea what everyone's talking about."

"Oh, no worries. If you have a question you can ask anybody. They don't care if you don't know. They just want people to come and have a good time."

"I was surprised to see tailgate parties. That was great."

"Isn't it? There's a place in Texas that only charges ten dollars a carload to see a match, and they're usually packed. People tailgate and make a whole day of it. Do you want to sit with us, Taylor? We'll make room for you."

"No, I'm going to stay here where it's closer. But where are you in case I change my mind?"

JaneAnn pointed to seats in the grandstand about halfway up, then turned back to Taylor. "Be careful down here. See that line?" She pointed to the fat wooden beams delineating the sidelines. "That's the edge of the field and sometimes they run right along it so be sure you stay back a few feet."

"I will." Taylor promised.

JaneAnn turned to leave and then stopped. "Oh, while I'm thinking about it, there's a tradition at halftime called the divot stamp. Anybody can come onto the field and fix the chunks of grass dug up by the ponies. So I might see you out there."

"Thanks." Taylor watched her leave then returned her attention to the field. Riders had lined up facing each other where the two mounted referees were standing and then one of the officials bowled a small white ball between them. Immediately there was a scumble of legs and riders on the ball and she lost sight of it for a second, then saw it launch downfield about fifty yards. Immediately the riders were after it, ponies pivoting on their hind legs and launching into a gallop. Catching up to it one rider leaned over and smacked it with her mallet, sending it toward the number two player who hit it toward the goal, but a player from the other team was tight on her side, almost bumping her. When she took her shot it was wide, sending the ball out of bounds. The mounted umpire put it back into play, although Taylor couldn't tell who was supposed to have the ball at this point or why. It didn't matter though; the game was moving on.

At the far corner of the field there was a momentary tangle of horses as one rider tried to take the ball from the other, using his mallet to make the grab. He was unsuccessful, missing the ball entirely but snagging the other's mallet instead. *That'll probably be a foul,* Taylor thought, but it wasn't. She was surprised when she heard someone nearby exclaim, "Ohhh, hooked him!" and the game kept going.

One of the next plays came her way on the field. She heard the ball make a wisping sound as it rocketed past her and then actually felt the ground shake as ponies and riders pounded toward her after it. For a moment she saw details in slow motion, taking in the churn of the horse's front legs and pull of their chest muscles as they powered her way. Following the surging movement of neck muscles upward she could see equine faces challenge each other, locking eyes in sidelong fashion. One pony shouldered the other, shoving him sideways and eliciting a bump in response as the other put his head down, stretching forward to gain an advantage. Then they screamed past her, steeds and riders following the path of the ball. She realized her hands were numb and her heart was hammering from a rush of adrenaline. She snapped to the right so she wouldn't miss a millisecond. The riders were intent on the ball, heads down and making moves as the horses battled. They were horse and rider in one, each knowing the other and doing their piece. One player whirled her mallet in an arc with such speed it was simply a dazzle of wood. The tiny white orb was sent between the goal posts with about eight feet to spare and people cheered, shouting out their favorite numbers or horses and then urging them on as the game resumed.

Taylor was mesmerized and feeling a little breathless. She'd never seen anything so powerful and alive in her life. The players seemed to be everywhere on the field at once. Pretty soon Taylor gave up trying to understand the rules and just enjoyed the spectacle of these incredible animals and the figures atop them, jousting and jockeying for position while charging around at forty miles an hour.

After three chukkers it was halftime and the announcer called for the divot stamp. People fanned across the field like a river spreading out in a delta, flipping the tiny half-circles of sod over with a toe or an instep and mashing them down flat.

JaneAnn came by and took Taylor by the hand. "Come on. You have to try this if you want to be a true polo spectator."

She showed her how to flip the little half-circles of sod over with a toe and mash them flat with a nice "stamp" of the foot. Taylor's thick Doc Martins made it hard to get a toe under the divots. JaneAnn laughed. "You have the opposite problem I do. I'm wearing stilettos and I can flip them over but can't stamp without skewering it. You've got the perfect stamping boots." They spent half-time together, her flipping and Taylor mashing, laughing together.

"I think I'll sit with you the second half and see what it looks like from there."

"Fabulous idea." JaneAnn was all smiles. "Come on."

The second half started and once more the players were after the ball in a rush of legs and mallets. Sometimes, when the ball was going in one direction with the group it was suddenly launched the other way. Watching closely, Taylor gathered that if an opposing rider could get a mallet on it, they could hit the ball backward toward their own goal while running the other direction. Then the whole cartel would tumble to a halt, turn around, and follow it again at a run. The ponies were nimble and powerful – really equestrian athletes. She watched a black horse come out of a dead run by planting its front feet, bouncing a few times until its forward momentum stopped, then turn left with the last hop and start down the field again without even pausing. One rider leaned so far out of the saddle to put a mallet on the ball that he unbalanced his pony and the two fell in mid-stride, him out of the stirrups right onto the ground. His stallion recovered, springing up instantly, but then stood staring down at its rider with a "what are you doing there?" kind of look.

It wasn't all blurred movement and daredevil antics, though. At one point the game came down field the usual way, riders in a dead-out gallop while launching the ball toward the goalposts. This time it hit a divot and ricocheted straight up in the air, falling lifeless on the ground fifteen feet from the goal. All eight riders converged and were mincing around it, each vying for the chance to extricate it from the scrum and put back into play, but they were packed too tight. Suddenly the little ball popped out of the group like a chip shot in golf and rolled leisurely through the posts with all eight riders standing and still looking around for it as the official waved his red flag, signaling that a goal had indeed been scored. The laughter bounced around the crowd and then swelled as everyone got the joke. The whole afternoon was fun and handsome to watch, and Taylor was enamored with the game by the time it ended. She didn't even care who had won.

Taylor and JaneAnn descended the grandstand looking for Olivia and found her with a group of patrons. They waited almost ten minutes for her to finish with them, then another few came along to thank her for hosting the match. JaneAnn knew it might take an hour for Olivia to wrap up.

"You know it will be a while before Olivia can leave. She'll be thanking people and chatting up the team – all that sort of stuff. Instead of standing around why don't you catch a ride with me?"

They told Olivia and soon were driving back across the 520 bridge into the setting sun, a beautiful sight of scarlet and salmon in a Tiffany sky, the puffy clouds from earlier now edged with molten gold. Jane-Ann was driving along, recounting some story about her and Olivia when Taylor cut in.

"JaneAnn, why did Olivia ask me to be her apprentice?"

"What do you mean? You have the talent, so she asked you."

"Does she even like me? She's so...harsh, sometimes."

JaneAnn sighed. "There's a lot more going on with her than you see."

"She's not like that with you. Or anyone else. Is it just me? "

JaneAnn looked out across the water a moment, then back at Taylor. "Okay...let's go somewhere and I'll tell you about Olivia."

Knowing Taylor's love of things retro JaneAnn took her to The Oceanaire restaurant downtown, and when they walked in Taylor thought it must be like First Class on a 1930's ocean liner. Big band music by Tommy Dorsey carved the air, warm woods wrapped the walls punctuated with brass fittings, and crisp white tablecloths matched the crisp white aprons on waiters in tuxedos. She almost expected to see the bartenders wiping glasses with a cloth. The place was packed, yet they scored a choice booth in the corner.

After they had ordered beverages JaneAnn flicked a privacy spell around them, showing Taylor how as she did so, and then addressed her question.

"Liv really is a good person – maybe too nice."

"What do you mean?"

"She used to have an apprentice. They were tight, very close friends. But something happened and now Olivia doesn't want another apprentice. It really hurt her to lose the last one and she doesn't want to get attached again."

"Then why don't you train me? She doesn't want to."

"She has to. There's a reason for everything, and you crossed her path, not mine."

"But so what? What if you taught me instead?"

JaneAnn shook her head. "Everything has to balance out...and you can't always tell which piece is the counterbalance. I'm not messing with that."

"Where's her last apprentice now? What happened?"

"Here, I'll show you." JaneAnn placed her palm against Taylor's cheek and the Oceanaire fell away, replaced by a vision of antebellum Louisiana.

Taylor gasped, looking around her. Huge live oaks draped with Spanish moss graced a plantation house nearby, the surrounding grounds were fragrant with magnolias and bougainvillea, a kitchen garden of corn and squash and tomatoes and muskmelons shared a fence with the horses on the other side. Then she was inside the house where Olivia and a younger woman were being dressed in frothy gowns with layers of petticoats, laughing together, gossiping with the servants about the social life in New Orleans. The scenes swept over her: riding in the open carriage to cotillions and dinner parties, managing the business of the plantation

and shopping in town. One treasured purchase together was a beautiful walnut dining table followed immediately by frequent dinner parties. And magic, of
course. They adored working it together and delighted
in each other's abilities, using it to heal the neighbors'
animals, and their children, and the neighbors themselves, all uncelebrated and unknown to the populace.
She could hear snippets of conversation with Olivia:
the young woman's name was Celeste.

Olivia was smiling as she sat on Celeste's bed.
"Tell me about this new beau of yours," she asked, and
listened to the dreamy retelling of a wonderful, romantic evening at *Antoine's* restaurant, just Celeste and
her new lover. Lots of romantic evenings followed and
daytime trysts as well, along with promises to introduce Olivia soon to the mystery man.

But in the next scene everything was wrong.
Olivia was frantic, looking for Celeste every way she
could think of, scrying to see her and failing, transporting to places of shared memories yet finding no one,
physically running from room to room until she found
her in the parlor, on the silken settee. Olivia crept in
slowly, a step at a time, horrified to see her beautiful
apprentice, her closest confidante, in scarlet-tipped
pieces set up like some ghastly, broken porcelain doll.

In a daze she took in the dismembered limbs,
the delicate face now slack and tipped back on the
slashed throat, the gashed and blood-drenched dress

hardly able to hold the pieces propped up so purpose-fully, all arranged for her to see. Taylor could hear her as she tore at herself, blaming herself.

"How could I have not known this! How could I be so careless and let him trick us like this? To pretend to be someone else. And a *romance* of all things, to get to her! Goddamn you, Dantin!" She knelt on the floor and sobbed, her arms thrown across Celeste's slim torso. "Please forgive me..." she disintegrated into grief.

The despair Taylor felt from Olivia was crush-ing. She wailed inconsolably and the servants dashed in to help her but stopped at the threshold. Voodoo belief was deeply held here; no one would cross it.

"*It is Ouanga!* Go get the *gris-gris* bags!" Some ran off to get their bags of charms to ward off the evil spirits that were obviously here. Olivia's most loyal houseman tried to coax her out of the parlor.

"Olivia, there is bad here. You have to leave!" He looked frantic. But she wouldn't leave, shouting at them to take their belongings along with their free pa-pers and find another life. Then she set the house ablaze, holding her palms out until everything around her was licked by orange tongues and she watched Ce-leste's corpse blacken, then fall into rubble along with the charred settee. Olivia had no doubt Dantin had taken her powers when he had killed Celeste, but she was damned if she would leave anything else for him to desecrate. Turning away, she walked through the flames and across the lawn into the bayou where she let the mist swallow her.

JaneAnn took her hand away and Taylor sat silent, too shocked for words.

"Now you see." JaneAnn took a sip of her wine.

Taylor was replaying the memory again when a thought hit her. "JaneAnn, that was almost two hundred years ago. How?"

"A witch can live for centuries. It takes magic, but as long as you give back you can use it that way. One reason for the charities and such."

"What about Dantin? Giving back doesn't seem like it would be his thing."

JaneAnn smiled. "No, it's not. He's a Blue/Black, the tint in his blood. Witches like him are stronger than us, and can live an even longer time with a chimera possessing them. They both crave adrenaline and sensation, cruelty and power. But they can also steal the essence of another witch to add to their power. They kill them and take it."

"Why such a vendetta between the two?"

"Dantin and his chimera had the perfect set up. He was an Inquisitor. He had all the power and luxury and torture he could ever want at the stroke of his pen; even a word could bring a dozen people to his prisons. Then Olivia and a few of her friends exposed him and he barely got away from the stake himself. His familiar had to rescue him. And on top of that, he desired Olivia, had sent her gifts and romantic tokens for years, but she wouldn't have him. The first thing he did after she ruined him was get rid of her lover. He had a weapon forged with his blood in the steel so it was magically strong – and he cursed it, too, but I don't know what else it can do. Then he tracked them, found them, and ran them both through as they stood in each other's arms. Pinned them together with one thrust and Tristan took the worst of it. Olivia still carries her wound." She shook her head. "Dantin and Olivia have been at this a long time..."

She narrowed her eyes, suddenly adamant. "Taylor, you watch out for Dantin. Don't you let *anything* happen to you." She crossed her palm over Taylor's and a vision appeared there. "This is what he looks like. Don't ever forget. And here's a spell you can use to see if someone is Dantin in disguise. I wouldn't put anything past him."

"I promise to be careful." Taylor was shaken, still fresh with the memory of Olivia and Celeste and all this new information. JaneAnn saw she was rattled so she lightened the mood.

"Hey, do you want dessert?"

"I've never been to a place as nice as this. What do you think?"

"I know just the thing." She caught the waiter's attention. "Could we please have two Château d'Yquem?"

"What's a Château d'Yquem?"

It's a dessert wine, about five hundred dollars a bottle. There are some things in life you should try."

Taylor could hardly believe the tiny glass of golden liquid was eighty-plus dollars. She took a small sip as JaneAnn had instructed and held it on her tongue a moment, letting it warm, then breathed out through her nose. The taste was rich, like mellow gold all swirling and meshing with the softest clouds of summer fruit. Peaches, apples, vanilla ... the barest whisper of tastes, rich and smooth. Her eyes closed slowly and she stayed suspended in the mouthful of feeling until it dulled and slipped down her throat when she finally swallowed.

JaneAnn smiled with her. "Magic comes in mortal forms, too, doesn't it?"

So nice to be home alone. There was something about knowing the house was empty that was soothing for Olivia. Stretching her arms over her head she arched her back, feeling the tightness loosen, then flicked her fingers toward the fireplace and a few cozy flames licked the wood. It would slowly grow over time, burning down to embers as fires do. Olivia pre-ferred the natural rhythm of a real fire to a magical one that stayed steady no matter what. She knew plenty of witches who cast a bank of flames from noth-ing and commanded it to stay until released, but she liked something traditional, attached to reality. The armchair next to it was distressed leather, like the old-est pair of jeans that fit perfectly, and she sat in it to stare at the flames.

Bailey lay on the carpet, the firelight painting his tan fur with gold. He looked up at her, dark round eyes encircled in black, like Egyptian eyeliner. When his ears were up he looked like Anubis himself. *Adorable boy*, she thought, and slid from the chair to sit on the floor with him, cupping his face in her hands and rubbing his ears. They were both content, half-drowsing when a burning pain hit her shoulder and she sucked in a breath. Bailey whined, a small distressed sound, his ears pressed flat against his head. Olivia immediately transported him to another part of the house.

Dantin.

The pain got worse, nauseating her, immobilizing her. She put her head down and tried not to vomit. Then a smooth, masculine voice breathed into her ear.

"Ahh, my beauty. I've missed you." His hand caressed her hair.

She gritted her teeth, grunting against the stabbing under her shoulder blade and looked sideways up at him. "Get away from me."

"Now why would you say such a thing to me?" He ran his finger languidly along her arm, cutting her. The skin curled open behind his touch and Olivia howled despite herself. Dantin removed his hand, letting her breathe as he watched her. Then he put his face next to hers.

"So you have another apprentice for me. Your pathetic Will-O-Wisps aren't going to keep me off her."

"Stay *away* from her!"

Dantin regarded her placidly. "That's a stupid response since you know I'm not going to."

Controlling her breathing with effort, she grimaced at him. "Why do we even do this? It's always the same."

False surprise painted his face. "Because it is so delicious to see you like this. Maybe I'll kill your friends, too, JaneAnn and Alejo. Just for fun."

"Leave JaneAnn alone. She's done nothing to you."

"Well, that's not the point, is it? The point is you care for her."

"They're both fully trained witches – too mature, too clever for you. You would have done it by now if you could."

"And you know that for sure? Why would I play all my cards at once when I can stretch out your misery? I got rid of that halfling lover of yours, Tristan. I killed Celeste; I swallowed her essence. Easily, Taylor will be mine as well. No one you care for is beyond my sight..." He oozed with gloating over her.

Olivia was furious. She hated this agony making her weak. Dantin was inches away. *God, what I would do to you if...*but she couldn't move without searing pain. Dantin saw it and smiled.

"Yes, I know; my glaive still bites you doesn't it? My blood is in it. You can't use it on me." He looked around. "I know it's here with you. I can feel it. Oh, Olivia, I love you helpless like this. My favorite toy..." He smiled and touched her cheek tenderly as he disappeared.

By inches the searing under her shoulder dissipated and she was able to breathe. She screamed in rage, a guttural, echoing sound filling the room. But it was pointless, she knew. Just a placebo, an impotent gesture.

She heard Bailey whine outside her room and let him in, reassuring him. Doobie came in, too, lying beside him on the carpet, and they watched Olivia together as she went to her closet and opened the doors. Against the wall on the floor was a wooden box, staring benignly up at her.

Kneeling before it she lifted the lid and stared at the medieval glaive inside, broken metal pieces sharp and shining, even in the half-lit room. Her blood was on it, the red with the silver sheen, and so was Tristan's pale celadon blood, the color still fresh as if yesterday instead of three centuries ago. Three centuries... She missed Tristan. Her chest was still tight with loneliness for him, and sometimes she couldn't picture his face, which pained her as well, but she couldn't bear to make herself forget her feelings for him.

Cupping her hand she willed magic to fill it with a silvery fluid, like mercury. Pouring the fluid on the carpet she smoothed it to a glassy surface and looked into it, finding her memory there.

She was with Tristan, sparring with swords. She didn't need more practice at that point; it was just something they did together, like hunting or dancing or riding side by side. He lunged and she protected, then whirled for a downcut as he leaped back to avoid her metal. She lunged again, and again he avoided her, this time so quickly he was a transparent image of himself for a split second and she caught him at it.

"You cheat!" she laughed. "Using magic to get away." He had, it was true, using his powers to flash an extra few feet away when he saw her sword would strike him.

He mocked a hurt look. "What do you want me to do? Let you pinion me? I don't feel like stopping to heal a poke when we're enjoying this so well."

He raised his sword again, pointing it at her chest and looking her in the eye. A challenge! The game was on … their swordplay was quick, like an old Errol Flynn movie but oh, so much faster. The stone walls reflected the sound of their game, metal strikes and panting, until both stopped suddenly, showing that Liv had her knee on his chest and her sword at his throat. She laughed aloud with the joy of it – he had certainly bested her many times before – and stood up, offering her gloved hand to him.

He took it and rose, breathing hard and looking her over. "You have a couple cuts, but nothing much. I can fix those." He touched her arm and the injury was gone, then pressed a palm against her ribs where his sword had cleaved the leather and blood drooled down her bodice, leaving drops on her leather pants. At each press both her wounds and battered attire mended, showing no sign of the fight. She did the same for him then turned her face up to kiss him, which he returned with a tenderness that would have surprised anyone who had come upon them *en garde* moments before.

Forcing herself to stop, Olivia scooped through the mercuric liquid and lifted her palm, watching the rest stretch upward to it. She willed it to dissipate and remembered her arm now, feeling the rivulet of blood that ran down it. She passed a hand over the wound to close it, feeling the sting as her arm repaired.

She looked again at the glaive in its box. How many times had she stared at it like this? She'd never yet thought of a way out... Then with a start her eyes widened. Suddenly she needed to talk, and to someone she knew well.

She tapped an international number into her cell. After only two rings a male voice picked up.

"Olivia!"

"Hi, Alejo. How are you?"

"Fantastic – just going out after dinner." She knew he would be up late; in Buenos Aries dinner never started before nine and the nightlife he loved ran even later. It was only midnight there.

"What are you doing tomorrow?"

"You tell me – what are we doing tomorrow?"

"Have lunch with me here? If you don't have previous plans?"

"Absolutely. What time? I'll come to your house." He was witch; it was easy for him to transport himself to her. They agreed on the details and then he had to hang up. "I'm sorry, but I'm with friends and the valet is just bringing the car." In the background Olivia heard voices urging Alejo to come away.

They said their goodbyes and Olivia returned to the metal pieces glinting in their nest, tapping her finger on the edge of the wood as she studied them. Then she closed the lid on the glaive and pushed the box back into the closet.

The Center atrium was open, a mezzalune column of air that cut through several floors bordered by shops, offices, and a huge wall of glass against the street. Palomino's embraced one side, displaying its décor for all to see. Alejo loved it immediately: the dark woods juxtaposed against white frosted glass, wide burgundy columns supporting a coved ceiling of soft pumpkin, the art pieces of tiger-striped glass. Sparkling halogen lights dusted everything with brilliance. It was a decadent combination of oversized and delicate and colorful, like twenty-first century baroque.

Local celebrities and professional athletes came here hoping to be seen as they indulged in the food, much to the delight of ordinary people at tables nearby.

A couple of women recognized Alejo, whispering that he was the man from the magazines, the one on the polo pony. He smiled at them as they sat down, causing a miniature stir at their table.

"You just can't help yourself, can you?" Olivia laughed at him and then spelled the table so they could continue talking candidly about Taylor.

"I think she's coming along well. She learns fast. I've loaded her up with every defense and protection skill I can think of."

"And how is she adjusting to all this?"

"Fine, I guess."

"You guess?"

"She's doing fine."

"You said she had a sister?"

She didn't want to get into details with him. "She hasn't said a whole lot and I don't want to pry."

Alejo raised an eyebrow at her. "Just teaching her magic and nothing else, then? Well, bring her to the match in October. We'll all want to meet her. You said the only other witch she knows is JaneAnn."

"Yeah...and of course she's been around since we started. They even went out for a drink last night, but mostly Taylor's been busy working her skills."

"Then it will be good for her to go to Houston and meet everyone. She needs to know her family. Has she ever been there?"

"I don't know. I don't think so. You know, I don't think she's been anywhere much." That suddenly hit Olivia, remembering what she'd seen when she and Eidolon had scryed her. "I'll fly her down and show her around Houston."

"What about JaneAnn?"

"She's going beforehand. She wants to visit with Beth and Marcus and Julia before everyone else arrives. She's staying with them at the Big House."

"So, today we are here for what, then? Just a nice visit suddenly?"

"No. Dantin graced me with one of his visits last night."

"Oh. Hell... Are you all right?"

"Nothing I couldn't fix, but no – I am not all right. I can't live like this. There has got to be an end to it and at this point I really don't care what I have to do."

Alejo was alarmed. "You can't do that; you're a Silver-Tint. We can only help or heal with our magic and revenge is not returning good. You don't know what the blowback will be, Olivia. Besides, you don't have anything that can kill him. He has gained something additional from every witch he has killed."

"I have the glaive."

"...and he can tell whenever it's around. And who knows what else it does; it's his blood in it. Besides, how could you possibly plan anything with him stalking you constantly? He must have spies or something. He always seems to know what you're up to."

"I know..." She looked miserable. "I wouldn't even know how to ask for help without him knowing." She reached across the table for his hand. "I wish I knew a way out of this..."

Alejo looked startled, glancing down to her hand on his hand. His expression softened. "I can't stand to see you go through this either, but..."

Olivia looked at him intently. "I just want you to understand me – where I'm at."

"I do." He studied her face for a moment and then took his hand away. "We're okay. Here, let's just eat." Their plates had arrived and he focused on his food. She'd slipped him a wordless plan through a charm when she had touched his hand. Damned clever woman. It might work if they could keep it secret – and if the magic behind it was sound. He could feel her resolve, too, when she touched him. She was done with Dantin tormenting her, one way or another.

Alejo was right. Dantin did spy on Olivia. Right now he was watching them both through the eyes of a man at the table next to them. It wasn't that hard; all humans had a little witchery in them and he could tap into it by sending his chimera to envelop them. It was such a weak connection they couldn't even feel it, but he could see what he wanted almost anytime, anywhere. It was hard to hear them through such a weak connection but he wasn't too worried.

The Silver-Tints are stupid, he thought. They could probably combine efforts and do him some real damage, but they had this pathetic code of only doing good with their powers for some reason. Still, they were weaker than Blue/Blacks. They drained easily unless they gave back to the logos and he was happy not to be one of them. He'd heard it had been different in the past, but that was so long ago the stories were just fragments, bits of legends that were so diluted they weren't reliable.

He was suddenly very annoyed. Olivia was one of those stupid Silver-Tints and yet he craved her. He was obsessed with her, wanted her, thought constantly of her day and night. He loved her; he hated her. He hated how much he loved her and she didn't love him back. He wanted to hurt her for it, destroy something she loved so she would feel how much she had hurt him.

He had plans for her apprentice.

Practice. Practice. Practice. Taylor continued to practice everything she had learned. In the meantime, the sun set earlier each night until it was dark by five. Day after day heavy grey clouds pressed down on the city, obscuring the roof of the Columbia Tower where only a month earlier they had stood in the late summer night. Even the Space Needle, at half its height, was wrapped in drizzle and fog. Water dripped slowly and constantly off everything, bending little branches and twigs with its weight and filling the rain chains suspended from houses. Little upside-down bells, filling with clear water that ran in rivulets to overflow into the next cup in line, all the way to the ground. At night, the water settled along bare branches and made little silvery slivers of reflected moonlight. Life seemed to slow down in a cocoon of mist and constant half-light.

Taylor saw less of Daphne and Chloe lately, ever since Olivia had tested her again with the chimera and found she could keep it at bay with little effort. Once she had learned to keep up a barrier, it was easy to maintain. Olivia told her to keep it that way until she was fully trained and wanted a chimera of her own. Still, her Will-O-Wisps flared up every once in a while to visit and proclaim aloud that they were still around, even if they couldn't be seen.

And of course, Taylor was out of the house to volunteer. She picked a few animal shelters to help at and loved the sweet little creatures, so deserving of affection. It floored her to realize that without giving back like that, living an indolent life of luxury and sorcery would be bereft of meaning, unfulfilling. The animals made her less lonely as she lay in her silken bedroom at Olivia's mansion, and now she could discuss volunteering with Karen on the phone, something Karen was also doing with her college friends. But Taylor felt she was drifting further away from her sister, who seemed to be having a magical experience of her own at school. Not only that, Taylor knew Jane-Ann had more in common with Olivia than she did, and although Olivia was marginally nicer lately it wasn't like they were friends.

She came home one day to JaneAnn and Olivia in the kitchen, having coffee as usual. They got together several days a week for this ritual, drinking and chatting away. Occasionally Daphne and Chloe were there, too, like today. They were sitting in the air as if on invisible chairs, flames cascading downward as they perched. Taylor sat down beside them on one of the slipper chairs, dunking her teabag in a cup.

"I don't mind the rain right now, but by New Year's I'll be ready to tear my hair out."

"Yeah, I know." JaneAnn agreed, "And it's dark all the time. Good thing there's the winter holidays to brighten things up."

"Hey, don't we brighten things up?" Chloe was pleased with her pun.

"Oh, you have the absolute worst jokes." Daphne shook her head.

Chloe ignored her, impatient to discuss something else. "Tell her, Olivia."

Olivia posed a question to Taylor. "How would you like to go somewhere warm?"

"Sure...but where? Like a vacation?"

"Like a vacation. We know a polo player from Argentina and his team plays all over the world. Next month they'll be playing a match in Houston and we're going there to watch. Have you ever been there?" She wondered if she'd been right about Taylor's lack of travel.

"No, never. When is it?"

"Last week in October."

JaneAnn cut in. "There's more, too. Since he's witch, a bunch of us follow his polo team and we're all going to a gathering beforehand at Marcus and Julia's ranch house. They have a huge place out by Lake Houston."

"How many? Are they all witch?"

"Almost all. There'll be over eighty of us there."

Daphne was tickled. "They always have the best get-togethers."

"I like JaneAnn's, too," Chloe argued with her. "But we had other plans in October..."

Daphne explained. "We thought with Taylor doing so well here, we'd go visit family."

"That's okay," said Olivia and JaneAnn nodded. "We'll all be there with Taylor. You go ahead."

The Will-O-Wisps were anxious to tell Taylor about Houston, but after a minute Olivia cut in with another surprise.

"So Taylor, you're going to meet more of us. But honestly, you can't go like that. You need a wardrobe and some sort of style." Her eyes traveled from Taylor's shoulders down to her feet.

Taylor knew Olivia never left the house without considering her attire. It seemed to be one of her greatest joys to choose fabulous cuts of clothing in fine fabrics and supple leathers to adorn herself. She looked down at her Doc Martens, faded jeans, and t-shirt and didn't know what to say. Taylor looked so uncomfortable Olivia couldn't help feeling bad for the once-over she had just given her.

JaneAnn quizzed her with narrowed eyes and a suspicious smile. "Olivia, where are you going with this?"

"Nowhere – she just needs something to wear in public."

"And you're taking her shopping. Lord help us." She turned to Taylor "No doubt she will disgust you with her extravagance. You know Olivia and clothes."

"JaneAnn, it's not a big deal. She just needs something more than what she has now."

"...and no doubt you have a whole day planned with a personal stylist and everything." She turned to Taylor. "She loves this sort of thing."

Taylor, wide-eyed and open-mouthed, simply looked at them both. Then she started to recover and thanked Olivia profusely, looking like she might even hug her. Now Olivia looked uncomfortable and tried to wave her off.

"Oh, it's no big deal. I just thought it would be fun..." She trailed off awkwardly.

Just then the greys sauntered into the room and flopped down on their big fuzzy pillows. For Olivia it was a perfectly timed intrusion. All three paused to watch as they curled up bonily and then Bailey, inhaling deeply after lying down, let out a long contented groaning sigh and closed his eyes. Doobie squirmed onto her back, feet up in the air, and feigned sleep, although her ears indicated she was listening.

"Well," said JaneAnn with a big grin, "saved by the bell, Olivia."

"Oh, Hell. JaneAnn, shut up." She looked at Taylor. "Be ready to go at nine-thirty tomorrow morning. We'll grab a latte on the way."

She picked up the book she'd been reading off the kitchen counter and disappeared into the living room. Taylor looked questioningly at JaneAnn, who simply burst out laughing.

In the morning, Olivia was already dressed and leaning against the doorframe of the breakfast nook when Taylor came down in jeans, Doc Martins, and her favorite Bettie Page t-shirt.

Liv looked her over. "Cute shirt. Could be adorable with a vintage jacket and some retro pumps. Do you mind?"

"Yours would fit me?" Olivia was smaller than Taylor, who was five-foot-seven.

Olivia looked surprised for a second, then: "Witchcraft, remember?"

Taylor felt a jacket enclose her arms and then her back. The shoes felt different, too. They were just...there. She looked down at them, marveling at the oval toe and t-strap. She fingered the sleeve of the jacket, loving the nubby soft material with little flecks of colored yarn in it. She looked in the mirror and

loved the whole casual-vintage-dressed up look immediately. The jacket nipped in at the ribs and had a little
peplum that made her waist look tinier, her hips
curvier, and her legs a million miles long. The jeans
and t-shirt kept it from looking too stuffy. "How did
you know?" she asked, looking at Olivia who now
stood with her arms folded and looking very satisfied
with herself.

"Bettie Page shirt. Dead giveaway. Ready?"

They spent the day in downtown Seattle shopping for Taylor. The stylist, Dara, asked her a zillion
questions designed to assess her needs and her style,
and then selected outfits which, although updated, had
a nod to the thirties, forties, and fifties. There was always an edgy piece to the look; studded suede shoes
with jeans and vintage jacket, or a laser-cut black
leather belt around an angora sweater and pencil skirt.
She loved the soft, rich fabrics and nubby textures that
would keep her warm and cozy in cold, drippy Seattle.
They also bought some basics: a dozen cashmere
sweaters in different colors, pants in both warm and
cool colors, three styles of jeans, some random tops for
a bit of fun, including a terrific Ramones t-shirt, and
narrow-waisted jackets in rich fall colors. Shoes came
next, and Olivia encouraged her to indulge her creativity. Adding to the studded pumps, she picked two different pairs of suede over-the-knee boots by Moschino,
each costing over a thousand dollars, some Marc Ja-
cobs ankle boots in red patent with a leopard fur lin-
ing, and Chanel pumps, one pair in black with

snakeskin embossing, and another in nude because Olivia said they would go with everything.

After dropping some really obscene money on attire, they hit an upscale salon which somehow made Taylor's own haircolor richer and gave her a sleek, full cut. Makeup, but not too much, finished off the look and she was amazed when they finally turned her toward the mirror. She never in a million days thought she could look this beautiful. Her eyes were huge and green and stood out with soft plum shadow that defined and enlarged the contours. The lashes were long and thick and the whole effect was gazelle-like. Creamy skin flowed smoothly over her face *Where did I get cheekbones like that?* and her lips were full but not overdone. She looked past her reflection to see Olivia watching with a contented smile.

"Come on. Let's have some lunch and show you off."

Olivia took her to Palomino's in the Atrium where they spent the next hour. Taylor was enjoying her new trappings. She felt polished and sure of herself for the first time in years – maybe the first time ever. *Amazing what a few ounces of cloth and leather can do*, she thought.

After lunch they walked back past the boutiques and through the revolving door where they were immediately stopped by rain. And more rain. It came down in misty waves that were separated by dots of rain in between. It made a spattering rumble on the glass awnings covering the sidewalk where several dozen people were ensconced, even ones with umbrellas. Seattleites were used to a soggy mess and constant drizzle, but this was rain mixed with wind that turned umbrellas inside out and blew up dresses and coats. Liv only stood a second, looking at the miserable sight before turning around and heading back through the revolving doors.

"The hell with this – come on," she said to Taylor. Scanning quickly she found a blind spot in the lobby caused by a short hallway and headed there, Taylor following closely. As soon as they were in the alcove they disappeared together, emerging in the hallway next to the concierge's desk at Nordstrom where they had stowed Taylor's shopping treasures.

"Why be a witch if you can't avoid slogging through a mess occasionally," said Olivia.

They picked up all of Taylor's new loot and were leaving the store when Olivia stopped them. It was still raining. "I'll take us to the car."

Taylor felt a familiar magical rush in her chest and suddenly they were on concrete in the parking garage walking toward Olivia's Mercedes. She felt woozy and nauseated and she stopped, shopping bags hanging at her sides.

"Will you let me know when you're going to do that? It's really unsettling if I don't know it's coming."

"Oh. Sorry. I'm used to either being alone or with an experienced witch. I'll try and tell you, but really, you get used to it fast."

"So now I know why people gesture; it lets you know something's coming."

Olivia opened the spacious trunk but not everything fit so they stuffed the back seat with their remaining cache, relaxing into the front seats as they started up the winding exit ramps. Taylor saw why they hadn't taken the Jaguar that day.

"Taylor, let's take a break from lessons," said Liv as they emerged into the grey light of the Seattle day. "Until Houston why don't you just practice what you know? Otherwise free time until then." She acknowledged Taylor's nod, and then turned on the windshield wipers as rain spatters obscured pedestrians in the intersection.

At home they dumped the packages on Taylor's bed for her to sort out and Liv left to change into something lazy and comfortable. Taylor settled into her own cozies – flannel pajama bottoms and an over-sized sweatshirt. Encased in haphazard comfort she pulled her beautiful new clothing out of the bags and laid it all out on the bed, fingering the soft fabrics.

"What do you think, Doobie?" She smiled down at the quiet black dog lying on the bed, nose just touching a pair of caramel-colored jeans and looking up at her with soft eyes. Taylor sat on the bed next to her, feeling her warmth while looking at the spread of riches. So many changes, so much that was new, Olivia's sudden generosity. It left her off-balance. She looked at her treasures for a while, finally putting everything in the closets and drawers. She left only some forest green heels out to decorate the dresser top; they were too beautiful to hide in a closet. Spooning with Doobie she reached behind her and pulled the comforter over them both, petting her warm fur as they both fell asleep for a welcome snooze while the rain pattered on the bedroom window.

At the other end of the townhouse Olivia hung up the phone after confirming travel arrangements. Watching Taylor made her remember that she enjoyed a life few people experienced. She didn't know if Taylor had ever flown, yet Olivia hardly thought twice about taking a private jet. She subscribed to an exclusive aircraft fleet with dozens of Gulfstreams, Dassaults, and Citations for her to choose from whenever she wished. She wanted Taylor to have this experience, to introduce her to everything out there. The girl had hardly had a life at all...her potential almost wasted except for a chance passing in the market by the two of them.

She had something else for Taylor, a talisman to give her. Looking at her desk she held her hand out and the drawer opened a crack to reveal a very old copper coin, a Barrowman's guilder from Antwerp, minted in 1546. It disappeared from its nesting place to settle in her palm, a soft shimmer tailing its movement. Holding it between her fingers she stared hard at it, concentrating, then palmed it and rested her cheek on her fist, staring into the fire. At first she was upset that JaneAnn had told Taylor about Dantin, embarrassed at her weakness, but then she was thankful she hadn't had to tell her herself. She also saw Taylor adopt a new earnestness about her lessons that impressed Olivia, and the spells JaneAnn had given Taylor eased her mind as well. In addition to the Dantin problem there were lots of things that would kill for the chance at a mortal life and Olivia was determined to give her apprentice whatever it took to protect herself.

She got ready for bed, glad to sleep late in the morning, but her night was spent in uncomfortable fits and wakeful moments interspersed with disturbing dreams, monsters, and things trying to grab her, but she could only move in slow motion when she tried to get away and could only mouth voiceless shouts at Taylor to run.

She finally couldn't sleep at all. *The worst time is the black, thick, middle of the night trapped with your own doubts, only your own thoughts and no one else at all who can help you.* She was afraid they were all on a closed-ended path.

Taylor stood next to the luggage in the entry waiting with Catherine and the greys, listening to Olivia upstairs as she took one last look around.

"Are these guys okay with Olivia leaving town?" she asked Bailey and Doobie's longtime pet-sitter. "I guess she goes off a lot, but they know you pretty well, taking them for their walks and all."

"Oh, yeah. We just hang. When she first got them they would look around the house for her when she traveled, but now they know when I come, special things happen. We go for car rides, to the park, once I took them to the zoo – they loved that."

Taylor laughed aloud. "Your clever ploy."

"Yeah," said Catherine. "They're two of my favorite clients – oh! I mean Olivia's one of my favorite clients."

Olivia came down and pulled her coat out of the entryway closet.

"I think we're ready. Taylor?"

"Yep. This is it." She pointed to her suitcases.

"Looks good – why don't we hang out in the kitchen until the car arrives?" She addressed Catherine, switching languages: *"Эй, Кэтрин, как ты сегодня утром?"*

Cath answered her without missing a beat. *"Я большой - две работы из-за этой неделе, однако. Рад, что остаюсь здесь один, где я могу учиться."*

Catherine attended college and this pet-sitting gig gave her flexibility with her school schedule. Olivia liked her because she was good to her greys, and more importantly the dogs liked her, so she always practiced a little Russian with Catherine when they saw each other. The three of them sat in the kitchen, Olivia and Cath alternating Russian and English until the driver came and put their luggage in the car for them.

Taylor remembered being astonished by the whole bag-carrying and being fussed over. She couldn't remember anyone ever opening a car door for her let alone carry her suitcase, and now here she was, was

sitting in a town car with a driver. She watched downtown slip away through the large windows, the Columbia Tower turning small and disappearing as they
traveled and then faced forward, settling back onto the
smooth leather and feeling rather special. She'd
brought her iPod and pulled out the earbuds as it was
a good twenty minutes to the airport. She didn't notice
as she spun up her music that they were already exiting the freeway, turning south to a mid-sized airport
bordered by small buildings and large hangars. When
the driver stopped and opened the door for Olivia,
Taylor was surprised they'd arrived already. Looking
outside, she expected to see the drop-off zone at the
commercial airport. Instead they were in a small parking lot with a posh looking lobby attached to the
hangar behind it.

"Where are we?" She was straining to see anything familiar.

"We're taking a private jet instead."

"You have a private jet? YES!" she burst out
with naïve abandon, giving Olivia exactly the response
she had hoped for. Olivia tried not to smile, watching
Taylor impatiently fidgeting in the parking lot as she
waited for the driver with her suitcases. The driver
couldn't help being amused, either, and he and Olivia
looked at each other, both enjoying Taylor's reaction.

"Taylor, you don't have to wait for him."

"Oh! Okay – where do I go?"

"Right through the main doors there. Give
them your name; they're expecting us."

"Okay." She walked up the steps so quickly she practically fell on her face.

Olivia looked after her indulgently as she pulled on her gloves. Then she smiled to the driver: "Thanks for the ride, Ben. Have a great week."

"Oh, I wouldn't have missed that for the world. Have a good trip, Ms. Phalen." He took the bags to the side door directly into the hangar.

Liv walked unhurriedly to the glass door and pulled it open, going from the concrete to deep pile carpeting. Two staff members at the front desk greeted her with professional warmth. "Good morning, Ms. Phalen. Ms. Moore is already in the club room. Any changes or updates before you fly today?"

"No, thank you. Everything stays as requested. How did Taylor do?"

"She's fine. We assigned someone to walk her through since it's her first trip."

Since it was a beautiful bright day, Olivia had requested they board the Gulfstream on the tarmac outside the hangar to give Taylor the full treatment. The jet had been pulled out and was warming up. They could hear the sonic whine of turbines as they walked toward the white plane, all slim lines and swift angles against the black asphalt beyond. Their luggage was being stowed in the aft compartment along with a square case that attracted Olivia's attention.

"I'd like that one up front with me, please – under my seat." She watched as it was removed and placed as instructed.

Olivia walked behind Taylor as she approached the jet and watched her, seeing her head turn to scan the jet from nose to tail. They both stopped a moment to drink in the sight, Taylor the aircraft and Olivia, Taylor as she approached and mounted the steps. Taylor stopped at the doorway and pressed her palm to the white enamel of the curved exterior.

For a moment Olivia was back in time, looking into an ornate *ormolu* carriage on a bright spring Paris day. As she had entered she had paused as Taylor did now, touching the gilded carvings beside the doorway, little rosettes and cherubs welcoming her into the tufted velvet interior bright with turquoise upholstery. She had gathered her wide satin skirts close to fit through the doorway and sit on the feather-filled seat. Looking around as the footman closed the door she had perused the little gold buttons holding the velvet in place, the delicate carved rosewood of the ceiling panel. She had heard the driver click the horses into a trot and the coach had started with a jump. She had felt ethereal and special being transported in such luxury, quite a change after the medieval years of hiding in poverty and the noise and filth of London. And now Taylor was stepping into this twenty-first century coach and looking around her in the same way.

Taylor gazed around the cabin as if in slow motion, taking in the lustrous wood interior. "What kind of wood is this?"

"It's burl wood." She waited and let her experience it.

Taylor touched the surface with her fingertips. "It looks like it's under glass."

"There's layers and layers of deep polish on it." The entire cabin was rich with wood, the curved interior panels all tan and brown swirling grain, glowing under the polish.

Liv watched Taylor as she moved through the cabin, looking at the caramel leather seats and long banquette set in along one side for sleeping or just stretching out next to the windows. "Flat screen?" She pointed to the plasma panel embedded in one wall.

"Yes, they set it up with some of your favorites. We can tap any channel or the movies or games they downloaded; I gave them a list of what you like. It's a long trip to Houston – three hours at least."

Surfaces glistened under halogen lights as she looked around. It was almost too much to take in at once. Then something broke into her dazzled vapor. "Look how big the windows are! They're huge – and round instead." She leaned over and looked through at the wide expanse of tarmac.

"You can see so much!" Then she sat on the banquette, looking right and left. "This leather is soft as butter."

"It is nice, isn't it?" The voice came from a crisp, well-groomed young man as he approached.

Olivia introduced him. "Robert is our attendant on this flight."

He looked down at the younger woman. "Nice to meet you, Taylor." He looked forward as the engine noise was suddenly muffled. "The crew just closed the doors, so that's my cue to make sure you're all buckled in. Taylor, could I ask you to change seats and move into this high-backed chair for takeoff? It's more secure."

After Robert buckled them in and went aft, Olivia leaned over to Taylor and whispered, "See? No different than riding in the Jag." That prompted a startled realization from Taylor; once riding in Olivia's Jaguar had been an unreal experience but now it seemed perfectly normal.

She looked out the window. Already the jet was taxiing out and clearance was prompt, one of the advantages of a smaller airport. Liv had asked for the tower/pilot communications to be audible in the cabin and they could hear what was going on between air traffic control and the pilots. They both liked the clipped, professional sounding pilots as they communicated with the tower. Kind of sexy, Olivia thought as she listened; it never gets old. A kind of audio porn.

After only a moment or two on the runway they accelerated, pushing Taylor back into the plush seat and bringing an adrenaline rush to her chest. The runup was short and the climb steep, taking them up and out over the Sound quickly before leveling out high above the San Juan Islands. The tower gave them clearance on their flight plan to Houston, then the compact airliner banked again to the southeast and they were on their way.

Settling in for the long flight, they unbuckled and stretched out in the cabin, Taylor lying down on the banquette and looking out though the large round windows at Mount Rainier below. Liv had the cockpit communication turned off, telling Taylor it was pretty boring during midflight. Then she picked up her purse. "I have something for you. A reward for working so hard all these months."

Opening the oversized clutch, she pulled a little copper coin from the side pocket. "It's a coin from Antwerp. Very old." She handed it to Taylor, who mouthed an "Oh" as she looked at it in her palm. It *was* old; Liv had not understated that. The copper was dull and slightly worn from all the hands that had traded the coin over centuries. One side was stamped "1546" over an image of what looked like two curved lines and a handle. A cart or something? She turned it over. A figure in flowing robes and the words "SANC-TVS ANDREAS" was stamped on the other side.

"What does it mean?"

"It's Saint Andrew. I don't know why he's on this coin, but I picked it because it's unusual. It's a coin for the Barrowman's Guild in Antwerp. In the six-teenth century the Barrowmen carted around all the materials to build the city by hand – without them it wouldn't have happened. Now it's the center of the world diamond trade. Here, I put it in a bezel with a bale so it can hang on your watch. You can wear it every day without putting on something extra." She took the coin, which was now locked to a sturdy link, and clipped it around the leather strap next to the watch face.

"I love it." said Taylor. "It's like a charm attached to my watch. I've never seen anything like it."

Olivia elaborated. "When people used to have watch fobs a hundred years ago they would hang mementos off them; today people hang charms off their purses. Same thing."

"Olivia, I love it! Thank you." She hugged Olivia, who looked startled but then relaxed.

"You deserve it." She tossed her bag aside and scooted down in the leather seat, stretching her arms out and up over her head with a yawn. "Look, let's kick back, do a whole lot of nothing on the flight, and then shop and feast in Houston before Julia's party."

They whiled away the long flight, Olivia reading and Taylor perched on what had become her favorite spot, the bench seat against the four large windows where she could recline and watch the ground pass by. The windows were huge, easily twenty inches across, and close together. Taylor loved the expansive view and how close the sky was through the glass. She could imagine being a bird.

Along the way the Rockies turned into high altitude plains, a broad swath of yellow and green earth stretched out below, then became irrigated patches of farmland in squares and circles of green as they descended, interspersed more and more with houses as they approached Houston.

Taylor had to give up her spot eventually, and reluctantly she returned to the high-backed seat and was buckled in, checked on, and approved for touch-down.

As they taxied to the private hangar Robert fussed over them, gathering up their possessions, asking how they wanted their items and arranging it all for them. He handed Olivia the square case she asked for and on their way out he gave them a warm good-bye.

The air outside was balmy compared to Seattle, which startled Taylor at first. She had forgotten that Houston was so far south and warm breezes came off the Gulf. The smell was incredible, all warm and green, but not like the northwest evergreen smell. This was grass and green sapling wood and warm water and... she couldn't describe it, but she could tell she wasn't anywhere near Washington anymore. The hotel had sent one of their limos to pick them up – another thing Taylor had never done in a day of firsts – and zipped them through tree-lined streets and into downtown. Taylor, with her window down all the way, enjoyed the semitropical weather.

Hotel ZaZa was the visual equivalent of an Austrian pastry display, textures and colors were eve-rywhere. Traditionally shaped furniture like Hepple-white curved-back sofas and Chippendale chairs were finished in metallics and modern graphic print or ani-mal pattern upholstery. Oversized crown molding painted in silver sat atop chocolate brown walls and

set off lush deep pile carpeting. Both women perused
the glory around them at length – Taylor because
she'd never seen its like and Olivia because although
she'd stayed here numerous times, she just plain loved
it. "Urban decadence" reviewers had called this. Too
right.

They each had a suite, different in style, on the
third floor. After they split, agreeing to meet in two
hours for dinner, off came their shoes and they fell
onto the furniture. Olivia immediately sank into one of
the zebra-print wing chairs in her sitting area and Taylor fell backward onto her bed, soaking in her surroundings. Heaven, she thought. Both luxuriated in the
fact that a fat week of balmy weather in a different
city with new experiences and no responsibility
stretched out ahead of them. Vacation mode was on.

They spent the next few days shopping at Nie-
man-Marcus and the myriad of small boutiques uptown, Taylor picking out lighter clothing for the
warmer Houston weather. Tops in gossamer fabric and
elegant embroidery, dresses in filmy georgette, and
pants of lighter cotton were her new staples. The cash-
meres and tweeds she had chosen in Seattle were uncomfortable here in the semitropical climate of the
Gulf.

The Museum District was everything Olivia
had said it would be and they spent hours wandering
around Hermann Park and visiting the museums. The
stainless steel exterior of the Contemporary Arts Museum was breathtaking, its sleek and kitschy contents

reminding Taylor of her suite at the hotel. The elegant Czech museum, with its delicate collection of crystal and beautiful baroque interiors looked like a palace, and the tiny Byzantine Fresco Chapel Museum was a miracle to be in. Simple white arches held up a tiny dome and apse from the thirteenth century. They looked up in silence at paintings almost a thousand years old, appreciating the intricate images and marveling at their age.

Lunch in an outdoor café afterward was a delight. They ate spicy barbeque and coleslaw which tasted nothing like their pallid remake in Seattle. Here secret spices were rubbed into the meat, followed by long hours of smoking the brisket or breast in a closed charbroil at low temperature, infusing it to the heart with dusky flavor. The sky above them was a deep blue bowl, and the Gulf air shimmered with rays of sunlight far more golden and direct than those that hit Seattle this time of the year. Ahhh. It felt buoyant and unrestrained. Nowhere like it, Taylor decided.

The next day there was the Houston Fine Arts Museum and the Meenakshi Devasthanam Temple, then the Houston Grand Opera at night. Olivia had asked the concierge to purchase loge seats for them at the opera and find out the name of the HGO's donations director. After a quick phone call and a $10,000 donation they were members of the donors club, a private room where patrons gathered during intermission and where trays of chocolates, hors d'oeuvres, and wine were passed out free of charge. Taylor was surprised she liked the opera as well as she did. The sets and costumes were beautiful, the music equally so, and it was easy to understand with the supratitles projected on a slim screen above the stage.

By the third night they were tired and hung out in Olivia's suite, watching old Marilyn Monroe movies and consuming popcorn and sodas that room service had fetched for them from a local theater. Nestled in big fluffy hotel robes they leaned back against the silk pillows that were threatening to overcome the padded headboard.

"So, Julia's house tomorrow night," said Olivia, popcorn in one palm and huge soda cup in the other. It made her look strangely juvenile instead of the usual sophisticated exterior.

Taylor asked over her Diet Coke straw, "What time should we be there?"

"It starts at sunset, around seven p.m. I'd like to get there a little later, like seven-thirty."

Wanting to make a good impression, Taylor asked, "What are you wearing? I don't have any idea what to expect."

"You can wear anything. People from every part of the world will be there. I've seen boubous, business attire, beaded dresses…"

"But you never look out of place. I'm afraid I won't really look right…what's the term? Putting lipstick on a pig?"

Liv looked surprised at that. "Where the hell did you get the idea that you aren't good enough to wear nice clothes?" She turned up on her elbow to face Taylor. "Listen, an old southern woman I used to know – she was mortal but so much common sense in her, the way those southern women are – would say 'It's not money that makes people high-class, it's man-ners.'"

She smiled at the memory, then shared the next thing the old woman would also say: "After all, you can dress up a really loud, trashy person and they act like jackasses, ruining all that dress-up. Now *that's* putting lipstick on a pig."

Well, she has a point... Taylor laughed aloud.

Olivia laughed, too. "Look, everyone will love you. Just be yourself, be polite, and you'll do fine any-where, anytime. It's a good rule to take wherever you go and trust me, I've been around the block."

Taylor smiled, relaxed, and leaned back on the pillows, feeling better. They finished watching *Gentle-men Prefer Blondes* and ate popcorn – just like any other couple of witches on vacation in a luxury hotel.

The next day was agony for Taylor, anticipa-tion eating her and making time drag. *What will hap-pen tonight? What will it be like at Julia's?* It was like waiting for Christmas.

She looked through her clothes that morning, trying to decide what to wear, laying out multiple out-fits, trying them on, discarding them, starting over. She finally settled on the wheat colored jeans and a garnet-colored silk top, her favorite caramel-and cream-colored cowhide heels and no accessories. *Oh great, I'm getting as bad as Olivia with the clothes,* she thought. But it felt good to have something in common with her mentor. She gave everything a last once-over. Feeling satisfied with her choices she went downstairs to get her hair and makeup done.

She was waiting under the hotel portico when seven o'clock came around and she watched Olivia walk easily through the lobby with long strides. They got their rental car from the porter and headed out to JaneAnn's, going up the Eastex freeway and taking the East Loop to the slower Beaumont highway so they could keep the top down. It was a warm October night, even by Houston standards, and the dusky sky was gorgeous. Pale greyish blue mixed with mauve, then turned scarlet at the horizon as they drove along, passing a variety of suburban, industrial, and finally wooded scenery.

They were long past Sheldon Reservoir and it was getting dark when Liv turned left up the Crosby-Lynchburg Road. A few jogs to the left and a turn off Main Street (is it a requirement that every town, city or borough have a Main Street?) sent them west toward Lake Houston, along South Diamondhead Road where the houses got larger and farther between until they were in a green expanse of trees. Olivia turned right on an unmarked, narrow lane.

The wooded drive up to the "Big House" as Olivia called it, was nondescript, if you didn't know where you were going you wouldn't know there was anything special at the other end. It opened into a broad meadow, and at the far side was a mansion lit inside and out with the obvious makings of a party. It was huge – a sprawling ranch house on two levels a quarter mile away through the tall grass. *They really do things big here in Texas*, Taylor thought as she looked around the meadow on either side of the drive. Subtle waves were visible in the grass from the evening breeze, created by the cooling twilight air as it settled.

There was a border in the green ahead of them, a kind of ridge she couldn't see clearly but the grass seemed to change, becoming perfectly still. Straining her eyes to focus she could make out a disturbance, like a mini-mirage, and as they went through it the feeling was electric, like the energy she pulled off Pioneer Square that night from atop the Columbia Tower.

"What was that?"

"It's a magic perimeter that JaneAnn, Julia, and Marcus cast for tonight's party. It's a pool effect – if you have a group of witches you can pool their powers and form a pretty handy privacy screen."

"I don't understand."

"Imagine an immense bubble over the house and gardens, one the ordinary world can't see into. It takes a lot of witchery to make one this big, but there are a lot of us here and it draws on everyone just a bit. From outside it looks like the same house and lawn. It's nice to relax and not worry some mortal will see your magic."

Taylor looked around as if the very air would be different, but no, it was just a beautiful Houston night. The trees ringing the meadow were just trees, the sky was filled with a bazillion simple stars. Looking to their left she could see a group of people standing in the knee-high grass. As they moved closer though, Taylor could see tiny glistening orbs bouncing in the air around the group.

She pointed. "What's that?" Olivia turned her head in that direction and then back to the road, completely blasé.

"I have no clue – could be anything in this setting." She kept driving.

Taylor continued staring at the lights, knitting her brows as she tried to figure out what was going on there. In her peripheral vision, Liv saw her staring hard and turned toward her, just starting to say: "Oh, you want to be careful about..." just as her little witchling disappeared from the car.

With a sigh and a smile Olivia pulled over quickly and parked. Then looking toward the little clan of witches on the lawn she disappeared as well, reappearing over by the little floating orbs. Sure enough that's where she found Taylor, looking confused.

"How did I get here? I didn't will myself here."

Olivia motioned around her. "With all this magic concentrated here, you have to be careful what you're thinking or it will happen, whether you want it to or not."

"Oh!" Suddenly she appreciated all those tedious hours of mental discipline exercises.

"No worries. There's very little that can't be fixed if you make a mistake. We've all been there. Come on – let's see what you came here for."

What looked like shining orbs from a distance were little winged horses each the size of a softball, glowing crystalline in the dark and making tiny whinnies that sounded like glass wind chimes. Taylor was enchanted.

"Where are they from?" She reached her hand out to one, not daring to touch it in case she hurt it.

"I don't know. I've never seen one." She asked the group, "What's going on with these?"

One of the witches answered, grinning wide about his creations. "Aren't they cool? They're not real. They're little toys I made up." He came over to Taylor, turning her palm upward and touching it. A horse appeared there, tossing its head and trotting up her forearm to take off into the air. It tickled her skin – she was surprised they weren't real – and she laughed in delight. They watched as a couple of them disappeared like a soap bubble, bursting into little sprinkling rhinestones of light that dissipated before they hit the ground, and instantly two or three more replaced them. They flew around and in between the people in the group, sometimes landing on shoulders or outstretched hands. Taylor thought she could stay here all night with these little charms.

Olivia was enamored, too. "All the things you'd like to do but that would be difficult or a waste in any other setting." She mused aloud while she watched the creatures, then touched Taylor on the arm. "Come on, let's get up to the house and see who else is there."

She looked at their car and it disappeared, popping up closer to the house where it now sat parked with the other vehicles. In the parking area was a combination of the sleek and run-down from the motor world, even a couple of old cars with rusty paint and a VW bus amongst the primping Maseratis and Austin-Healys. *Comforting to see*, Taylor thought, less intimidated by who would be inside the mansion doors. Still, her curiosity was so intense it was like a dry itch in her chest.

"Let's pop up to the walkway." said Olivia, her way of warning Taylor she was going to flash the both of them. Taylor had to admit she had been right during their Seattle shopping trip. The more they did this sort of thing the easier it was for Taylor to reorient herself in the new location. Only rarely was she surprised now or stumbled as they hit new surroundings. They appeared on a wide curving path of concrete carved into a perfectly manicured lawn with Olivia leading the way, obviously at home here. The double front doors were wide with a cut glass transom over the top and matching sidelights. Taking ahold of the curved handle Liv opened the door and walked in with Taylor a close second.

The living room was large and expansive, designed in tone on tone shades of grey and cream, yet
not at all monotone. A profusion of different textures
and patterns in shades from pearl to charcoal made the
living room lush and guests mingled in groups and
pairs on the curved sofa and overstuffed chaises. Taylor wasn't sure what she had expected, but the scene
looked like a perfectly ordinary social gathering to her.
The little crystal horses were the most excitement
since they had arrived. But while Olivia scanned the
room Taylor began to see subtle differences between
this and any other party. Murky patches, like haze or
smoke, intermingled with guests. Some people were
translucent...she could see through them if she paid attention. She knew what the murk was. She had seen
Eidolon often enough by now that she knew this was
how he appeared if he chose to, but what were the others?

"Look, there's Alejo." Olivia pointed at a tall
and very good-looking man standing amidst a cluster
of people. He was bronze and lean, with a ready smile
and outspoken cheekbones set atop a clean jawline. His
espresso hair looked like it needed a cut two inches ago
and was pushed behind his ears but the effect, along
with his friendly manner, gave him more of an ap-
proachable, dazzling look instead of aloof and too
handsome. Wow, thought Taylor. He was quite animated, making sweeping motions with his hands and
bending his knees for added effect as he told a story to

the cluster around him. Liv smiled and turned to her novice. "Let's see how long it takes him to notice us."

"You don't want to go over there and say hello?"

"And wade through the scrum to try and get his attention? Pffft. Screw that." She folded her arms, relaxed, and stared at him. It wasn't very long before he looked up from his admirers and saw them across the room. Recognition lit up his face and he waved. Olivia smiled and raised her hand in return, then pointed to her right at Taylor. Alejandro excused himself from his group and came over to fold Olivia up in his arms and lift her off her feet.

"So good to see you again!" He was truly happy to see her and there was an ease that told of old friendship with no pretense. He put her down and then stood in between both women, taking each by the hand and introducing himself to Taylor.

"So you are the newest of us." His Latin accent made his R's and T's sound softer and rounded, sensual to her ears. "Olivia says you are doing well." Taylor smiled and shrugged, and enjoyed the compliment. She felt petted and welcomed by his reference to her as one of "us."

Olivia continued the discussion in a way meant to include her. "We've been working your skills for, what, almost six months?" and looked at Taylor for confirmation. Taylor nodded, casting about for some-

CATHLEEN DUNN

thing clever to say but found nothing, so after a moment of looking at her Olivia went on to fill the gap, turning back to Alejandro.

"Have you seen Julia?"

"Only when I first came in. I was here a little early."

"So, what does she have in store for us tonight?"

"Nothing too dramatic, I think. I didn't talk to her very long, though."

"Well, I'll look her up later and visit awhile."

Alejandro turned to Taylor. "Have you ever been to one of these?"

Taylor found her voice. "No. I'm really excited to meet everyone. Olivia says there could be all kinds of magic and you never know what could happen."

"True." Alejo agreed. "Not nearly as exciting as it used to be though. For a while we used to try and outdo the time before but that got out of hand, I think."

"What do you mean?"

Olivia answered. "Crazy things like mythical animals and doorways to other dimensions. Neither is very safe."

"Why?" Taylor was intrigued.

Alejo answered. "Well, the animals got too outlandish. At first dragon rides were exciting and dangerous, but they seemed silly after a while. Plus it uses too much magic to create anything like that. The more power it takes to maintain something, the less stable it

• 134 •

is over time, of course. Especially the doorways, they're not as reliable as they used to be. What if someone gets trapped on the other side when the door closes?"

"Wow." Taylor considered. "I never thought of that."

"Depending on who got trapped, that's not a bad idea. I wish I'd thought of that before." Olivia said craftily. Then she turned wistful. "But it's not like it used to be. The magical world and this one used to be a lot closer. There was a bridge between the two and people used to mix. Elves and all that."

"What?" This was more than Taylor had expected.

Alejo had some sage advice. "You'll find there are several realities; the oldest stories are often the truest. Just go with it."

He looked across the room where someone was trying to get his attention. "I'm afraid I have to go meet some people there." He pointed. "For the team charity. Can I catch up with you two later?"

"Sure – we'll look around and see who's here." Olivia kissed him on the cheek. "Find the gang and you'll find us probably."

"Of course. Wait, don't go yet. Here…." He produced three tall champagne stems out of thin air. "Let's drink to welcoming our newest into the fold." He raised his glass to Taylor's, chiming the rim on hers and then Olivia's.

"Thank you..." Taylor was secretly thanking Olivia for bringing her here as she took a sip. "We'll see you at the match tomorrow."

"Oh, you're coming to watch me play?"

"Handy, don't be a boob – you know damned well that's why we're all in Houston instead of getting together somewhere else." Olivia was looking at him the way she'd look at an obnoxious little brother. He ignored it and laughed.

"Yes, I know, but it's more polite to sound surprised when people talk about me. Of course I'm so pleased to have my friends here to watch. You like polo, Taylor?" He looked at her intently as if he'd waited all day for her alone to talk to.

"I've only seen one game, but it was very exciting. I've learned more about it since then."

"Good! The game is always an adventure for me as well. I never get tired of it."

Olivia cut in. "You never get tired of being the center of attention. Be careful of him – too many girlfriends," she said to Taylor in a way that told she was jesting. She obviously was fond of him.

"You see how mean she is to me?" Alejo's attention was still on Taylor and he was feigning hurt from Olivia's attack on his character. They reminded her of siblings who tortured each other constantly but would step in for sure if someone else teased one of them. She loved their silliness.

"Come on, let's drop this loser." Olivia walked Taylor off in a pretend huff. "I'll see you later," she threw over her shoulder at Alejo, who was looking fondly after them before going to the man who had called him a few moments ago.

They left the great room and entered an adjoining, more intimate one. It looked like a library, with its rows of books, coffered ceiling, and leather furniture. There was classical music wafting through the air and they stopped to listen with the other guests sitting there, beguiled by the harpsichord quartet who played for them. Looking in that direction Taylor could see the music came from figures in period costumes, but they were an image only, transparent like the people she had seen in the main room.

"What is going on?" she asked Olivia, who motioned her to the back of the library so they wouldn't disturb anyone.

"That's Vivaldi and Paganini playing. Do you recognize *Summer* from Vivaldi's *The Four Seasons*?"

"I've heard of Paganini. Isn't he the guy they say sold his soul to the devil so that he could play the violin better than anyone? Is that really him?"

Olivia shook her head. "No, they're just shadows...their music carries their imprint. They can manifest in form like this if there's enough magic around, but it's not really them; it's more of a haunting."

"So those are their spirits?"

Liv shook her head again. "No...usually once a person is gone they dissipate into the logos and their energy becomes part of everything else, but..." she thought a moment. "Not all witchcraft is the same.

Those two have magic like you and me, but they can't use it to do the things that we can. Their magic came through them in the gift of music, and the compositions, when they're played, still hold their essence."

Taylor was rapt, watching the figures touch harpsichord keys and finger strings on their instruments, a deep well of emotion showing in their transparent movements. Liv went on to explain, still whispering, as if a louder tone would be sacrilege in the library.

"Their magical power infused their compositions, slipping beyond mortality to a higher level, into the logos, which is why people say they feel transported listening – they are momentarily. Sometimes, who they were can materialize through their music and they can perform, but I've never seen them talk with anyone, only play...so I believe it's only the memory of who they were, suspended in the music."

"Ohhhh..." Taylor's eyes went dreamy as she looked at the phantoms. She listened for a while longer, closing her eyes. "So beautiful..."

The music was so sweet and pure of line it didn't seem real. She knew why the others in attendance were so captured by it. She was a piece of the music itself, feeling the notes suspend her and carry her along. As she floated on the music, totally engulfed in it, visions came to her of rooms long past, and she saw them through the artists' eyes as they worked on their compositions. Vivaldi sitting at his *scrivania* and writing centuries ago, the window open over the sunny courtyard where he worked at the *dell'Ospedale della Pieta*. She could hear children playing on the *terrazzo* tiles between the garden beds as she watched him writing notes on yellowed vellum. The individual notes came alive, swirling off the page as they became sound. And there were Paganini's long fingers on his violin, a blur over the strings they moved so rapidly. Then they moved slowly, pulling love and longing and every other emotion from the strings to tell the story in the notes. She saw him then, trying out new combinations of notes on a cloudy fall day. Playing to audiences in Munich and Warsaw and Vienna and Strasburg. The gambling and the women, and a vision of a masquerade ball glittering with hundreds of candles in the crystal chandeliers, all of it reflected in floor-length mirrors. It was an entrancing way to hear the music and she was loathe to leave when Olivia touched her arm. She put her off for the moment, and after experiencing a few more pieces like the wild *Le Streghe* by Paganini they left the room and went outside. Taylor was astonished to hear the notes did not carry past the threshold. There was different music outside, but it didn't clash with the music inside although the door was wide open on this warm night. Taylor couldn't resist leaning back through the door and then out again to test. Within the room was the entrancing violin and harpsichord; when she leaned forward it was replaced by a contemporary band, its dark rock mixed with classical overtones and ethereal vocals. Stepping away from the house and looking across the back yard she could hear it coming from a young woman with long black hair and pale eyes sitting at a keyboard on the other side of a swimming pool. She and the other musicians were lit up by the refracting turquoise light that ascended from the water. The effect was ghostly but Taylor couldn't see through them, the light definitely reflected off their skin and clothing.

She and Olivia drifted through the garden toward the music, stopping under a lattice of jasmine to listen. The combination of vocals and fragrance and the night sky was heady, the deep bass and drums were palpable and the voice lustrous, almost shimmering as it flowed through the air. It was like seeing the world with her sorceress eyes for the first time, only now it was music instead, showing her its depth and dimension. The desolation was forefront in the deep thrums of the bass guitar while the vocals soared with intense beauty, describing pain and darkness in the words. She understood the term "hauntingly beautiful" for the first time.

In awe she pointed at the band members. "Are they real? Or are they dead?"

"No, not dead." Olivia reassured her "Not at all – she has the gift, like Vivaldi and Paganini and she's definitely alive." She pointed across the yard. "Why don't we go sit down by the French doors on the patio?"

Now Taylor couldn't help how much she stared as they strolled through the back yard. She'd never

seen such a profusion of magic. Shooting stars enliv-
ened the night sky and points of light clustered over
people, suspended in the air to illuminate their conver-
sations. No bulbs, no cords, simply points of white
light in little flocks that undulated in the soft air cur-
rents as people passed.

Olivia surveyed the scene. "Apparently the
theme for tonight is exotic pets."

Taylor pulled her gaze from the lights to sweep
the garden. A dozen oversized animals were sprinkled
throughout the yard amidst clumps of people who were
dwarfed by their size. Some stroked the deep fur of
silky foxes and rough-coated wolves that had been created, lounging with them as if it were the most normal
thing possible. One russet-colored vulpin was curled in
a ball, tail wrapped around the person tucked against
her hip, another lay upright and cleaned its paws with
little licks while a guest reclined against it and chatted
with friends. A massive wolf lay on his haunches with
forelegs outstretched, looking regal and watchful and
lupine, dominating the guests sitting in the grass there,
and a black jungle cat stared at her with citron eyes
while the man next to it scratched its ear languidly.
Extraordinary birds in all kinds of colors with long tail
feathers and shimmering plumage preened and appeared or disappeared next to guests, depending on
who had treats at the moment.

There were no seats left at any of the outdoor
tables on the patio, so they stopped in an open spot on
the grass next to two men discussing the merits of

scrying versus using runes to get information. As they stood, two wrought iron patio chairs with deep cushions appeared and they sat down in them.

"I love parties at Julia's...her house knows what you want and when you want it." She sank into the upholstery and stretched out her legs to take full advantage of the night air.

Looking around to see what she meant, Taylor noticed that drinks and appetizers seemed to be cropping up randomly, like a tray of crostini with goat cheese and roasted red peppers which appeared next to the two men. They looked delighted, stopping their debate to reach over for a treat off the platter, followed by closed eyes and murmured approval.

Taylor was confused. "Can't everyone make their own stuff happen?"

"Well, sure but we can do that anytime, and we're not surprised when we get what we asked for. A party's about seeing what your host will turn up for you and not having to do the work."

"What else have you seen at these? Is it always animals?"

"No, I've seen dimensional tag, where invisible doorways flash you twenty or so feet away, but you never know when – and you never know where you'll disappear from or go to. Imagine almost catching someone and then suddenly you're somewhere else – or running away and all at once running toward your pursuer. You never knew where you were going to be at any moment." She laughed. "We had a few crashes, but no one got hurt. Another time we created an invisible maze. You could see all around you but couldn't tell where the turns and blind ends were. Everyone looked like a bunch of mimes walking around and feeling their way along. People were falling all over themselves, hysterical at watching each other try to figure it out."

Taylor looked out into the yard to imagine the maze Olivia described, smiling at the ridiculousness and thinking it would be fun. She looked back at Liv, still interested.

"What else?"

Olivia had been watching Taylor, enjoying her reaction. At the question her gaze softened. "Snowflakes," she said dreamily, tipping her head to the sky with serene eyes. "Imagine drifting snowflakes. Beautiful in any setting, but these were delicately lit from within as they lofted to the ground. Hardly a glimmer of light in the palm of your hand. And the drifts on the ground...soft, glowing drifts." She was engaged in the memory, then looked over and smiled at Taylor, a deep breath bringing her back into this moment. "Incredible times...I'll show you how to do it when we get home."

She held out her hand with the empty champagne glass, which disappeared, then leaned back to look at the shooting stars overhead. "What if we stay out here for a bit and then go inside to introduce you around? I'd like to listen to this group for a while if that's okay with you."

"Sure." Taylor had no idea what was okay with her – everything was all so fascinating she couldn't have decided what she wanted if you'd stuck it all in a police lineup and said "pick one." Underneath, however, was a smoldering curiosity to see what other rarities she would come across tonight.

She didn't need to wait long. Within ten minutes an older man came over and sat down next to her in the chair that appeared for him. He was transparent, like the people she had seen before in the great room and the library.

"So this is Taylor... are you enjoying your evening with us so far?" His eyes crinkled as he smiled at the girl. A good feeling came off him, waves of calm and kindness. Something vaguely familiar...

But then Taylor was startled, realizing they hadn't been introduced. *Does everyone know about me?* She eyed him as she answered, trying to gather information. "Yes, but I'll have to admit that I keep wondering if I'm missing something somewhere else."

"Undoubtedly you are. But don't try to rush off to the next thing so quickly or you'll miss what's happening where you are now."

Taylor broke into laughter, disarmed now. "Somehow that made sense. So you know who I am, but who are you?" She didn't know what she was expecting.

"I'm Ethan. I'll be right back." He disappeared. Taylor looked at Olivia, completely blank, then confused because her companion was smiling.

"What was that all about?"

"That was Beth's familiar. I imagine they'll be out here in a moment, or we'll need to go inside and find them now that they know we're here."

"Who is they? Wait, that was a familiar? I thought they looked like –" but she was interrupted by four figures that appeared next to them, three women and Ethan.

"He was right. She was out here listening to that damned artist she loves so much. Pay up." She turned to the woman on her right and held out her palm.

"Are you serious? There's not a thing I could give you that you can't summon up for yourself."

"I know – it's the principle of the thing because I'm right." She fluttered her fingers in a "gimme" gesture and the other crafted some sort of certificate from the air with a flourish, putting it into the outstretched palm.

"Thank you." She smugly put it into her jacket pocket. The other pretended an exasperated look but a smirk took over. She turned to Taylor.

"Hi, I'm Jolene." The soft drawl from the South was unmistakable and her smile was genuine as she touched Taylor's arm in welcome. The winner turned to Taylor as well.

"Akinyi." She offered her hand. Hardly an accent at all but a way of speaking she couldn't place. Very faint Southern syrup and clipped P's and T's mixed in together in a way that showed she knew several languages. She was creamy espresso, tall and curvy and slender, with beautiful long features that were Somali in appearance. Taylor wanted to just look at her, she was so beautifully crafted.

Obviously, they had all known each other quite a while. Olivia stood, putting her arm through Taylor's to introduce her to the two remaining figures. "This is Beth." She pointed to a diminutive woman with a long mane of blond ringlets. "And this, as you know, is Ethan." They both turned toward him, where Taylor could easily see the pool and its pale uplighting through his form. It was a little disconcerting; she kept looking through him instead of at him and felt inconsiderate but couldn't help it. The effect was just so peculiar and foreign.

Taylor concentrated on his face. "Beth's familiar, right?"

"Right."

"But I thought you appeared as smoke. Eidolon always appears as smoke." She looked at Olivia and then around the circle of witches.

"Oh, we can appear as almost anything but not a solid form. Smoke or mist is easiest because it doesn't take extra energy to define edges or make multiple colors." He faded to a pale fog, then dissipated, then returned again, this time as a young girl. Beth held out her hand, beckoning Ethan and he disappeared into nothingness at that point.

Taylor turned to Liv. "Does Eidolon do this?"

"No," she said. "We keep it pretty simple."

"Has she seen blending?" Beth was addressing Olivia.

"Not yet. We haven't gotten that far. She's had her scare, though."

Taylor heard sudden murmuring sounds and looked around, seeing they were all glancing at her with empathy. She picked up bits of sentences: "Oh, I remember when that..." and "Oh, God, it was ghastly," and "I couldn't believe..."

"What are you talking about?"

Olivia explained. "The day a chimera tried to possess you during lessons. We've all had that happen at one point or another."

"We know it can be pretty horrifying," said Akinyi. Everyone else nodded assent, eyes on Taylor. Almost a resigned agreement to it all, as if normalizing it like that was supposed to make her feel better. *Well, it doesn't. Feels worse, thanks.*

Beth leaned in and touched her arm. "It doesn't have to be that way, though. If it's someone you trust you can let them in. It's like being one with your best friend or someone you love." She turned to Olivia. "Do you mind if I show her?"

"What, right now?"

"No, Olivia, I didn't mean right now, but..." She was taken aback, surprised at Olivia's sharpness.

Then the others were talking again, discussion sweeping around the small group. "Oh, she needs to know." "Beth and Ethan have such a good partnership." Nodding together. "That's pretty basic if you're going to..." Taylor wished she caught the rest of that one. *What is going on?* She felt apprehensive because she didn't know and her name was in the middle of it.

"No one's doing anything to me." She broke in, a little loudly, and they all turned to her in surprise. "I'm standing right here, you know. What are you all talking about?"

"Sorry, Taylor," said Olivia, turning to her, "Beth is asking if she can show you her and Ethan together so you can learn about it."

"What do you mean 'together'?"

"If you have a familiar you can blend with them and share experiences. I didn't think it was time to show you yet, especially since your scare with it before."

"That was a long time ago. I'm good at rebuffing them now." Taylor wanted to show she was capable and find out what this was about, learn something new, be part of the discussion, but Olivia was having none of it.

"It's not safe yet." She turned to the others. "Give it a rest. I want her to have a break."

Beth stepped in. "That's all right, no harm done. Olivia's right, not everyone does it. Besides, this is a B&S. Let's go inside and see what we can bog into."

"What?" Taylor thought she heard her wrong.

Akinyi interpreted. "This is a party. Let's go inside and see what there is to eat." She shook her head. "She's Australian." She said, as if that explained everything, then looked at the others. "Everyone, just relax instead of jumping all over Taylor to see what she knows and what she doesn't." She waved them off and turned back to her. "Sorry, Taylor. Apprentices don't come along very often."

Taylor was still hooked on the blending subject and wishing it hadn't been dropped, but like a mind reader Beth came back to her as they walked along. She leaned in close with a conspiratorial whisper. "I'll tell you more about it later," she said, like a favorite aunt who let you sip their drink when no one else was looking. Taylor smiled, mollified. She loved Beth's curvaceous accent, words almost put on their side by her Aussie pronunciation. "...a B&S – let's gai inside and see what we can bog inoo."

Jolene's soft voice lofted over the group. "I'd rather stay out here and find a spot where there's not a noisy crowd so we can chat." Akinyi agreed, and Beth liked the idea as well, so outside it was. They all ambled over to a spot further out in the yard where it was quieter, next to a raised flower bed, and stood talking and laughing while they waited for the furniture to arrive.

"Have you guys been here long?" Olivia was looking around at everyone as a cushioned lawn chair appeared behind her.

"Beth's been here the whole week of course, but we got here about half an hour ago." said Jolene.

Olivia turned to her apprentice. "Of course she and Akinyi arrived together. They were childhood friends and have been business partners for decades."

"Are you going to narrate everything we do tonight?" asked Jolene.

"Well, I kind of have to at first, don't I? It's not like she's known everyone for the last three hundred years." She perused the group. "Anyone seen JaneAnn?"

"Yeah, she's here somewhere." Jolene was arranging herself on a chaise. "She's catching up with everyone, and you know how she likes to cruise around on her own for a while."

"Where are Marcus and Julia?"

"Oh, God knows – hosting this thing could put them anywhere."

Olivia turned to Taylor. "Julia and Marcus are Jolene's parents." She gestured in the air between them and a portrait arose, a couple facing Taylor with him in back and her in front, his arms around her and the side of her head tucked into his cheek, her long dark hair spilling over her shoulders. A brown-eyed, handsome couple. "They could look older now, I don't know if they've allowed that or not."

"Not really," Jolene answered, "they look the same."

As they conversed Olivia provided more images to explain the stories that bubbled up. Beth and Olivia kept up the nuggets of information, popping in a few comments here and there as she or someone else showed Taylor a picture of the story – "So when they say Cornelia they mean Akinyi when she was really little. Akinyi was called Cornelia before she changed her name in the 1930's after a trip to South Africa." Taylor gathered that Jolene and Akinyi grew up together on a Louisiana plantation around 1803. "Akinyi's mom was mortal, but when Akinyi showed up with powers, Marcus and Julia took them both to their mansion to live as family…"

Later the conversation wound up a different path: "Beth is from Australia. She owns a big sheep station in the Kimberley region there, just off Fitzroy Crossing…" A picture showed. "She has a great penthouse in Sydney, too. You should go there in person sometime." They presented a beautiful view of Sydney Harbor from an obscenely huge penthouse.

And later to Taylor's quizzical inquiry about one of Beth's stories: "No, a bushranger isn't like a Texas Ranger here. A bushranger is an old-fashioned Australian term for an outlaw, and Beth thought this guy was exciting and dangerous and sexy." Jolene smiled at Beth: "You like those bad boys."

A purring response. "So? What could I possibly have to be scared of?" Taylor admired her confidence and the big, expansive stories she told about life in Australia with its variety of legends and superstitions from the Outback. After Beth finished regaling them with her tales the subject settled back on the other two witches, Jolene and Akinyi, in snippets contributed by everyone.

"... back then it was a huge scandal in Louisiana when Julia and Marcus gave the plantation to Jolene and Cornelia, then up and left to vacation in Europe for over a year... a year! Oh, it was the talk all up and down the river! But it wasn't unusual for their family to do odd things. Before the war they gave out hundreds of freedom papers, to everyone they purchased. The other landowners were furious at the volume, but no one could touch them for doing it. And then to go and leave the whole works to a couple of girls barely in their twenties! I know it happened with young men all the time back then – they lived in *garçonnières* by the time they were fifteen and oversaw things by eighteen – but this was different, both women and one of them black, no less! It wasn't done back then...just wasn't done! Oh, there were lots of attempts to ruin them, vicious ones, but no one could. It seemed whenever there was an opportunity to be had, anticipating bad weather and avoiding floods or the fevers, nothing ever seemed to happen to their household. People certainly did talk about how that could happen. Half of them said it had to be voodoo and half said they were the luckiest two people they had ever seen."

"That's not so unusual." Akinyi was laughing. "Right, Beth? I seem to remember more than a few bushmen and swagmen going on about strange things at your station..."

On it went, the stories and retellings, and catching up on what was new. Then Olivia stopped for one of Taylor's occasional questions.

"What do you mean, what about Marcus and Julia? You mean before Louisiana?"

Taylor nodded.

"That's hard to tell. They don't say too much about their past."

"How old are they?"

"I don't know." Olivia gestured to get Jolene's attention. "Hey, how old is your mother, Jolene?"

Jolene looked blank. "I don't know. Why?"

Liv turned back to Taylor. "She might even be older than me, but she's never said. I don't know if Marcus even knows."

"Are there very many witches older than you?" Taylor asked Olivia, who shrugged her shoulders.

"I don't know. I never really thought about it."

Taylor pressed more, looking at the two on either side of her. "Aren't you curious?"

"I'm not." said Beth. "What difference does it make?"

That was a good question. What difference *did* it make? Taylor was trying to orient herself to this new society. "Well, don't they know the most? You would go to them for answers, right?"

Now Akinyi was interested, too, uncrossing her long legs and leaning forward to get into the conversation. "Not really. Everyone has different experiences and we share. But a familiar knows more than one of us possibly could, so why would it matter who knows the most or who's the oldest?"

"Well, who's in charge then?"

"In charge?" Akinyi looked like she just had seen some spit on the sidewalk. "No one's in charge of us...we just live life and be what we are. Witch. I can't imagine anyone telling me what I can do. Mortal society already has its restrictions. I don't want another layer of that on top of me." All around her were nods from Beth, Olivia, and now Jolene. Taylor tried to get a handle on the concept.

"So there are no rules you live by? You just do whatever you want?"

Olivia raised an eyebrow. "*Can* you just do what you want? Especially if you use magic? And what if you're cruel or malicious?"

Realization bloomed across Taylor's face. "Ohhh – karma. What goes out comes back, one way or the other. Those rules of magic keep everyone in line."

Akinyi nodded. "Right, it's a self-maintaining system. No need for a 'queen of the witches' or something ridiculous like that, and it weeds out the jackasses real quick." She snapped her fingers.

"Unless you're a Blue/Black." Taylor made the statement innocently enough. The group fell silent, then Akinyi answered.

"Not exactly. They're stronger, because their tint makes them aggressive, bolder. They bend the rules and augment their powers through killing. So they seem to stay just ahead of karma, but there's a huge price they continually have to pay for it. Sooner or later karma catches up with them, too."

"And in the meantime they keep hurting everyone else while our hands are tied." Olivia was smoldering. No one answered her.

"I'm sorry..." Taylor stammered, but Jolene rescued her.

"It's okay. They're good questions, Taylor." She nodded approvingly and then changed the subject. "Hey, you guys said you saw Handy in the living room, surrounded by all his minions. Should we get him out here to visit with us?"

They were trying to decide who was going to go find him when a pale sparkle in the air between them sidetracked the discussion. As they watched, small columns of golden champagne slowly appeared, suspended in the air, evanescing by themselves.

"Well, how are we supposed to drink *that*?" drawled Jolene.

Beth answered her. "I suspect it's not finished yet. You know Julia does things with *panache*."

And of course, tall crystal flutes took shape around the floating pools. A low coffee table faded into their midst, followed by a tray of canapés, and on Taylor's corner a sudden flash left behind a tall glass of sweet tea with crushed ice, her favorite.

Beth was tickled with the diminutive show. "Marcus and Julia are such a great hosts. Even their drinks appear like a Broadway dance number."

Olivia took a flute from the air and leaned back
with it, looking across the lawn into the dark. The
glow from the champagne was good, not too much al-
teration. She could choose to block the alcohol with
magic but didn't, preferring the discipline of drinking
it slow, like a mortal. She looked around the group,
dissociating herself for the moment. There was always
the worry of Dantin where any of her friends were concerned. Oh, God, why in the world had she taken Taylor shopping and on vacation? She was sure Alejo had
been right. If he was not around he still somehow knew
what was going on. Well, at least she could tell when
he was close by, and Taylor had spells so she could detect him. She closed her eyes.

Beth leaned forward to sample an endive from
the tray and then turned to Taylor. "So, how did you
and Olivia meet?"

"She just came up to me on the street one day
and started talking."

"Just like that? Had you ever met before?"

"Well, we lived in the same neighborhood, kind
of. I knew her by sight but that's it."

"So you already lived there. Did you grow up in
Seattle?"

"Yep – a Washington native." She was hoping
Beth wouldn't ask about her past because she'd grown
up so poor, but Beth took a different path.

"Liv hasn't had an apprentice for quite a while,
and you've been living with her the last five months.
You two must be pretty close."

Taylor hedged the question. Quite frankly, she wasn't sure what to say about her and Olivia so instead she asked, "Akinyi said apprentices don't come around very often. Are there any more here?"

"A few, I think. You're the only one in our group."

JaneAnn came along just then. "What do you think of our little party?"

"It's nice, but so far I've only been in a couple rooms and met your friends."

"Hey, thanks." JaneAnn pretended hurt feelings and Taylor apologized but JaneAnn laughed it off. "I get it. I'd want to look around, too." She sat down to visit with Jolene.

Taylor turned back to Beth. "I'd like to hear more stories from Australia."

"What do you want to know?"

"Well, everything, I guess. What about magic there? Olivia says it's different in every culture."

"Well, in Australia the Aboriginal magic is natural, just a part of life. They don't have witches burned at the stake and all that baggage from Europe. Us blow-ins brought that with us, the warding off evil spirits by keeping boots in the attic and such. But that's not so interesting. Now the Outback stories, those are fun Big-Notes to tell."

"What?" Taylor still didn't know all the Aussie slang.

"A blow-in is a transplant, an immigrant. Big-Notes are stories you tell about yourself. Could be

called bragging, but most people want to be enter-
tained. Hey, why don't you and Olivia come to my
station for a visit? I can tell you stories all night, but
you never really know until you've been there."

"Well, we could see what she says." Taylor had
her doubts about Olivia taking her on a visit to Australia, but Beth seemed to assume they were friends.
She asked Beth about her.

"What's Olivia really like?"

"Well, we're all careful to stay low-key but
Olivia's really private. She never says a whole lot to
anyone about her personal life, and we've known her
longer than most, I think. She's fair dinkum, though."

"What's that?" Taylor was getting used to the
Australian accent finally.

A fair dinkum …. a true dinky-di. It means the
real thing or genuine. Olivia might keep to herself, but
she's not phony. She's probably the best friend you
could have." She flipped her long curls back over her
shoulder with one hand as she spoke. "Don't let her
bother you. That's just the way she is. Most of us are
happy to lair it up with our stories given half a
chance," she said with a laugh. "But what about you?
Are you having fun?"

"I didn't really know what to expect tonight."

"What's your favorite thing so far?"

Taylor looked around. "How do I pick? Here,
I'll show you the first thing I saw when we came in...it
was a bunch of little crystal horses that were really

cute." She produced one in her hand and gave it to Beth.

"Well, isn't that just about adorable?" Beth was watching the little figure as it trotted around on her lap throwing its head and whinnying. It flew up and around the two of them, then landed back on Beth's lap to curl its legs under it and lie down, the wings folding as it did so. She petted the neck with her forefinger and looked back at Taylor, smiling. Ethan appeared next to her – or she assumed it was him – as smoke, curling around her.

Seeing this, Taylor jumped on the opportunity. "Earlier you were talking about blending. Tell me more about that."

"Okay." Beth adjusted her petite frame and the crystal pony flew off so it wouldn't get jostled. She waited until it settled in again, this time in the crook of her arm. "Well, I can tell you about me and Ethan. No one could possibly know me any better or be closer to me." As if to punctuate the point, Ethan coalesced from smoke draped over Beth to a transparent copy of her, sitting so close their legs and shoulders were touching. Beth the witch turned to smile at Beth the familiar.

Taylor pulled back. "I get what you're saying, but I'm not used to this yet so seeing two of you, and one transparent, is a little creepy."

"Well, it all depends on your point of view – you said Eidolon always appears as smoke so that's just what you're used to. Blending with your familiar can be the best experience of your life – there's nothing like it."

Taylor was intrigued. "Can you show me?"

"Sure, but you won't see much by looking. I'll still look like me. It's Ethan that feels the difference – all the sensations of a mortal body. You'd have to experience it."

"Liv has never told me this much about it."

"If you want to know more I can show you, but you ask Olivia first – she got all shonky about it when I mentioned it."

"Shonky?"

"All dubious, unsure about it. Sometimes she thinks I'm too open about the whole thing. But I just meant showing you how it can be done." Her hair had slipped back over her shoulder again and she let the pony fly off so she could use that hand to sweep it behind her.

Taylor watched the little horse disappear over the bushes. "Thanks, Beth."

"Sure. Anything you need I'm happy to help."

Just then Alejandro came out through the patio doors, looking for them. He didn't have any hangers-on with him, but as he came through a few people stopped him to talk. He obliged them patiently, although you could tell he was trying to wend his way over to where they were sitting.

It's funny, Taylor thought, *this is no different than mortals fawning over a professional athlete or a movie star, even though we can live just as lavish a life*. She wondered if he liked all the attention. It looked like one would need such patience with all the people around, not a life for the faint of heart.

It took him quite a while to meander over to the women clustered on the lawn.

"Hey, Handy. Here." Beth gave up her seat on the bench to go sit by Akinyi.

He sat and turned to Taylor, smiling in that way he had. "Having a good time?" He could have been a toothpaste ad, he was so brilliant.

"Look, you." Olivia stepped in. "Forget about doing that. You're with us now and you can just sit and stare for all we care. Relax." Alejo eased up visibly and Taylor realized she had been right. It wasn't really a party for him, this was work.

Alejandro stretched out his long frame, resting the back of his neck on the seat and gazing at the sky while the others talked around him. Taylor noticed that while he was still handsome and radiant, he seemed a little tired and quieter, not as animated as he had been with the others. He was just...a nice guy. She liked him for it.

They talked and lounged for the next hour and a half, listening to music and watching the magical tri-flings others were doing to show off. They discussed to-morrow's match, how long they would be in Houston, where they were staying, how often did they see the others, discussing old times and reminiscing, usual party conversation. Taylor was getting bored. These were other people's memories, not hers. She wanted to see what else was happening, to be alone for a while and move through the crowd without any strings.

She stood up. "I'm going to look around. I want to see what else is going on."

Olivia put down her glass. "Do you want me to show you around?"

"No, please. I just want to be on my own a little. I can come back and find you in an hour or so."

JaneAnn looked at Olivia. "The poor girl has been stuck with us all night."

Liv shrugged. "Okay. While you do that I'll find Marcus and Julia."

"I'll go, too." Alejo stood up.

"Fine. You and me then." She turned to Taylor and traced a gesture on the back of the girl's hand. "Here – now you can find me tonight without looking all over. Just touch it and ask it where I am."

Taylor stared at her hand, which didn't look any different. "You can do that?"

"It's temporary. It only lasts a few hours."

"Thanks. How long do you want to stay tonight?" She was hoping for late.

"I don't know. Find me with the charm around eleven-thirty or twelve and we'll decide what to do next."

Alejo shooed her off. "Okay. You have the charm, either you find us or we'll find you. Go look around while you have the chance. Gatherings like this don't happen often."

Taylor was elated, independence at last. She walked toward the house that was all lit up with the affair going on inside.

Alejo turned to Olivia after Taylor entered the mansion. "Let's go find our hosts." He dropped his hand to the hollow of her back and turned her toward the house. After they were out of earshot he whispered to her, "I found Schmidt. He'll do it."

Olivia said nothing but nodded as they walked toward the house. Schmidt was an experienced charmsmith, one of the best in the last thousand years, it was said. After a few more steps she turned to him and took his hands, looking up at him.

"Thank you so much. I know you don't…" She looked down at the ground and then back up at him. "Just thank you."

He put his arm around her indulgently. "I think you're a selfish toad for getting me mixed up in this, but you're welcome."

"Yes, I am, I know, but…" She returned his hug.

He held on to her when she tried to disengage from his grasp. "That doesn't mean I'm not worried. If we can find a different way…" He shook his head and released her. "Come on, let's go find Marcus and Julia. But I don't want to look all over for them; give me something to scry in."

Olivia summoned an abalone shell filled with water and Alejo held it as they looked into the pearlescent interior. It was a perfect medium and they watched as the surface coalesced into a scene of Julia in the game room upstairs, next to a billiard table. They didn't bother looking around the house to find their way, they simply disappeared and reappeared next to Julia where the scry had shown them. She didn't react as the two appeared; she was answering a question from one of her guests. When she was finished she turned to Alejo and Olivia.

"Hey." She was casual, pacing herself tonight. Almost a hundred guests in your house could wear a person out. "What's going on?"

Alejo sat next to her on the edge of the pool table. "Catching up with the usual crowd. Liv's novice Taylor is around here somewhere, looking around."

"Sitting with us at the match tomorrow?" Olivia hoped she would.

"Of course. And I made reservations for the Loft at Mark's after. I want to visit with y'all but don't have time tonight with all this going on." The upscale restaurant in an old gothic church was a favorite among Houstonians. The Loft was a semiprivate room overlooking the main dining floor.

"Perfect. The Loft to ourselves."

"Plus the food... oh, my God." Alejo was right; the food was famous all over town. "I'll be starving after the match. Can't eat too much before spending a couple hours on a pony."

"When do you have to be there?" Julia knew it was getting late and he was playing tomorrow. The match was a fundraiser and tonight was kind of a pre-schmoozing event.

"Between noon and one. I have to be in the tent for press."

"Well, good luck tomorrow. I'm sorry we can't talk longer, but I'll see you both there." Julia had to turn away. She couldn't beg off the people waiting to talk with her.

The game room was in a huge overhang above the living room and Alejo and Liv went to the railing overlooking the crowd below. Olivia perused the scene with satisfaction. "I knew Taylor would enjoy this. She hasn't been much of anywhere at all."

"Where have you taken her so far?"

"No place really. Here to Houston, and she wanted to go to Tibet when we first met."

"So did you go?"

Olivia laughed at the memory. "I had to – it was to prove magic to her."

Alejo smiled. He'd had that kind of experience as well. They stood at the railing a long while, quiet, enjoying the view of the party below and through the big picture windows into the back garden. No Dantin here tonight, a gathering of Silver-Tints wasn't the smartest place for him to be. *It's almost shocking to relax like this*, Olivia thought. As they stood and watched a few guests left, followed by several more and they could see the crowd start to prune down a bit.

They made their way down the stairs, chatting with people on the way, to the open study just off of the main room. Fewer guests there allowed them to sit in comfort and chat. Intermittently, people came over to wish him luck in the match as they continued dribbling out the door in singles and small groups, and the two talked for quite a while that way, waiting for twelve o'clock and Taylor to come find them.

When they split up Taylor walked into the house and through the vaulted family room off the kitchen, past little pockets of people laughing and talking. She looked around, she knew no one, didn't know her way around JaneAnn's. Self-consciously she stood a few moments, looking at the ceiling beams and the furnishings, pretending great interest while she decided which way to go. She finally decided left, which turned out to be through the swinging doors into the kitchen.

Taylor had wondered where all the food was coming from, but it certainly wasn't the kitchen. The galley was pristine, clean and not a speck of use in sight. Probably a big spell or something, but it was beyond what she knew. It had to be centralized somewhere to be organized and staged like a clearinghouse. It would have been too complex to keep track of everything in its separate pieces. She tried to figure it out, but of course logic was only partially helpful. This was magic, after all. Somewhere the catering was running itself, food and beverages appearing and disappearing, fleeting dirty dishes or messes before they disappeared, but where? The sight was shocking, almost. A party here and not a living soul in the whole galley. Unfortunately, the puzzle was only interesting for a second so she meandered back out the door and further into the interior of the house.

The first hallway she found sent her upstairs to the wing of guest rooms. Party sounds and conversation receded behind her; even her footsteps were silent on the carpet as she moved along. It was a long hallway with doors on the right and left, but they were shut and Taylor wondered, of course, what was behind them? Probably guests, she told herself sensibly. But the doors at the end! A set of deeply carved pocket doors, like something from a Spanish hacienda of the 1800's, were partially open. She approached them and stopped, fingering the curves and cuts in the wood. Peering inside she could see it was a whole suite – on the left there was the bed with its sumptuous pillows and coverlet, to the right an adjoining private bath. The thing was huge, furnished with a couch and reading chairs along with occasional tables, like a small apartment. No personal effects were on the dresser, no luggage in the open closets, the room was alone in the quiet with only Taylor as company. She slid open the doors, spreading them wide and they disappeared smoothly into the walls. She came into the apartment slowly, looking around, to sit on the couch. Lying her head back on the cushions, she stretched her arms along either side of the seat back, imagining this was her house. Unbelievable a scarce six months ago. *When I am on my own will I have this much? On my own.*

She wondered when that would be, but had no idea how to tell when she was ready. Lately it mattered.

She prowled the rest of the suite, examining, imagining, stopping finally at the far wall with its massive window seat and knelt on the cushions to look at the garden scene below. She could see the party through the floating lights, like sparkling plankton suspended in an invisible sea. There were fewer people out there now. She looked at her watch with its dangling charm. A quarter to eleven. She'd been up here alone a half hour already. Suddenly it was important to get back downstairs.

Retracing her steps, she came back to the kitchen, turned a different direction, and found herself walking into a huge formal dining room. The high ceiling and bank of windows gave way to a massive round table that would easily seat twenty people. The room was empty, cavernous almost. Her fear that the party was breaking up seemed to be happening and she had missed so much of it! She walked through the dining room to a hallway on the other side. Maybe there would be people out there.

The hallway turned out to be a wing facing the east with an entire wall of French doors. It was a sunroom, where garden furniture and plants made a cozy, informal escape, and a few couples sat there talking together. She cruised down the walkway and smiled at a few people when they looked up at her. She wanted to enter a conversation but didn't know how. She didn't have the nerve and furthermore, didn't know what to say. *Taylor, of course no one's going to stop you out of the blue, you have to talk first.* But she kept walking, not knowing what else to do until she had to stop; she was at the end of the atrium and had to go back.

She spent another twenty minutes wandering the house before she found herself back where she and Olivia had first come in, the library with the classical music. The notes from the strings and harpsichord were still there, enticing her, but fewer people listened now. Taylor didn't want her growing disappointment, this lonely feeling to be part of her memory here; earlier it had been so beautiful. She peered into the garden where they all had sat earlier but only Jolene and Akinyi were there, talking intently. Finally Taylor ended up in the vaulted family room where she had started. The whole gathering was different now. It was past eleven and the party was crumbling. Feeling really self-conscious now, she wished she had a drink or something in her hand. As she thought it, a glass of iced tea, a flute of champagne, and a bottle of water faded into view on the counter next to her. She smiled at Julia's considerate house and selected the bottled water.

"Thanks, house." She gave it a half-hearted smile and watched as the other two beverages disappeared.

Sitting in one of the overstuffed chairs she twisted the top off her water, picking at the corner of the label as if truly engrossed in removing it, listening to the group next to her talk about their latest travels, exotic places Taylor could go to with her new powers but didn't want to alone. *This* was a bust. She'd waited weeks for this night and now what? She looked down at the new shoes she'd decided to wear. She'd certainly had a different scene in mind when she'd chosen her outfit and pictured herself at this gathering.

She was still looking at them, hoping they wouldn't always remind her of social failure and mulling over whether or not to find Olivia when a voice came from behind her.

"Nice kicks." Then a smiling face surrounded by short platinum hair popped into view as the voice continued.

"Hi, I'm Nicole. You look like the only other person here that doesn't know anyone." She looked younger than most of the guests, a round, teenage face with full cheeks and lips. Almost childish-looking.

Taylor was startled, looking at her wide-eyed for a millisecond. "Oh! Hi. Yeah...I was with some people, but I lost track of them." *No need to be obvious that I have no friends.* "How about you?"

"I heard about this so I came to check it out on my own. I don't have the nerve to break into someone else's conversation so I've spent most of the night by myself just looking around." The blond cherub was still peering down at her.

"And I wanted to look around, but by the time I got to, it seemed to be over. Here, sit down. I'm Taylor."

"Hi." She sat.

"How did you find out about tonight?"

"I can't remember. Word gets around."

Taylor was jealous of that. Nicole knew enough of the magical community to find out about tonight through the grapevine. Taylor considered telling Nicole she came with her mentor but opted out of it. The girl seemed so in charge of herself.

"So you're here. What do you think?"

"Really?"

"Really. Tell me."

"I think it's a snore." Nicole was under-whelmed.

Taylor laughed. "Yeah. I know... me, too. Why do you think so?"

"Well, I thought I'd come and it would be great. You know, a lot of witches from around the world. I thought I'd meet some people, have discussions, learn something, but it's like any other party aside from the magic tricks. I mean, there was a crowd and all and some cool stuff, but mostly people wanted to sit and visit with people they already knew."

"Yes, exactly!" Taylor was on her page.

"I also heard that famous polo player Alejandro Whatever-His-Name-Is would be here, and there's always fun around him, you know – maybe dancing and wildness, people jumping in the pool with their clothes on, I don't know, just … more. But I haven't seen him at all. And I've been looking."

"I know him!" Taylor wanted to impress Nicole for some reason. She wanted Nicole to want *her*.

"No, you don't."

"Yes, I do."

"You actually know that guy? The one from the magazines." She was between believing and not.

"Yes. I'm serious."

"I'd love to meet him. Can you introduce me?"

"Yeah, for a few minutes. I just left them and I don't really want to go back and end up staying." This was half true. She wanted to give Nicole something to like her for but didn't want to end up back with Alejo and Olivia. She wanted Nicole to pay attention to her, not him. "I'm supposed to check in with him and a friend before I go anywhere, though."

"Then what's the problem? We don't have to stay there unless he's got something going on, but what we have here is boring." She said the last word in singsong, like a doorbell. *Bing-Bong.*

"Okay, come on." Taylor stood up. "I don't know exactly where he is, but I have an idea." She touched the back of her hand, wondering how this would work. Then Olivia and Alejo on the sofa in the living room popped into her head as if it were her own memory. She could see them clearly but didn't know exactly which room and she had to concentrate. Maybe the great room where they first saw him? Or the study on the other side of that room, opposite the library. Yes, that was it. The study, it simply took a few seconds for her to feel which room it was. They walked through the house and up behind them. They turned around at their names.

"Hi, Taylor." Alejo and Liv looked from her to the blond girl.

"Hi, Olivia. This is Nicole. And Alejo." She pointed to her new companion, "She didn't believe I knew you."

Alejo looked at Nicole. "Oh, I've known Taylor a long time. We're good friends." Then he smiled warmly at Taylor. Nicole was suitably affected, looking at Alejo as if he were made of gold and satisfying Taylor's need. Taylor was ecstatic inside. Oh, I just love you, Alejo. Thank you!

Olivia looked away to hide a smile and let Alejo do his thing. He asked Nicole a few questions, told her how wonderful she looked, and then asked Taylor if she was finished for tonight.

"No, not yet. I want to spend a little time with Nicole." She looked at Olivia and got a nod.

"This is Olivia. I came to Houston with her." Liv nodded hello and asked Nicole the usual pleasantries about her evening. Taylor ratcheted up her nerve and asked Alejo:

"Hey, is it too late to get her a ticket for tomorrow's match? How do I do that?"

Olivia turned to him. "Is it?"

"It's not too late. I have extra comp tickets. VIP tent, too?" Alejo obviously had experience with people wanting a piece of his world. Taylor felt fleeting guilt for using him even though he knew what was she was doing. She promised to make it up to him somehow, if she could.

"If that's okay, that would be great."

"That's okay." He was almost offhand. "I'll let them know. They will have them at the entrance." He looked at her companion. "Nicole, right? They will be under your name."

"Yes, Nicole. Thank you!" Nicole was preening inside because now she knew someone famous. Taylor could tell she wanted to remain here with Alejo's group but couldn't think of how to ask. Taylor didn't want to stay, though. She wanted to know Nicole on her own.

"Alejo, what's going on with you guys? Just kicking back?" She hoped he would know what she was trying to do. He did, picking up her cue right away.

"Yes ... just winding down for a little while before I go back to the hotel. You promise to come and check in with us before you go? We'll be right here."

Taylor was relieved. "We will. What time is it now?"

"Almost twelve. We'll leave around one." Taylor felt a prick of disappointment. Just over one hour. Not very long, but Nicole would be at the event tomorrow. *Hey, twenty minutes ago I was going to leave on my own. What am I complaining about?* Turning to leave she motioned Nicole to join her. They were energized about tomorrow but still unsatisfied with the evening. Neither wanted it to end now.

Taylor sighed. "I wish there was still magic going on. I liked the shooting stars and everything else.

That band by the pool was really good, too. The mix of dark notes and rock in it."

"Yeah, I heard she's got powers but not strong, or something like that?" Nicole had heard bits here and there so Taylor filled her in.

"They're mostly wrapped in her music. My friend Olivia said that maybe she could develop and gain more powers, but you never really know for sure."

"That's harsh. Can you imagine having a little bit of magic and can't do everything you want? That's like seeing the feast but can't touch it."

Taylor had to agree. She could hardly remember life without magic although she used it sparingly. There was something about being able to have what you wanted, whether you used it or not. It felt safe and comforting.

Nicole saw it differently. "Doesn't it seem a little weird that here we are with all these powers and don't really use them to have a good time?"

"Yeah, but how long would that be fun by itself? There was plenty of magic here and we were bored to death because we didn't have someone to talk to." She leaned toward Nicole conspiratorially. "Hey, what if there's some kind of secret rule that if you're a witch you can't act wild? What if everyone wants to cut loose but are forced to live a dull identity to hide the truth – like Superman and Clark Kent?"

Nicole laughed. "Hilarious. What an idea." She looked around. "Like that woman over there." She pointed at a dowdy-looking woman in a flowered dress and utilitarian shoes laughing with her friends. Nicole began to talk in a low-pitched, official voice, like the narrator of a grade school educational film.

"That one" she referred to Dowdy, "is secretly a spy for a terrorist organization sent here to infiltrate us and capture a witch for study. They will try and copy our magic ability through cybernetic implants but first need to experiment on us to discover how our powers work. If that fails the plan is to use one of us for some nefarious deed, perhaps as a WMD. That blowsy woman is trained in Aikido, Jeet Kune Do, Marine Corps Combat fighting, and Egyptian Stick Fencing. She wears a fat suit to further hide her true identity as a sleek, athletic, and fully conditioned deadly weapon."

Taylor laughed in delight. "Egyptian Stick Fencing? Really." Then she looked around, pointing out another person. "How about him?" The target this time was a handsome, clean-cut man. Nicole hardly missed a beat with her story.

"That one is well-known in scientific circles. He masquerades as a nuclear physicist. Decades ago he was on the team that built the first atomic bomb and his assignment was to interfere and prevent its creation, but he failed miserably as we all know. For that mishap he was relegated to the basement of the particle accelerator in Switzerland, where he spends his days cleaning the tunnel of dust specks with a tiny brush while he keeps an eye on their progress and reports back to his magical handlers. He secretly wishes for an arms dealer to attempt a heist of the radioactive nuclear isotopes used in the collider so he can thwart the crime and redeem himself. Of course, that is un-likely as there is no known use for such low-level radio-active isotopes in destructive weapons applications. So his wish to be a hero and save the world is, sadly, doomed to failure."

Taylor smothered her laughter. "That just made no sense." They snickered together and then Taylor pointed. "What about her?" Their next victim in a long velvet dress and costume hat with an ostrich feather was totally unaware of the drama played out on her.

Nicole narrowed her eyes and looked at Taylor seriously. "Ah, that is truly a sad story. Although she appears crazy she is actually is a very accomplished witch, going on lecture circuits around the world as a motivational speaker for poor insecure souls in the witch community. She holds workshops called "Build-ing Your Magical Skills" and was the subject of a fea-ture article in the much vaunted "Better Brooms and Cauldrons" September issue. But she yearns to throw away all that success and stress in order to have a sim-pler life selling fake potions and herbs to tourists in Sa-lem, Massachusetts."

Taylor could hardly breathe, she was laughing so hard. Her ribs hurt from trying to hold it in so no one would know how they were dissing the guests. So nice not to be so serious about their craft all the time! She said so to Nicole, who agreed, exasperated.

"God, that's true. They're all so stuffy with their 'Be careful of this or that,' and 'Watch Out' all the time. So much doom and gloom. Half of them are clinically depressed for one reason or another, I swear!"

That caused Taylor to peel off another laugh and she had to wipe tears away from her eyes. This girl was ideal – unfettered, no one to account to, and clever.

She was dying to know. "So how did you learn about magic? Do you have a teacher? I know it's difficult on your own."

"No, I don't have one. I have a familiar that teaches me."

"How did you find a familiar when you didn't know magic?"

"When I learned I could move things, or set them on fire, or make them appear and disappear, I tried to do more, but I wasn't very good at it. I was trying to concentrate harder and focus like I'd heard people talk about. Then one day I was outside myself, like in another world. Taylor, it was amazing. It was like flying places and seeing multiple colors in everything and secret creatures around all the time. It was beautiful."

Taylor cut in. "I know what you mean. I've been there, too. But my mentor showed me and since then it's been a lot of time and work trying to handle it, and here you do it by accident."

"Well, don't let it sound like it was all that great. I lost my way and couldn't get back. It seemed like days I was floating out there and was really scared I'd done something I couldn't fix. Then one of the chimera out there helped me find my way home and how to get back into myself."

"What happened? I was told it's almost impossible to find your way back once you slip out."

"It was. If it hadn't found me I don't know what would have happened. But it said if I wanted to, it would teach me magic, and it did. I've seen things I never dreamed could possibly exist, but I can't do it all yet."

Taylor was thinking of her experiences and how much more she'd seen tonight. "How long have you been using your power?"

Nicole shrugged. "I don't know…a little while."

Taylor could feel herself identifying with Nicole – so much in common and not one so far ahead of the other like Olivia and her friends. It was great to be on the same footing as someone and not be the newbie!

Nicole sat forward in her chair, ready to get up. "Hey, let's go look around. There might be something going on still."

"I don't know. It's after midnight at this point and it looked pretty dead when I came through an hour ago."

"Well, I'm tired of sitting here. Maybe we can make some fun."

They moved through the house and went outside. Jolene and Akinyi were gone now, along with almost everyone else. The house had already removed the lawn furniture. Gone were the animals, the shooting stars, and only a few guests remained, maybe ten at most. It was quiet out here now except for a low hum of conversation from the die-hards that stayed.

"Yeah, this is done." said Nicole. She tapped Taylor's arm and started off across the lawn. "Come on. I want to show you something." Taylor followed her into the tall grass of the adjoining meadow, wondering what they were doing. Once they were there Nicole crouched down and Taylor followed, obscuring them both from the view of the leftover guests.

Nicole nestled down in the grass. "Think of something good – of the warmest, most wonderful feeling you can – and hold that thought."

"What? Why?" Taylor had no clue.

"Just do it. I have a surprise."

Taylor did, picturing herself lying on the sugar-white sand of a Tahitian vacation poster she used to keep in her room. She'd always dreamed of going there. She imagined the sun hot and soothing on her skin and the ocean breeze keeping her the perfect temperature at the same time it brought exotic fragrances.

Nicole eyed her. "Are you ready?"

Taylor nodded, looking at Nicole and wondering what was next.

Nicole reached her hand toward Taylor's face, palm flat. As she watched, Taylor saw another hand reach out from Nicole's, a chimeral palm that flexed and shone as it touched her forehead. *She was blended with her familiar!* She hardly had time to capture her own thought. As they touched her a burst of wonderment raced into view, then rushed down to encompass her whole body. Not only was she warm and stretched out on her sandy beach, she was the sun, and the sand, and the perfumed air. All of it and a thousand times more flowed through her. She was no longer restricted by her limiting skin. She was made of fragrance and heat and breeze. The feeling was exquisite, exotic, it was too much and not enough at the same time. She gasped at the beauty of it all. Then it was gone.

Nicole took her hand away and sat looking at Taylor, who was completely still with her mouth hanging open. Taylor didn't want to move and disturb what she had just felt, afraid it would go away. Saying nothing she flicked her eyes to Nicole, who was watching her, silent but with anticipation.

After only a few seconds Nicole couldn't stand it anymore. "Well?"

"That was incredible." Her whole body was vibrating.

"I know!" Nicole was delighted.

"What was that?"

"A hit of magic. My familiar showed me. You think of something you want amped up and it will go into you and increase the feeling by about a zillion times. Isn't it awesome?"

"Wow." Taylor was thinking how different this was than her first experience out in the ether with the chimera. That one seemed to try everything at once, choke her, take her over. This was different, didn't feel threatening. Was this what Beth was going to show her? Why was Liv apprehensive about it?

Nicole was anxious to share with her new friend. "Try something else."

Taylor tried the other end of the spectrum. Instead of the beach she pictured herself on top a mountain – yeah, that gigantic rock in Yosemite that was cut in half by ancient glaciers. She pictured what the vista would be like from there, the mountain sky, what it would sound like and feel like to perch there and absorb the view. She opened her eyes and nodded to Nicole.

"Okay, go ahead."

The glowing palm touched her face again and the vision slammed into her like the chill of mint in her mouth on a cold day, only it wasn't cold. The temperature was completely comfortable, but the feeling itself was breathtaking and crisp. The bald granite spanned a thousand feet below her and she gaped at its grey beauty. Then it was suddenly beside her. She swept over the speckled face of the monolith as if she were an eagle flying along the sheer wall. From her perspective she could see the tiniest rodents below, could hear deer drinking from the pristine lake, the scratch of pine needles against each other in the centuries-old evergreens. She was the brisk brilliant air itself, was everything and everywhere at once, and she could hardly breathe in enough of the delicious wind that rushed through her. She wanted to cry, the feeling was so expansive.

It didn't last nearly long enough, a few seconds and then gone. "Why doesn't it last?"

"My familiar just rushes through you to give the feeling."

"Do it again." It was like waking from a dream and wanting to go back to sleep immediately to continue it. She was surprised that she wanted the cliff wall back again instead of her island dream. She pictured herself where she had left off to see if she could expand on it.

"Okay."

Nicole was smiling, nodding. "I knew you would love this." She palmed Taylor again and watched as her face went taut with the exhilaration, then slack from pleasure. After a few seconds she expected Taylor's eyes to open, but they didn't. She stayed as she was, so still that Nicole was concerned.

"Are you okay?" She was afraid her new comrade wasn't coming back to her.

Eyes still closed, Taylor said, "Yeah, I'm fine...just trying to make it last."

Relief washed through Nicole. "Oh. Dammit, don't do that!" She laughed. "Do you want some more?"

Taylor opened her eyes to Nicole. "Duh. Yeah."

"Pick something different. What else do you want to do?"

Taylor immediately thought of sex. Magnified like this, what would it become? Nicole wouldn't know what she was thinking, would she? Taylor picked a fantasy and then nodded at Nicole. "Okay, go ahead."

As the hand touched her she felt the glow of magic coming on, the arrival of power once again. It was sinuous feeling, sensations warming her toes, then ankles and then snaking up her inner thighs and through her entire core. Lust and movement and slippery soft erotic feelings burned through her, filled her to bursting. Her breasts were cupped by glowing palms and every orifice had incredible sensations. It was uncontrollable, she wanted more. She heard a long groaning noise and then stifled laughter. Then it was gone – but sooner this time, she could tell.

"Why did you take it away?" She looked at Nicole, whose eyes were wide, her hand over her laughing mouth.

"Because you were making so much noise! God, you could wake the dead with that. You need to be quiet or we need to go somewhere private."

"You could hear me?" Then Taylor realized she was lying in the grass with her back arched, knees up and apart, facing the night sky. She was mortified, hoping her hands weren't somewhere embarrassing. She had no idea what she'd done while inside the dose of magic.

"That's okay, it happened to me the first time, too. You learn to maintain control. But isn't it great?"

It was, but Taylor wasn't sure about how far it had gone. To lose where she was, not able to control herself... Still, what a rush, and what else was out there she didn't know about? "Yeah, it was pretty awe-some." She was speaking carefully, hoping Nicole would think she was dazed instead of unsure.

Nicole was delighted with her new acquaint-ance. "I'm so glad we met when we did, I was about to leave when I found you. I didn't feel like I had any-thing in common with the others here, people already knew each other..."

"I know. I was thinking the same thing." Tay-lor really was relieved at having a friend of her own and intrigued by the fun she was coming up with. It made her feel solid, like she had a place in the witching world.

Nicole looked at her watch. "Hey, it's almost one in the morning. Weren't you going to check in with Alejo and Olivia? Then we could go find some all night clubs in town, I'll bet."

Taylor didn't want this to end but didn't feel like she could just leave on her own to some random place. "I came with my friend Olivia and don't want to abandon her so I need to take off. We're both going to the polo match tomorrow, so why don't we meet in the VIP tent?"

Nicole was disappointed but didn't push. "I could do that. Let's trade cell numbers." As Taylor pulled out her cell, intending to enter the number Ni-cole touched it, and there was her name and phone number in the contacts.

That's pretty slick, thought Taylor. *I was think-ing of the old way to do it. This girl uses magic for everything.* On the fly, she gave her info the same way when Nicole held out her cell.

Then Nicole asked, "Where are you staying?"

"Hotel ZaZa."

"Nice... I'm at the Icon. Cipriati suite. You know, we could just go to the match together tomorrow."

"I don't know if Olivia's expecting me to go with her, but..." Taylor didn't want to lose momentum with her new acquaintance. "Why don't you come over to my hotel room for coffee beforehand, then we'll all go together?"

"That sounds great! What time, like ten o'clock? I don't want to get up too early."

"Perfect. Come on – let's go find Alejo and Liv." She started off through the house, back to where they had left them. When they got there Alejo was already saying his goodbyes.

"I'm going back to the hotel now. Nicole, you know where to pick up your tickets, right?"

She looked at Alejandro and nodded, then turned to Taylor: "Are you sure you don't want to stop somewhere for a quick drink or coffee? It's only one."

"Nicole, I would love to, but I can't. For sure, though, ten tomorrow morning, my hotel."

Alejo smiled at them both. "Do you want help getting home?" That soft Latin accent again warmed his voice.

"What about the car?" Taylor looked at Olivia.

"I'll take care of it. Let Alejandro send you, he likes to do that sort of thing." She turned to him. "Show-off. You're a wicked child."

He laughed. "Where are you going?" He was looking at the two girls as Olivia faded beside him, already on her way.

"I'm at the Icon, she's at ZaZa." She could tell Nicole was still dazzled by him. Everyone was. She wondered if he had wrapped himself in a spell or carried some kind of charm or whether it was just him.

"Okay." He held up a palm toward each of them. "See you tomorrow." He smiled as they disappeared.

The pale colors of Taylor's suite flashed into view and she stood a moment, orienting herself, before walking over to sit in the chair and flip off her shoes. She'd seen so much that night. She just wanted to curl up in the little upholstered nook and replay it all. She was excited to have met Nicole, to have a friend of her own in this community. Everything was wonderful. Even the slow blobs moving in the lava lamp were wonderful as she watched them and relived the night. Alejo and Olivia were wonderful. And tomorrow would be wonderful. Oh, yes. Being a witch was terrific.

Many blocks away, Nicole materialized next to her bed with its soft blue and brown paisley bedding, now neatly arranged in contrast to the disarray of this morning. Nice to have any remnants of the night before all straightened out by someone else's hand. She always tipped the room staff well and they took good care of her. The zipper on her top undid itself as she walked through the bathroom to one of the sinks. She turned the water on to warm it up and stared at her image in the mirror as it ran. Looking at the room in the reflection, she spoke.

"No." It came out a little hesitantly, not what she intended. The marble and porcelain gave back silence.

She repeated a little louder. "No." More forceful this time. No change in the room reflecting back at her. But the nape of her neck tightened, the prickling sensation going up and down like baby spiders. She pressed her lips together, pinching the bottom one between her teeth and feeling the sting. It steeled her.

"I cannot do it!" She almost shouted. This time a response...she heard pale whispering, layers of transient hissing repeated in different strata.

"Oh, but you will..." The voices slurred and she felt a caress on her arm, the lightest touch going from one wrist to the back of her neck, a vile unwanted lover's touch.

Trepidation flooded her. The backs of her knees trembled and fear watered her mouth. She gritted her teeth and closed her eyes until the feeling went away, hanging her head over the sink for several long minutes to regain her composure.

The water still flowed, clear and forgotten. With hollow movements she reached out her hand to gather soap and washcloth but changed her mind. Shutting off the faucet she went back to the bed where she curled up, pulling the thick padded coverlet over her entirely. Closing her eyes, she thought a command and the lights went out, leaving her there as a mound in the fabric with the murky form of her familiar draped tightly over her.

The pounding of hoofs on the hard-packed turf was almost musical; multiple quick strikes that over-wrote each other in cadence. The sound broke up as the group turned, riders and ponies braking from gal-lops to turn and follow the little treasure now rolling in another direction. The noise from the crowd fluttered with occasional shouts when the action was slow, be-coming an uproar when they all went flashing down the field at full-speed toward the goalposts.

Taylor was peering into the stand of slim legs surrounding the little sphere, all moving and jostling closely in the pack. Turquoise and red shinguards flashed through the action, identifying who was on which team in the quest for control of the ball.

Barely an hour ago they had all been in the VIP tent, watching Alejo as he was being interviewed by the local TV station. Both he and another player, Thomas, had been tapped to publicize the event. On the way over Liv had tried to explain the volume of photographers that would be around Alejo and his team. She hadn't been kidding. From Taylor's perspec-tive it had been staggering, a flashstorm of publicity which was now tapering off. She was surprised to find she didn't like the experience, even watching it. How many times in the past had she fantasized about being rich and famous? It was not the way she had pictured it.

Alejo and Thomas had been doing interviews since one o'clock. They were splendid in their simple livery: turquoise polo shirts with a diagonal black stripe and crest at the left shoulder, the European cut making them look slender and broad-shouldered at the same time, their white jeans tucked into simple black riding boots.

"Look at them. They both look like royalty with the photographers and all." Nicole was wowed.

Akinyi had a puzzled scowl. "Why are they carrying their hats for interviews? They don't usually do that." She and Jolene both had on broad-brimmed hats, but they were designed for fashion, not a piece of protective hardware to take off and carry.

Beth answered. "Oh, that's nothing. The publicity people wanted them to wear shinguards for the photographers, too. Handy told them that was too much and would look fake, like the hat; they only wear them during the game. Then the promoters wanted the hat, too, so finally they compromised on stuffing their gloves in their back pockets and carrying the hats." She had come here with Alejo earlier and had watched it all play out.

"The gloves are okay, but who really believes carrying around your hat all the time?" Akinyi still thought it was stupid. "Whatever."

Jolene was standing with her, of course. They were always together. Jolene had her face close to talk in Akinyi's ear. Taylor watched the two women scan the room, picking out different people and commenting on who they knew and what they knew. They used single words, half-sentences, sometimes a look to communicate. They made Taylor think of her and Karen.

She turned to Nicole. "I guess we're all going out afterward. Come with us?"

Nicole waffled. "Do you want to do that or go somewhere else? I feel like dancing."

"Depends. We could probably do both. Go with them and then find a club." She turned to Beth on her right. "Beth, where are we going after the match?"

"Mark's restaurant." Beth replied. "It used to be an old Gothic church. Built sometime in the 1920's, I think. Julia says we have the Loft reserved."

Taylor turned back to Nicole. "I want to see it, at least."

Olivia came up just then. "I'm going up to our seats now with JaneAnn. You know where they are?"

"I'll come up with you now. These guys are almost done." Beth waved her hand at Alejo and the gaggle of press. "I need to get away from the buffet, anyway. I keep eating when I'm not hungry. Hey, I heard Julia and Marcus have one of those cabana tents close to the sidelines?"

"They do. They invited us over for a couple of chukkers, but I like the grandstands better; it's up higher where I can see all the action. Being in those cabanas is like being courtside at a basketball game. Are you two coming up soon?" She looked at Taylor and Nicole.

Taylor nodded. "Yeah, soon."

Olivia nodded. "Well, whenever you get there, we're in the center, halfway up."

In the center, halfway up was where they were now, trying to see which player out on the field was Alejo in the knot of riders and horses competing for the ball. It was hard for Nicole and Taylor to tell – at least five players between both teams had his dark good looks, as if it were a prerequisite to be attractive and from somewhere like Argentina in order to play polo. They knew for sure he was number three on the Cambio team in the turquoise jerseys.

The ball broke away from the tangle of horses, shooting down the field. Two of the players were already after it, matching stride for stride in full gallop. The Cambio player caught it first, long-handled mallet reaching out and tapping it to the left and bouncing it across the grass as they sprinted toward the goal. The red-jerseyed rider reached over his horse to put his mallet between them and steal the ball, careful not to come in at too sharp an angle and foul the other player. But the Cambio pony shouldered to his right and bumped off the red team horse as the other riders closed in behind. They weren't close enough, though. The Cambio player leaned forward and swung his mallet under the horse's neck, smacking the ball hard and off to the left so it sped ahead of the pack of riders and through the goalposts. The announcer shouted a goal was scored, but the crowd was already roaring approval and drowned him out. Taylor turned around to slap a palm with Beth, then with Nicole to her left.

Taylor could tell these teams were far better than the ones she had seen in Seattle. The game was faster, and riders used their mallets differently. More shots under the neck were taken or sent between legs. The riders hardly handled the reins at all, giving commands with their legs or letting their well-trained mounts follow the action of their own accord. They were obviously competitive in their own right, bumping and riding off their opponents with no apparent urging, and the crowd was abundant in shouting their love for the ponies, the game, and the thrill of it all.

The first two chukkers were over far too quickly and during the second break Taylor and Nicole took a better look at their surroundings. This was more elaborate than Olivia's horse property, a real country club. A neatly trimmed hedge ringed the field and grandstands, separating the parking lot and massive clubhouse from the inner sanctum of the polo field.

"Wow," said Nicole, "It's hard to believe there are tailgaters with their barbeques and cowboy hats right over there in the parking lot, and across from us it's all Mercedes and Veuve Clicquot champagne in the awards tent." She pointed at the latest model of the luxury car right next to the table of trophies glittering silver in the rich afternoon sun.

Taylor smiled back at her, enjoying her pleasure and feeling supremely happy about being here. The day was golden and semitropical, the air redolent with the gulf breeze richness and perfume that she had by now fallen in love with. Spectators were milling around and laughing, the air palpable with fun and excitement.

"They really take this seriously here...look at this place." Nicole was gawking right and left. "There must be three thousand people here."

"And it's bigger in Florida." Olivia put in. "And in Argentina, a polo field is practically sacred ground. Taylor's already been to a match back in Washington, and she's gotten very good at understanding the game."

Taylor offered an additional tidbit. "Some places around Miami they play on the beach. I've seen videos of it on YouTube – all the white sand. It's really cool."

"In Europe there's snow polo, too. I've been to a match in St. Moritz with JaneAnn."

"Really?" Both Taylor and Nicole were impressed.

From behind them, JaneAnn kicked in offhandedly. "You can go around the world attending these things. They're in India, England, Dubai...Marcus and Julia and I went to the Southeast Asian Games a few years ago."

"Wouldn't that be fun?" Nicole sounded almost wistful. "Just go around the world doing this. So is it just polo at this club?"

"No, they have other horse shows, dressage and jumping, or rent the club out for weddings, corporate gigs, and such." Movement on the field attracted her attention. "Oh, look. They're coming back on the field."

They watched as the teams lined up midfield and the referee threw the ball in between them. Immediately after it was chopped out of the group, Alejo raced downfield toward the posts. A Cambio rider gave it a hard slam Alejo's way so he could get a mallet on it and send it toward the goal but didn't hit it far enough and now he needed to catch it. Two riders from the opposing team chased him at a full run, horses flattening out for maximum speed. They caught up with the Cambio rider and he had to restrict the ball by using short taps in an effort to keep control.

"That's Alejo, setting up by the goal posts!" Taylor shouted. She pointed him out to Nicole. "See number three? That's Alejandro. He's waiting for the other Cambio rider to shoot the ball to him."

Two other red players pressed in close, but Alejo avoided them by cutting to the right and they galloped past him. His teammate passed the ball to him at the last minute and he cracked it across the goal line with inches to spare. But he couldn't veer off in time to avoid the goalpost and both horse and rider crashed into it, breaking it loose from its moorings and

CATHLEEN DUNN

sending Alejo and the bundle of cane rolling across the grass.

A huge gasp rolled around the crowd, but Alejo got up immediately and the crew came out to repair the post. The pony stood off to the side, agile enough to sidestep a fall but launching Alejo from the saddle.

"I can't believe he didn't get hurt! He broke the goalpost!" Nicole was all disbelief.

"Oh, he's okay." Olivia explained. "Those posts are meant to break. They're a bundle of light stuff, like cane or cardboard or something else, and it's meant to snap off when it gets banged into. "

"Oh..." Nicole was relieved. "It looked worse than that."

"Nah, it's okay." Beth joined in. "See? They're fixing it already and everybody's fine."

Indeed, after only a few minutes, the post was back up and the action resumed as if there had never been a crash. The game went back and forth for an-other few minutes of play, the stationary scrambles for the ball alternating with mad dashes to the goal lines. Right now there was a lull in the game; apparently one of the players was taking a penalty shot.

"What happened?" Nicole was lost. Taylor helped her out, hardly believing that she could explain.

"One of the players did an illegal hook – that means he hit the other rider's mallet from behind when he was coming up on him. He can't do that, so now this guy gets a free shot from sixty yards. See how the others are down at the goal now, setting up in front of it? They'll try and block his shot."

To their left Olivia kept her eyes on the field and smiled behind her sunglasses, listening to Taylor's command of the game.

The crowd watched as number three for the red team set up his penalty shot. It seemed to take a long time. He kept rolling the ball with his mallet, a foot forward, a few inches in this or that direction. Then he circled his pony completely around the ball, tapping it from the other side.

"Olivia, what's he doing?" Taylor looked across Nicole at her.

"He's balancing his shot. He'll try to get the ball up on top of the grass, like on a golf tee, so he can get his mallet under it a little more. He needs to get it up and over that line of defenders in front of the goal."

Nicole and Taylor looked at each other. *That's pretty cool.* They watched as the player trotted off a way and then cantered back, wrist flicking to swing the mallet in a huge circle to strike the little ball. The ball launched up and away in a long arc, going just over the head of the last defender, but hit the goalpost and ricocheted back to the ground, bouncing back onto the field instead of behind the goal line. A drooping "Aaaaahhh..." sighed from the red team fans. All the players except two, one from each side, loped toward the other goal in anticipation of the next play. The two left waited for the ball, which the referee bowled back onto the field, and the game was on again until the chukker ended.

During the break between chukkers three and four, Taylor and Beth took Nicole onto the field to be part of the divot stamp while Olivia and the others stayed in the grandstand. JaneAnn moved down a row so she could converse with Olivia on a level setting. Jolene and Akinyi decided to join Julia and Marcus in their cabana, so they headed that way. A cabana was similar to having a private box, more room to stretch out, more "exclusive" surroundings, picnic supplies, and shade. Jolene had insisted on going, and of course Akinyi went with her.

JaneAnn was in partial agreement as they watched the two descend the bleacher steps together. "I can't blame her at all for that. Those cabanas can be pretty plush. Still, I love being part of the crowd. It's so exciting. I'm happy right here."

Olivia responded. "Me, too, but you know Jolene. She's not one to indulge in sun on her skin. She likes to keep it pale."

"I don't understand that." JaneAnn shook her head slightly. "She can make it whatever she wants."

That prompted a smile from Olivia. She leaned closer to JaneAnn, lowering her voice. "I'll tell you what she told me once. She said sometimes she misses being a plantation daughter. She misses the idea that ladies stay out of the sun, misses going to cotillions, big fluffy hoop skirts, and carriage rides pulled by horses. She liked the fancier, simpler life back then."

JaneAnn looked back at her, aghast. "Oh, my God, does she miss outhouses, too? And getting water from a well? And in New Orleans, all that marshland and mud... Oh, and typhoid! Is she crazy?"

"No, I think she forgets... and she used magic for everything when she thought she wouldn't get caught. You usually love the culture you grew up with. It's human nature."

"Yeah? Well, I remember whole families wiped out from typhoid and no one left to claim the last person who died. There are whole cemetery walls in New Orleans filled with people who were the last to die, and there they've stayed over a hundred years. No one to put them in the family crypt because there's no one left."

Olivia wrinkled her nose at her friend. "Okay... hmmm. Morbid. Let's just forget all that. It's a beautiful day and we're outside at one of Handy's polo games." They laughed together and looked out at the field for a few quiet moments.

JaneAnn looked at Olivia in her Chanel sunglasses, the mellow afternoon sun painting her hair copper. A far cry from the gray day on a filthy London street where they had met centuries ago. *Times do change, don't they?* she thought. *Life goes on. Olivia has another apprentice finally. It must be doing her good; she hasn't mentioned New Orleans like that in decades.*

"Hey, don't forget we're having brunch tomorrow with Julia and Marcus so they can get to know Taylor," said JaneAnn.

"Sure. In fact we're having it in my suite. I already told them."

"Okay. Ten-thirty still?"

"Yep. Ten-thirty." Turning away, Olivia saw the spectators being ushered off the grass by volunteers, accompanied by the announcer over the loudspeaker.

"Ladies and gentleman, Chukker Four will start in just a few minutes."

As she watched the crowd return to their seats, Olivia saw Beth on the sidelines talking to someone. She felt the blood drain from her face when she realized it was Dantin.

She curled her fingers around JaneAnn's wrist, squeezing.

"Owww..." JaneAnn plucked Liv's hand off her. "What?"

"Dantin." She pointed. "Talking to Beth."

"Where?" She followed her friend's sightline. "That's not possible. You would feel him. And there are Silver-Tints all over the place – he wouldn't be stupid enough to show his face here."

JaneAnn scanned until she found Beth, but she was talking to a tall man in a cowboy hat. "Who, him? With the hat?"

"No! He's not wearing a hat."

"Olivia, I'm looking right at them and that is not Dantin!"

Olivia couldn't rip her eyes away. There he was, big as life, but JaneAnn couldn't see him. Was she going crazy? "Test him – get him to take off that hat if it's not him."

JaneAnn shook her head. "If it is him, I don't want to call attention to myself." She was trying to think. "You know, the right way to do this is test Beth when she returns. I'll see what she was really doing."

Olivia didn't answer. While JaneAnn was talking she watched the man look right at her and smile. She watched silently as Beth, followed by Nicole and Taylor made their way back up the bleachers and sat down.

JaneAnn queried Beth about the stranger. "Hey, who was that guy you were talking to? I didn't recognize him." She put her hand on Beth's wrist as she did. It was less likely Beth would know she was charming her since she was already answering the question. JaneAnn would pick up what she really saw down on the field. She felt like a shit for being so underhanded, but Dantin wasn't one to be trifled with.

"Just some guy, asking how to get a membership here. I gave him a couple of names to contact."

JaneAnn looked back and nodded at Olivia. Beth was telling the truth. And Beth didn't know, but it had been Dantin.

This was the worst possible news. Why Beth? And what was he up to? Dantin never did anything without intent, and usually with a twist. She didn't want to see a repeat of Celeste.

"JaneAnn, could you keep tabs on Beth? Just watch her for me."

"Of course." JaneAnn knew Olivia couldn't do it herself in this situation. "What do you think he's doing, Olivia?"

Slowly, Olivia shook her head. A dozen scenarios ran through her mind. It took incredible effort to look nonchalant as she focused on the field again. When the next chukker started the action was fast, driving first toward one end and then the other. It occurred to Olivia she felt the same way right now.

Nicole turned to Taylor, looking lost. "I can't tell which is which. I thought the red shirts were driving toward that goal." She pointed at the near end of the field.

"You're right, but they change it every chukker to make the chances even. Last chukker that was red's goal. Now it's where Cambio will try to score. I know it's hard; I can't always tell from the colors because they're all running in the same direction. You just have to remember at the start of each chukker."

Nicole smiled broadly at Taylor. "This is so much fun. You know, I'm so glad we met at Julia's. Thanks for inviting me to this." She turned back to the game, leaving Taylor basking in their new friendship as the action continued in front of them.

By the beginning of chukker six, it was Alejo's team with thirteen goals and the opposing team in the red shirts with twelve. According to Beth, this was a high scoring game because the ponies and riders were so skilled. She was going on about how the red team was also a world-class string of ponies and players, and that one of their riders had a ten handicap. Apparently he was one of the best in the world, playing position number two.

They were all focused on him then as he came on the ball at full gallop, then slowed and slapped the ball lightly with his mallet, bouncing it vertical. Then he positioned his mallet under it, bouncing it off the wood repeatedly. *What is he doing?* Taylor couldn't imagine.

She was shocked to see that he continued bouncing the ball off the upside of his mallet and resumed a full gallop toward the goal. He made lithe adjustments in the saddle up and down, forward and back atop his mount, staying under the ball with his mallet and keeping total control of it in the air. She couldn't see how the others could possibly defend against it and sure enough he drove through the goalposts without ever letting the ball touch the ground in the last hundred yards. The crowd went absolutely insane.

"Is that for real?" Taylor looked at Olivia in disbelief. Olivia was glad for the break from thinking about Dantin.

"Oh, yeah, he's one of the best. It's called dribbling the ball. You bounce it off your mallet instead of hitting it across the ground."

Nicole turned to Taylor. "He has to be witch. He must be using magic."

"Do you think? I mean really – I'm not being sarcastic." Taylor was still amazed.

Nicole shook her head as she continued to watch the player in the red jersey, her mouth open. "Has to be. How else could he do that?" She thought for a second. "Do you think Alejandro uses magic when he plays?" She looked at Taylor.

Olivia leaned forward between them and whispered, completely expressionless, her eyes still focused on the field. "Don't talk about it so blatantly around other people." Then she straightened and went back to the game as if she hadn't said anything.

Both Nicole and Taylor looked at each other, feeling chastised. Nicole was wide-eyed. "Do you think she's upset with us?"

Taylor gave Liv a furtive glance. "I don't know, but she's right." She'd never made a mistake like that.

Liv leaned forward again, in close earshot. "Just remember who's around you. Why don't you ask Alejo about it at Mark's? It'll be just us there."

"Okay." Nicole and Taylor both nodded and went back to the game. It was thirteen to thirteen and only three minutes left. The Cambio team couldn't score and ended up fouling one of the other players. The resulting penalty shot put the opposing team over the top in the last few moments of the match.

"Well," JaneAnn tried to soften their disappointment, "at least it's not a season game so it won't affect their international standings." They were all watching the players ride up to each other on the field and shake hands, congratulating each other on a good game.

Olivia wanted to leave right away, but Beth wanted to stay and watch the ceremonies. "Let's see how much money we raised. The last I heard it was over two hundred thousand dollars."

She was right, the match was a success and each rider was given an engraved silver Taghauer watch as a thank-you. They all stood together, displaying the watches for photos. After that, Alejandro and Thomas each grabbed a bottle of champagne, spraying it all over the red team in congratulations. The resulting scramble from everyone doused by the wet bubbles ended the "formal" part of the ceremony and most of the crowd scattered, trickling out to their cars.

"Come on." JaneAnn pulled Beth along with her. She wanted to make sure Alejo would show at a reasonable hour. He was often hung up after events with well-wishers or others catching him on the fly since he was in the vicinity. They all went down to the presentation circle and she reminded Alejo about Mark's.

"I'll meet you there in an hour, definitely."

"One hour." JaneAnn eyed him pointedly. "In the Loft. If you don't show up, I'll come and get you." She wasn't kidding. She'd done it before by grabbing him when he had a second of privacy and transporting him elsewhere, change of clothes and all. He actually loved it; to be surprised like that was nice. He laughed and turned toward the stables while the other witches headed for their respective rides uptown.

They were standing around chatting in the Loft at Mark's when Alejo mounted the stairs. He'd actually arrived around the same time they had, having used sorcery to change and get to the restaurant after a hot shower. A genuine hot shower, magic wasn't a good enough replacement for a real one, the soothing, pounding spray of water that he could stand under and let run down his skin in little rivulets. Now he was standing at the top of the stairs with the others, refreshed.

He and Olivia were with JaneAnn and Beth, watching Taylor and Nicole from across the room while their table was readied. Both Olivia and Taylor had used JaneAnn's charm on Nicole to make sure she wasn't Dantin in disguise, and an additional spell to see if she knew anything about Dantin. To their relief both came up negative so the girl was safe.

"I'm sure that she has a familiar." Alejo was watching the girls, arms folded.

Olivia agreed. She sensed the same kind of dual entity in Nicole as in Beth, except that Beth was powerful, deeply trained, and had a well-developed sense of self. Nicole felt a little pale, blurred around the edges, but being diluted like that wasn't unusual for a novice, Olivia knew. And with the others around it was hard to tell where they left off and Nicole began.

"I think Nicole can benefit from being around the rest of us, and Taylor certainly seems taken with her. It's good for her to have a friend of her own."

JaneAnn shook her head, wondering if Olivia would push Taylor to independence too soon instead of keeping her close where they could protect her. She was about to ask, knowing she would start an argument, when the *maître d'* announced to them that their table was ready.

After they sat, Nicole turned to Alejo. "Do you use magic when you play? You're so good at it."

He shook his head. "No, I really love the hard work. There's something about working hard and having practice after practice until everyone is in unison and the team is performing well."

"But couldn't you up the performance of the team if you tweaked it a little bit?"

"Yes and no. I could do a few individual things, but it's best to play as one with my teammates and my pony. I shouldn't manipulate their skills, and I can't outstrip them or it's not a team. We all need to play at the same level to succeed. And to do it the easy way wouldn't feel as good."

"But then you wouldn't have crashed into the goal post today."

Alejo looked surprised at Nicole, and then around the table at the others. "She certainly doesn't step into a conversation softly, does she?" He smiled with humor and looked back at her.

"Yes, I could have avoided that, but where is the excitement if I control everything that's going to happen? And when I play well, then is it me that plays well, or am I only good because I cheat with magic? I don't want to do that – I'd rather work hard and feel like I accomplished something and know that it's truly me who is good at it. And if I crash and am hurt, well, I can take care of that."

"Well, if that's the case you really are good. How long have you been playing?" Taylor asked.

Alejo calculated back for a second. "Mmm...just over two hundred and eighty years."

"What?" Taylor and Nicole looked at each other. Even Akinyi and Jolene were fazed; that was longer than they'd been alive.

Julia tagged onto the conversation. "That's nothing. He's been on horseback for over six hundred years – his family in Spain has always owned horses. Alejo loves them and of course he had to bring a bunch with him when he sailed to South America in the 1500's."

Alejandro was quietly proud. "I can think of no other way to live. Life without my horses? My ponies are my family." Then he looked around at the others at the table. "Well, in addition to you all, of course, but you don't live with me and I can't ride you." His last words elicited a huge burst of laughter from the group.

"Hey," As the laughter died Beth turned to Olivia. "I've got a great idea...why don't you guys lob out to my place for a visit? We can stay in Sydney for a couple and then go out to the station." She was referring to her huge sheep ranch in the Kimberley region of Australia.

Olivia mused. "Maybe that would be nice. I love your big backyard." She referred to the outback, a big expanse of wild territory that made up most of the continent.

"That's right." Beth coaxed her friend some more. "I'll take you out there and you can soak it up all you want. 'Roos, cricket, and beer. What do you say? Bring those greyhounds. They can chase jackrabbits and get some exercise."

It sounded pretty good...she found herself smiling at that. A month or two in the big Never. Still, Olivia hedged, not wanting to commit to anything regarding Taylor. And it was irritating that everyone assumed they would be close, just because.

"We'll see."

Smiling to herself, Beth took a sip of her wine and leaned back, satisfied she'd planted the seed. She would work on Olivia until she had her way.

Taylor turned to Nicole. It didn't sound like the invite applied to her new friend and she didn't want her to feel left out. "Hey, that's a great idea. Why don't you come to Seattle and visit us? I've got some stuff I'd love to show you." She was thinking of the little neighborhoods there, like Wallingford and Queen Anne, and of sharing the Columbia Tower experience with her.

Nicole's eyes lit up. "That's a great idea – I would love that."

Taylor was planning aloud. "Christmas is barely two months away. You could come early and we could spend the whole midwinter holidays together, maybe meet my sister if she comes back to Seattle. Unless you have somewhere else to be." She didn't know if her sister was coming back for the holidays, and suddenly she thought Nicole might have other friends or family commitments.

"No, I'm good. I could come out mid-December and stay through New Year's if you want."

It was an awkward moment. Taylor couldn't offer Nicole a place to stay when it was Olivia's house, not hers. "We only have one guest room at Olivia's, though."

"That's totally fine." Nicole answered, "I like to stay at a hotel where I have privacy and room service."

"Perfect." Taylor was mentally planning the itinerary already. She got Olivia's attention across the table. "Nicole is going to be in Seattle around the holidays. We can continue lessons together." She wanted to make sure Olivia knew she didn't plan on slacking off.

The exchange didn't escape Julia's sharp notice. "So, Nicole, I gather you're new to magic. Do you have a guide or someone teaching you?" *The girl is adorable*, she thought, *she looks like a little porcelain doll. We could use some new people in our crowd.*

Nicole swallowed a bite of appetizer before answering. "I have a familiar helping me."

"Well, if you want another person to practice with or are curious about different things, I would be happy to help you."

Gratitude was obvious in Nicole's face. "Oh, that would be..." She stopped, as if her words couldn't make their way through a choked throat. She took a breath and then appeared calmer. "That would be wonderful. Thank you. I'll call you."

Julia could tell Nicole was thankful, but she felt something else, too. Was it loneliness? She didn't seem to know anyone else, and she hadn't talked about anyone else. Empathy flooded her. "Well, the offer is open anytime. Just let me know. You know where I live."

"I will." Nicole assured her.

That assuaged Taylor's feelings about Nicole not being included in the invite to Australia. The conversation around the table thickened and for the next thirty minutes they ate and talked about the party the previous night and that day's match. But then the discussion turned to more reminiscing, and then Akinyi and Jolene describing their upcoming vacation plans. Nicole bumped Taylor's foot under the table with her own.

"Let's go clubbing," she whispered. She was antsy and wanted to get away with Taylor. Taylor agreed immediately.

"Hey, Olivia. Nicole and I are going somewhere else. Maybe Edloe's or somewhere with dancing."

"What, just the two of you?" Liv regarded the both of them, forcing herself to remember Taylor had JaneAnn's charm.

The others voiced their opinions around the table. "Olivia, they're in their twenties, or at least almost." Or, "Oh, let them go, what can happen to them?" Someone else added, "They'll be all right. I'd like to see some human just try and take advantage of them."

Olivia tried not to look annoyed. "Fine, have fun. I'll see you in the morning. Brunch is at ten-thirty."

Nicole stood up and Taylor did, too. "See you later, everyone." They descended the stairs and left Mark's.

Jolene looked around at everyone after they had disappeared. "I should go, too. I've hardly started packing yet."

Akinyi turned to look at her. "What are you talking about? You fill a few suitcases by magic and then conjure or buy whatever else you need along the way."

Jolene was put out. "Yeah, but I always start with a suitcase list and then conjure it all at once. I haven't written anything down yet."

"Why don't you use the same list each time? We're always going off someplace or another."

"Not the same place every time. I need different stuff."

Julia interceded. "Will you two quit quibbling about it?" The two stopped and Julia turned to Marcus. "For the love of God. I just know at some point I'm either going to have to spell them to shut up or kill the both of them to stop their bickering. Sheeesh."

The table roared with laughter. Everyone knew the two were best friends and they argued for fun. Then Marcus and Julia announced they were leaving, too. "It's been a long week for us, what with the party and all."

Olivia turned to the others. She wanted to get some time alone with Alejo and this was her opportunity. "I need to leave, too. I'm beat and I want to get up early and have coffee with Taylor. We haven't really talked for a couple days. She's mostly been with Nicole since last night."

"You might end up with the two of them tomorrow morning," said Julia. "They seem to be pretty tight."

Olivia fingered a leftover crumb on her plate. "Yeah." She nodded. "I feel a little bad about not including Nicole for brunch. I don't think she knows anybody."

JaneAnn reminded her. "Yeah, but brunch is for Taylor. We just met Nicole. And what happens when you two go back to Seattle? Take her with you to live?"

"Oh, heavens, no. Just thinking aloud. I can't help but notice she didn't seem to know anyone else."

JaneAnn smirked at Olivia and said under her breath: "...and you didn't even want the first apprentice. You're really a mush inside."

"Oh, shit. JaneAnn...shut up." Olivia stood up to go while JaneAnn laughed. Alejo rose with her, pushing his chair back.

"I'll take you back to your hotel and we can visit."

"Thanks, Handy." He'd spent the last few days in Houston with JaneAnn and Beth, but he and Olivia hadn't told the others they'd had lunch recently. She slipped into her jacket and waited for him as he said his goodbyes.

"Well, come on then." She stood there, pretending impatience. "You'll see them for brunch in the morning, you know." She wanted to tell him about seeing Dantin, or at least thinking she saw him.

Now Beth and JaneAnn decided to leave as well, since they were the only ones left. It always intrigued Olivia, this phenomenon: if a few people left a party it was amazing how fast the whole thing would break up and end, just like that.

The group exited the restaurant into the early dusk. It was barely seven o'clock and the setting sun reflected off the Gulf to warm the fading skies with gold. They turned to enter the cove outside between the nave and façade of the old cathedral, where they could see the whole street and be assured there was no one else around. Without further words the eight and their respective vehicles disappeared as if they were never there.

Olivia and Alejo materialized in the Black Label suite at ZaZa where she was staying and he looked
around.

"I haven't been here before. Plush."

"It's on my favorites list right now, the only
place I'll stay in Houston. I love the unexpected look of
it." She took off her jacket and walked into the bedroom to change her clothes.

Alejo moved through the expansive sitting
room with adjoining dining area and back again, looking at the décor and admiring the combination of classic and *avant garde* materials. Mocha-colored walls
throughout were set off by layers of crown molding in
a beautiful dusky vanilla, heavy looking to be up
against the ceiling but giving a richness to the suite
that was matched by ornate baseboards. He liked that
the furnishings were unusual, too: two wing chairs upholstered in faux zebra skin played off a simple couch
in charcoal grey linen. Small pillows in burgundy, navy
and plum silk made a surprisingly understated accent,
and accessories were mostly metal. It was a visual
feast.

Olivia came back into the sitting room to make
herself a drink.

"Do you want something while I'm at the bar?"
She liked the ritual of making it herself, shaking the ice

and vodka in the container, and creating her little salad of olives on the pick to go in it.

"Scotch rocks is fine." Alejandro came over to watch her, his six-foot-two inches making her five-foot-three inch frame look tiny next to him. It always amazed him, how small she really was after taking off her heels and padding around in pajamas. She handed him his drink.

"At the game I saw Dantin talking to Beth."

"What?" He couldn't believe he'd heard her.

"I'm sure it was him. I saw him clearly. Jane-Ann looked right at him and saw some stranger in a cowboy hat, but when Beth came back to our seats she checked and it was Dantin, no doubt."

"She asked her?" That would have surprised him; Olivia told very few about Dantin. Only Julia, Dan, JaneAnn, and he knew as far as he was aware.

"No, with a spell. Beth doesn't know what he looks like."

"What did he say to her?"

"He asked her about getting a membership, that sort of thing. But you know it's not an accident."

"*Como si no fuera poco...*" Sometimes he reverted to Spanish when he was rattled. "You want me to keep an eye on her?"

"No, JaneAnn is going to." She was pointed in her look at him. "You have other things to do."

"*Como Dios manda* – everything is going fine." He wanted to reassure her. "You know how he is. He does things so you can't forget about him. Half the fun for him is the mind game. But just to be sure, why don't we tell the others so they can watch out for him?"

"No. We've had this talk before. If they know, Dantin might focus on them to get to me."

"And if not, they don't know enough to protect themselves."

"But not as likely. And I don't want to scare them, either."

"Olivia, we really need to let them know."

"Handy, I'm not telling them and that's the end of it. Just leave it alone."

Alejo knew that what she didn't say was her fear they would ostracize her. Not a good thing to be friends with someone who had a Blue/Black after them. *But she should know us better*, he thought.

"All right then. We can't really do anything until we know more, so we stay calm and think it through. JaneAnn follows Beth, we check everything that happens, we put the information together, and we figure out what he's doing."

Olivia nodded and he could see the edge come off her a little. He used his pet name for her to ease her mood further.

"Come on, Livy, let's sit down and have our drink." They went into the sitting room where Olivia crossed to the hide-covered chairs, setting her drink on the side table next to them.

"I'm going to move these." She pulled her chair forward.

"I was thinking the same thing. Face them toward the window?" He pulled the other chair and turned it around until both chairs were next to each other in front of the glass, side tables repositioned next to them. Taking off his shoes Alejo stretched out, feet against the floor-length windows. Olivia settled into the chair next to his, curling up between the arms but then changed her mind, stretching out her legs toward the window as Alejo did. They sat quietly together for a while, the broad chair arms just inches from each other, and looked at the streetlights in the Museum District park below.

"Like sitting on the veranda in Saint-Domingue." Alejo was picturing the lush green foliage and tropical blossoms of the jungle, barely fifty feet off the porch of JaneAnn's plantation house there.

Olivia was immediately in the moment with him. She could see the carved latticework of the veranda railing, so expensive and rare in the islands, brought from Europe by ship in the 1730's. They used to put their feet up on that railing for hours, watching the birds in the jungle, the locals coming out to work the cane fields or moving around the house to do domestic chores, crossing the strip of lawn to fetch water, or beating the dust from the carpets brought out to hang there.

"Oh, I loved that place. All those beautiful birds! I think I loved the Cuban Tody best. The pink wings and powder blue throat..." Then she turned to him. "Do you remember the Toucan that nested in the veranda overhang? Those babies were so ugly when they first hatched!" Olivia laughed aloud.

Alejo knew she didn't really think they were so horrible. "Oh, but they grew up so beautifully."

"They really did, didn't they? I don't know whether I was sorry they left after they learned to fly, or excited about watching them disappear into the trees. Such a treat."

"I couldn't believe they nested that far north. But the whole place was magic without any help from us. Even the most ordinary things."

"Like JaneAnn's goats..." Liv turned to Alejo with an expectant smile. He didn't disappoint.

"My God, yes! She planted grass around the house and then let all those little goats roam the yard to keep it mowed for her! She could have used magic to keep it short..." He trailed off laughing at the thought of it.

"Yeah, but she liked them...and it was more sensible to pay the farmer for them so he had some income and not use up magic on the lawn all the time."

Alejo didn't give her an inch. "You are so full of it. You adored those things, too. We all did." He watched her shoulders draw up as she smiled at the memory, a little self-hug that told him he was right on the mark. Saint-Domingue was a favorite place for them both.

"Funny how we try to recreate it whenever we can. Look at us now. Here we are in a hotel room facing outside, chairs next to each other, and feet out in front of us." For several minutes they reminisced and then he turned curious.

"Livy, why don't you teach Taylor something besides protection, defense, and work, work, work all the time. Let her experience blending with a chimera. Teach her something fun."

"Not yet – I don't want to take any risks."

"How is that risk? The more she knows the better she can handle herself. I was surprised she didn't even know about the finding charm you put on her hand last night, and that one's so simple."

"I want to be careful with her. I think she could be very powerful and I don't want to do a half-assed job on this. And she's such a great kid, Alejo. I want her to be safe."

"So why can't she learn more skills at the same time if she's so smart? Let us show her how to have a little fun, too. The rest of us can teach her those things if you don't want to."

"Jesus, Handy, she's not a kitten to play with. She's my apprentice."

Alejo found that amusing but wasn't put off. "And it will give her more confidence. She's going to need more than just you teaching her. You might have a lot of experience, but you don't know everything."

"I have to do this. She's my responsibility."

"Livy, that means take her in and do most of the education. It doesn't mean you can't let a few trusted friends give her a couple lessons."

"I want to protect her from him. No one knows Dantin like I do." She narrowed her eyes. "He'd love to get ahold of her; she picks up fast. I mean scary fast. She transported the two of us halfway across town one night after she'd only studied a few months."

"But you can't control everything. You can't plan for every possible thing that could ever happen to her. You can only give her as much skill as possible before you let her go."

Let her go. Olivia hadn't thought that far yet but he was right. "Yeah, I know..."

"And you can't protect us all. You might have gone too far already."

"I don't think I have a choice."

He had no answer for that. *Goddamn that guy,* Alejo thought. *I'd like to punch Dantin right in the face. Just grab him by the neck and smash my fist into that face about a dozen times for doing this to Olivia. Now that would be satisfying.* Of course that wouldn't solve Olivia's problem. Dantin would take it out on her somehow and Alejo knew if he killed him outright the logos would unleash some unexpected results on both of them. Somehow, Olivia had to be the one to close the loop on Dantin's vendetta. Besides, she would see his urge as overprotective, as if she were weak. She'd unleashed on him once for doing it and he didn't want to stand in that spot again. But he couldn't help wanting to protect her or at least stay close to her somehow.

"Livy, I wasn't planning on playing the winter circuit or in Argentina this year. I'm going to travel. Why don't you and Taylor come with me? We'll show her different countries and teach her the more difficult skills. We'll give her a true continental education and we can both watch over her."

"Alejo, that's a whole world of new places. I won't know how to protect her when we're constantly somewhere different. I don't even know what's going to happen when we get back to Seattle. "

"That's ridiculous. You know as well as I do that magic isn't about where you are, it's about what your abilities are."

"I don't know... I can't lose someone else..." She paused and then looked miserable, confused suddenly. "I'm really starting to love that kid, Handy. I don't want to, but she's been through so much and is so sweet even though I've been pretty tough on her, cold in fact. But you know what? She's not angry at me for it, just hurt when I'm like that. I can see it and it kills me. And when JaneAnn told her about Dantin she didn't accuse me of hiding anything or putting her in danger. She just worked harder and never said a word to me about it."

"Oh, Livy..." He started to come over and comfort her, but she waved it off.

"No..." She was trying to prevent tears. "A hug isn't going to make it all better you know."

"Livy, just because you're an adult doesn't mean you have to be tough all the time. Quit being superwoman for one minute."

He waited, but she didn't respond so he reminded her of something else. "You know, you've been doing this dance alone for so long you forget we all used to depend on each other to watch our backs. Don't isolate yourself from everyone because you think you're protecting us from Dantin. For all you know that's what he wants you to do."

That stopped Olivia cold. Could he be right? It was an alarming thought.

"Come with me. Bring Taylor."

"Maybe you're right. Let me think about it."

"Good. You think about it and let me know before you leave Houston. And don't you dare make up some excuse for not going."

She shook her head at him. "I won't," she said seriously. Had Dantin isolated her as Alejo said? But she knew her friends couldn't be around every second. They lived all over the world. Then again, they could flash to each other in a nanosecond. And now she was about to do something that might get them all killed if she failed. Maybe she *should* isolate herself... *Holy hell,* she thought, *how did I get to this point? I don't want to pull Taylor into this with me.*

"You're right about Taylor. Feel free to load her up tomorrow – whatever you all want to do."

Alejo was relieved he'd gotten through to her. He watched her look out the window not talking, staring down at the Museum District below, light from the streetlamps reflecting off the cars as they drove by. Alejo studied her face in the half-light. *My God those huge brown eyes are beautiful,* he thought, *even unhappy as they are right now.*

Olivia felt him looking at her. "I'm sorry, you must be as tired of this as I am. Let's just sit here and finish our drinks. And then I'd like to get some sleep."

"Fair enough." He was fine with that. He glanced at the wall where the light switches were and the room darkened, silhouetting their chairs against the ambient light outside. He picked up his glass and took a sip. Both were silent as they sat in the darkness holding their glasses. Such a soothing, sociable ritual, he thought.

He picked up movement in his peripheral vision and looked down to see her hand reach over to his, her lacquered nails reflecting in the dark as she placed her palm on the back of his hand. He spread his fingers to catch a couple of hers in his and they continued to look out the window, wordless, but her touch was like electricity. He couldn't remember when it had changed for him, this wanting to protect her, comfort her, cover her with himself so that nothing could harm her. She certainly could hold her own in a fight; she, Tristan, and he had been in situations where she had been the deciding factor. The three of them had been tight companions, Olivia and Tristan a couple and Alejo their

• 224 •

closest friend. After Tristan was gone they had kept him alive through each other. But that was three hundred years ago and now it was different for him...but was it for her? He couldn't tell and was almost terrified to mention it in case it ended what they had now. He was elated and miserable at the same time when he was with her.

He was lost in his thoughts, in memories of the two of them and didn't know how much time had passed when Olivia spoke.

"Alejo, it's eleven o'clock and we have brunch tomorrow. I'm getting sleepy." Magical power didn't preclude human requirements. "Everyone's coming at ten-thirty."

"Give me a hug goodbye then and I'll see you tomorrow." He stood.

"You can come earlier if you want." She stood to put her arms around his waist and let him enfold her, the feeling familiar and soothing. Then she backed up a step to see him go.

"Bye..." He let go of her hand and faded out of the room and back to his own hotel, watching her as he disappeared. *God, she can be a handful,* he thought. And he absolutely, totally loved her.

Around eleven p.m. Taylor flashed Nicole and herself back to the Cipriati suite at Hotel Icon.

"I love doing that! Maybe someday it will be old news to just jump from here to there, but so far it isn't." She was tickled to show off her powers for Nicole. Nicole had confessed to Taylor that although she could do some things on her own, she usually needed her familiar to help her and was impressed that her friend didn't.

"Especially if you've only been doing this for a little while." Nicole had said. "Can you imagine what you'll be like with practice or if you get your own chimera?"

They had been to quite a few clubs that night, Taylor transporting them easily from one to another after they'd done a quick turn in each to see if anything interesting was happening. If they didn't like what they saw, they left, taking only minutes to assess the scene. After all, the next place was an instant away – a simple command and they were gone. Nicole liked to call it "Club Jumping." Another thing she especially liked was being invisible in groups. It turned out that she was addicted to practical jokes and had played some low-key ones at a couple of bars. Taylor was delighted to see someone having fun with her powers. Olivia was almost reverent in her use of them.

Now Nicole was leaning on the sofa with one hand and pulling off her shoes with the other, tossing them across the room.

"It's not all that late. Why don't you stay awhile and we'll watch TV or something? You could even spend the night." Nicole hoped Taylor wouldn't leave her alone here.

Taylor hadn't considered that option and did a quick assessment in her head. "Maybe... I'm supposed to meet Liv in the morning, remember." Since they appeared to be in for the night, she wanted out of her party attire and in something more casual. Passing her hand over her clothes she replaced them with her softest pair of old jeans and her favorite "Ramones" t-shirt.

"Great shirt." Nicole gave it an approving once-over.

"Thanks. It's my favorite. It's getting old and I keep forgetting to make a copy of it. I only remember when I'm out wearing it, not at home." A thought stuck her. "Hey, I'm just going to make two of them right now and since you like it, one of them is yours." She held her palm over the bed and in moments there were two of them – one in Nicole's size. She picked it up and gave it to her.

"From me to you. Hope it fits. Don't let me forget to take the other one with me."

Nicole immediately tried it on. "It's perfect. I love it. Thanks, Taylor." She looked in the mirror, admiring her gift and pairing it with sweatpants before relaxing on the sofa.

"You're welcome – just don't wear it at the same time I do. Don't want to look like twins."

"Yeah, obviously." The Ramones were instantly replaced with a different top. "So what do you want to do? We've had a full day and I could lax out and do nothing, but I'm not ready to hit the sheets yet." She turned on the television and muted the volume. "Tell me about Seattle. When I get there where should I stay?"

"Well, that depends on what you like." Taylor had been in the lobbies of few nice hotels in Seattle but of course hadn't stayed in any of them. "I don't really know a lot of fancy places there – or anywhere for that matter. I just started living like this when I met Olivia." She could hardly believe how unguarded she was with Nicole. The few stories Nicole had shared about herself made Taylor think they must be alike in many ways. In the brief time they'd spent together Nicole had never judged negatively anything Taylor had told her, and she realized with a sense of relief that she wouldn't mind telling her so many awful things, even a little of her home life. It was liberating.

Nicole was typically offhanded about the hotel. "Well, I can always look on the web or call a travel agent. If you know a couple decent ones close to where you live just give me the names."

Taylor pictured the city around Olivia's house. "Downtown is nearby, so anything there is okay. There's the Four Seasons or Sheraton, or the Hilton..." She thought about the time that Olivia had taken her to lunch in a beautiful old hotel on Capitol Hill, close to where they lived. "Oh! There's a really cool old one, higher up on the hill – The Sorrento. It has this really great lobby with heavy carved wood and forest green velvet upholstery, Victorian furniture, and lots of

palms. And we can have coffee there next to the fireplace. I think they serve tea in the afternoons. It's old-
school kind of lavish. Not as modern as the ones downtown."

"That sounds great. I like something with a little vintage to it. I get tired of modern hotels. That's
why I picked this place." The suite was furnished with
wallpaper and a mix of furniture that looked like it
had come from an antique auction.

"Don't you have a place of your own?"

"Not really. I'm still city-hopping, seeing
things. I don't know where I want to settle down yet.
So why buy a house if I'm never in it?" She got up.
"I'm going to hit the bathroom. Be right back." She
got up and walked through the bedroom into the adjoining bath and shut the door.

Taylor sat on the couch, stretching out her legs
to put her feet up on the ottoman. When she'd
changed, she'd put her clothes on the corner table, but
now she concentrated on them, along with the new Ramones t-shirt, to send them back to her suite at the
ZaZa. As she felt the magic flow through her, another
feeling intruded, something … repulsive, predatory. It
made the flesh on her scalp tighten, the roots of her
hair tingle. Sitting still, she moved her eyes around the
room to see if she could tell what it was, but nothing
presented itself. The silken drapes hung softly on either
side of the window, unmoving. The overstuffed chair
across the room looked silently back at her, nothing
unusual there. But the feeling was claustrophobic. It

pressed on her, petrifying her – she had the distinct feeling that if she moved she would be vulnerable. She remembered once, when she was eight years old, her sister had reached into her room and snapped off the light, shutting the door so she was enclosed in complete darkness and she had been instantly terrified. Unknown monsters residing in the blackness froze her, and she had been afraid to move toward the light switch or the door, or to make any movement at all lest she alert one of the dangerous things she knew were out there, in that dimension of dark. And the feeling was back. She couldn't tell what it was, or where it was, but something was here with her. Behind her.

She looked into the mirror across the room. Could she scry in it to find out what was here with her? No – she didn't know what she was looking for or how to scry for something like this. Immobilized still, she heard whispering behind her, multiple voices sibilating unclear words at her... She looked reflexively in the mirror again and this time there was something sooty-looking, like coal dust, moving down the wall behind her and curling out into the room...

"Hey!" Nicole came back into the sitting area, which became miraculously empty and normal again. "How about..."

Taylor spun around quickly, emboldened now that Nicole was here, and saw nothing on the wall. Of course. Just wallpaper and cove molding.

Nicole looked at her, then at the wall. "What's going on?"

"Did you see that?"

"See what?" Nicole looked back at her, then again at the wall.

"Do you feel that?" But it was gone, or mostly, anyway. Taylor hardly believed Nicole couldn't tell something had been there. It had been so strong...

"No ... what? I don't feel anything. What are you talking about?" Nicole looked absolutely blank.

Taylor was remembering something Olivia had told her about a signature left behind when something intense happened in a location. Something bad or anguish leaving more energy in a place...

"Do you know if something bad happened in this room? Is there a history here?"

Nicole shrugged, shaking her head. Her eyes were wide. "I don't know. It's just a hotel room."

"There is something really nasty in here. I can't believe you don't feel it."

Nicole looked completely clueless. "Well, your skills are better than mine. Maybe we can ask my chimera?"

"No... I think I want to leave."

Nicole was alarmed. "Well, don't leave me here alone! Stay with me, and tomorrow I'll get a new room. There'll be two of us – you won't be alone."

"Why don't you come and stay with me at ZaZa?" Taylor preferred that idea to staying here with whatever it was she had just encountered.

CATHLEEN DUNN

"No!" said Nicole. "I mean... why would I? I haven't had any problems. Maybe something just drifted through, or it wasn't as bad as you think. Has anything like that happened to you before?"

"No."

"Well, then, see? So you don't really know what it was, or if it's still here, even." Nicole tried to instill some calm.

"Maybe..." Taylor still wanted to go but didn't want to be rude to Nicole. "That creeped me out."

"I guess. Look, just stay a little while and see if it happens again. I'll bet it doesn't."

Taylor still hesitated and Nicole tried to dissuade her, wanting her to stay. "Maybe you only thought you saw something."

"No. It was here. And it was really rancid, whatever it was." She was adamant. Nicole gave up and tried to divert her attention.

"Okay... Of course you don't have to stay overnight. Can you stay a little while, though? We've only got a few days left. What do you want to do with them?"

"I don't know. I should spend time with Olivia. After all, I came here with her and I've disappeared to do things with you."

"Yeah, but only since last night. And you're doing that thing with her and the others tomorrow." Nicole couldn't mask her disappointment. Taylor felt the same way.

"I know. I wish you were going to be there. I guess they want to get to know me. I don't really like the idea of being grilled by a bunch of relatives." Even though she didn't think Olivia and her friends were actually related, they certainly knew each other well enough to seem so. She didn't know what to expect the next day. Some kind of test or something? It felt weird, and suddenly she did want to stay with Nicole a little while longer.

"Maybe there's an old movie on, or we can find some comedy on TV…"

"Or maybe we could do a few hits."

Taylor only considered for a second. "Yeah, okay." Her apprehension of last night, her surprise at losing control doing magical hits, had lessened now. Nicole was probably right; you learn to control it. She just needed practice. She sat forward on the couch, rubbing her palms on her thighs.

"Who wants to go first?" She had watched Nicole's chimera do the trick on Nicole the night before, thinking it was beautiful how a shaft of prismatic light had seemed to occupy her for an instant. Nicole's ecstatic expression had fascinated her as she remembered the feeling she experienced doing the same thing just moments before.

"You go ahead." Nicole was generous. "I can do this anytime and I like watching you." She raised her palm. "Let me know when you're ready."

"Okay. Give me a minute to decide what I want." She cast her thoughts over the last twenty-four hours, thinking she would pick one of the her new experiences and then let the chimera intensify it. The ghostly music in the library? That was so intensely beautiful, what would that be like? She realized she didn't want to touch that memory. It was perfect the way it was. What then – the animals? What could they do with that? No, she decided. But then, even as she thought it, before she and Nicole got started, she was seeing through the eyes of a predator, a cat stalking its prey, catching it and biting into it, feeling the squirming animal in her teeth. She shook her head violently to clear it away. *Where the hell did that come from?*

She took a deep breath and settled down, trying to think, but couldn't concentrate. It was as if she couldn't connect with her own thoughts. Images and memories came but in milliseconds flitted beyond reach. And then a horrific scene flashed in front of her, a burned-out place and charred bodies. Just for a second, and then it was gone. She grimaced, feeling the distaste in her mouth.

"I can't do this. I think that creepy feeling is sticking with me a little and I don't want to take a chance on mixing that with my fantasy." Suddenly she wanted to be in the same building as Olivia.

Nicole's lower lip poked out a smidge, but she was sympathetic. "I'm sorry about that. I wish it would go away." She didn't want her to be uncomfortable. "Should we just give it up?"

"Yeah. I think I really do want to go home. It's getting late."

"Are you sure?" Nicole was trying not to show too much disappointment. *Just be cool*, she thought.

"Yeah." Taylor stood up. She couldn't leave quickly enough. "I'll call you. Let's do something tomorrow, but I don't know if Olivia will want to come with us. I'll let you know."

"That's okay. I like her. I like all of them, but then they weren't all over me like they were you."

"JaneAnn said you could call her anytime for advice."

"Yeah..." Nicole's smile was happy, remembering that. "I might, too."

"Okay." Taylor hugged Nicole goodbye. "So we'll call each other tomorrow and make plans."

"Don't forget your Ramones shirt."

"Got it. I already sent my stuff over ahead of me." She disappeared.

As soon as Taylor left Nicole turned a furious voice on the room. "You were here! I saw you trying for Taylor, hoping she would want to see you. But she's too smart, isn't she?"

The whispers returned again to answer Nicole, the ones from the night before, but this time raspy and more distinct. "Smart? She was frightened. She's weak like you."

Nicole was humiliated at having to say it. "No, she's not like me. She's stronger because she's been taught. She knows better."

"Well, we will see…we have what she wants…"
The slimy, guttural, shooshing voices were falling over
one another yet speaking together. "…and she has what
you want."

That horrified Nicole. "Leave her alone!" She
whispered her shout, afraid other guests would hear if
she was too loud, and she didn't want to use energy to
craft a privacy spell just so she could shout.

"Leave her alone! Leave her alone…" They were
mimicking her, like bullies on a playground, and they
didn't stop there, accusing her of treason during dinner
that evening.

"You were going to ask that witch for help!
That Julia person…"

Nicole was silent, trembling, afraid to go too far
in her push back.

"Answer! We know you were trying to ask for
help! She offered to teach you and you were going to
blurt out everything. You even tried to!" The tone
turned mocking. "*You were going to cry… waaaahh.*"
The babyish imitation was unnatural sounding.

Nicole defended herself. "I didn't say anything
– nothing at all!"

"No, because we cut you off."

"You don't know that. I wasn't going to say
anything."

"LIAR!" The voices were vicious and so loud in
her head that Nicole covered her ears. But there was
more they were angry about.

"...and you let Taylor leave. We came here to find another. Two of us, two of you. That is our agreement."

"I remember." Nicole went over her dilemma. Two familiars possessed her. One chimera had been hard enough to handle. At first it had been fun, trading instruction in magic for hedonistic experiences. Then it wasn't enough for it simply to play – to swim and eat and make love and lie in the sun. Soon it wanted constant stimulation and forced Nicole to glut herself with food and drink, making her vomit and then go back for more. And it was fascinated with sex. It drank in her embarrassment at what it made her do, thrived on it, thrilled to it.

Now she had two. Curiosity drove them to demand more unusual "entertainment," like killing her while skydiving. They refused to let the chute open as Nicole plunged toward the ground, flailing, screaming "No! No! No!" and anticipating the impact and horrible crunch of her striking the dirt. But only feet before sure death it flashed her backward, uninjured, and high enough this time to open her chute safely. Somehow even sex was worse now. No kink was too much for them. The more disgusting and degrading the act, the more strident her pleas for it to stop, the more she was humiliated by what they made her do, the more they possessed and controlled her. She knew her misery and terror fed them yet couldn't help it. One she could fight occasionally but against two she was helpless, fully controlled, submerged into them if they so decreed. How could she do that to another person? But how else could she escape her predicament? Then her night took an awful downturn.

"So now we seem to have time on our hands," the voices slurred "and we are bored. Some amusement is required." They'd learned subtle sarcasm from their experience with mortals. *Oh, God.* Nicole hung her head, looking at the floor and trying to think. They'd find their fun, no matter how late, no matter how spent she was. Only exhaustion, physical incapability prevented them. What argument against it would work now?

She reminded them of a commitment. "You said not while we were here. I need to be able to find someone suitable and gain their trust."

"You found someone, and you let her go."

Nicole tried to buy time. "It's hardly the second day. She's not stupid. You think she'll just open up to you? She's had training."

"And if she were ours now, you'd be doing this for only one of us. We're going out. Get dressed." Her clothes, ready for a night of relaxation dissolved away, replaced by a spandex dress so tight it looked like an Ace bandage wrapping her torso. It was short, stopping just below the soft cheeks of her bottom. She felt the air, cool on her tender flesh. No panties.

Fear pierced her because what she knew was coming. They'd forced her before, trolling for strangers who would satisfy their bestial hunger through her, and there was punishment when she tried to resist. Sudden rebellion filled her, infuriated her and gave her nerve. She tried to make a demand. "No! At least let me cover up more, put on more clothes!" There was no answer. They'd had this argument before. It was all part of the humiliation they craved, her embarrassment at being so exposed. Drinking feelings through her that they couldn't have on their own. It was one reason they let her rebel; they didn't care what emotion she exhibited as long as it was intense.

She tugged at the spandex, trying to remove the hated dress, pulling it up and over her head before she was stopped by the unseen chimera. She could feel the familiars using her to come through to the material world, controlling her movements though she fought and twisted blindly with her arms in the air looking like a headless, half-human thing writhing in the room. Then pain and pressure began, hot searing jabs in her back and her thighs, making her stomach twist and throb. Resisting one would have been a balanced argument; against two it was useless to fight them. She gave up and complied, pulling the dress back down and stepping into her heels before plucking a jacket from the closet as she left her suite. Passing a hand over her defeated face she added a generous amount of makeup, heavy shadow, and glossed lips. If this look could attract sex faster it would be over for her faster as well, especially if she complied.

It was a decidedly casual brunch this morning. The six were in Olivia's suite, all in jeans or sweats and no makeup, and JaneAnn and Olivia both had their hair back in ponytails. Taylor had never seen Olivia's hair in a ponytail. She was sitting in the zebra chair next to Olivia on the ottoman while they ate. JaneAnn was picking fruit off the plate in her lap with her fingers while Alejo lounged at the other end of the couch with one leg crossed over the other, knee out, drinking coffee. So far the talk had been mundane, how did Taylor like Houston, where had they been, what did she like best, and all that, until Julia took a magical turn in the subject matter.

"So you're through the basics, transporting and invisibility and controlling a few things, the rules of using and all that."

"Yeah. And scrying. We talked about spells and potions, but Liv wanted me to learn without relying on that."

"They come in handy, though, especially at a distance, or if you want a delayed effect. You can't be everywhere at once. Do you speak any other languages?"

"I only took a little French in high school. I was going to ask Olivia to teach me because she knows both French and Russian. She and the pet sitter speak Russian all the time, but I decided I might as well learn French because I know a little."

"Oh, here... I can do that right now." Olivia put her plate down.

Alejo queried her. "You haven't given her language or even explained how to do it?"

"I didn't realize she wanted to know." Olivia ignored the look he was giving her.

Taylor felt the need to respond. "Well, of course I didn't say anything; we haven't had time. We've been so busy with magic I didn't want to ask you for French lessons, too. That would mean a couple more hours every day in practice."

Olivia's answer was a surprise. "No, it wouldn't, you can do it with magic."

"I can? How?"

"Here." Liv turned to face her. "Now, look into my eyes. No, not at them, into them. Look past them, as if you were looking into my mind. That's right. Okay, now think about the language that you want and open up a little to let me give it to you."

Taylor nodded, wondering if she would hear Olivia's thoughts or something.

"No, but I can hear yours." She smiled at Taylor's startled look. "It's okay. That's all I heard. I've been doing this a lot longer so it's easy for me. Just concentrate on accepting the French, Taylor. And relax – try being a blank slate in that part of your mind."

"Okay. Just a second." Taylor took in a breath and let it out, shaking her hands to loosen up. Then she looked back into Olivia's eyes. "Ready."

The sounds crept up on her, like background noise at first and then more distinct. She could hear syllables in her mind, then words, the swooping, lilting sound of French... and she understood! She understood it all. There were sounds, and they each meant something. She had to try it out.

"Puis-je parler français?" She heard it come out of her mouth and turned to Alejo.

"Suis-je parler français? Suis-je le dire non?"

He laughed and nodded to her. "Yes, you're saying it right. You're speaking French."

JaneAnn couldn't help being tickled as well. *The moment of discovery never gets old,* she thought. *"Alors, que pensez-vous?* What do you think?"

"Oh, mon Dieu, c'est incroyable! Merci, Olivia!" Taylor hugged Olivia, who laughed. This wasn't so bad after all.

"You're welcome. If I'd known it would make you this happy I would have done it sooner."

Julia observed, "You know she's going to be walking around speaking it all the time until she's used to it. You're going to have to brush up on yours."

"I'm okay with that," said Olivia. "It's French after all, not like an annoying tin horn or something that she's honking all over the house."

Taylor still could not get over the wonderment of it, speaking softly and pointing at things in the room. *"Fauteuil – miroir – rideaux – moquette."* She turned to the others. "So how do you do it?"

Marcus answered her. "Lots of ways. Someone can give it to you, or you can pull it from text; although, if you do that you'll be able to write it but probably get the pronunciation wrong. If it's an emergency you can pull it from someone's consciousness without them knowing it, but be careful about invading their privacy like that."

"I know. Olivia told me. Forcing someone or tricking them, like a love spell."

"Good, you know then." Marcus looked at Liv. "She pulled that French in fast."

A brief smile crossed Liv's face. "Smart as hell."

"Show me how to learn writing," Taylor asked, and Julia demonstrated two different techniques while Alejo and Olivia watched. Easily, she was able to pick up Spanish from Alejo, and another dialect of written French from an old novel they conjured up. She didn't have to be shown twice.

"What else can I do?" Taylor was eager.

"Anything you want – almost. Become gifted in any talent, turn into almost anything, look like anyone."

"What do you mean?"

Alejo answered. "You can remove your flaws and be more attractive, make others think you look totally different, change into anything."

"How different?"

"Anything. Making others think you look like something else is a glamour, a feint, or a trick. Actually becoming it is different magic. "

Taylor was fascinated. "Show me."

"What do you want?" Alejo was curious to see what she would choose. "An actual transformation or a glamour?"

"Either. Wait, a transformation." Taylor was loving this. Oh, I wish Nicole were here!

Alejo nodded. "Okay, what?"

"Something big, scary."

Immediately he morphed into an enormous tiger. He was huge, his head nearly two feet across from ear to ear, body eleven feet long to tail tip. A deep, rumbling purr, almost growl-like, came from him as he sauntered over to Taylor and rubbed his head against her. She had to raise her hand to stroke him; he was that tall.

"Some ear rubs would be nice." He startled Taylor with that and the others laughed. It was weird to hear Alejo's voice coming from this cat. She complied and he asked her, "What do you think?"

Taylor laughed now, taking his huge head in her hands and rubbing his whiskered cheeks. "I love it, Alejo."

"Or would you prefer a Sumatran tiger to a Bengal?" He morphed again, slightly, the fur on his cheeks becoming longer, and the stripes on his head a little shorter, almost like oblong smudges instead. Taylor watched, captivated.

"Or a white tiger?" Under her hands the color changed to a beautiful milk with black stripes. She was overcome with the same wonderment she had felt in her early days with Olivia, learning new magic every day.

"Oh, this is wonderful!" She beamed at Olivia. "I want to try it!"

Liv nodded back at her. "Go ahead." Foremost in her mind as she watched was the discussion with Alejo last night. It was amazing how much she was enjoying watching Taylor learning and having fun at it.

She and JaneAnn watched the other witches become a few creatures. They took on different visages as Alejo showed her the difference between glamour and transformation. Taylor tried several different morphs, only bobbling slightly once or twice. She was a keen study, and the others praised her generously. Three hours passed like nothing. Taylor was a sponge, drawing information and skills from them so fast it alarmed Olivia. She forced herself to loosen up, irritated at her own caution because of Dantin. She now felt she might have been holding Taylor back.

Beth was talking. "You're quick and usually get it right the first time. I'd like to see how advanced you become in one sitting."

At that point someone had conjured a harpsichord and in wonderment Taylor was watching her own fingers play. The spinet notes wafted delicately into the air and floated away as they listened. After a few arrangements Taylor stopped. "Can I compose music? How would I learn that?"

JaneAnn answered. "You can gain an ability by magic but you're only drawing in what already exists.

Originality, creativity, and talent are something you need to be born with if you want to come up with something new."

Taylor had another pang of wanting to share with Nicole. She wished she were here, too, learning all of this. She found herself wondering what her familiar had taught her and what their relationship was like. She excused herself to the ladies room, and then called Olivia off to the side on her way back.

"Liv, I feel bad leaving Nicole off by herself while I'm learning all this. I don't think she knows anyone in town. I'm going to call her and check in."

"Okay." Olivia understood about Nicole. It was never pleasant to be the outsider. "Tell her I said hello."

"I will." Taylor went to get her cell phone. "Thanks."

Olivia returned and stood next to Alejo at their desecrated brunch spread. "Where's Taylor?" he asked.

"She's calling Nicole."

"I'm not surprised. They're the same age, I think..."

Taylor came up just then. "Nicole says she's got a few errands to run and we're going to get together later. We've only got a day or two left before you and I leave."

"Okay. And I think we're done here. Just look at everyone." Indeed, the other witches were lounging all over the room. Marcus looked like he could go into a food coma any second and Alejo announced he had some things to do that afternoon. They all said their goodbyes to Taylor and she left, followed shortly by Dan, Julia, and Alejo.

"Beth's leaving and I'm going with her." Jane-Ann picked up her sweater. Olivia nodded and the both of them shut the door behind them, leaving Olivia alone in her suite.

She was exhausted. She hadn't slept the night before because Dantin had been constantly in her head. This was supposed to be a vacation with less worry about him because of the other witches around. What could he be up to? But she was so sleepy she could hardly concentrate. She went to her room and fell into bed, still wearing sweats.

Her arm had fallen asleep. When she tried to move it she could feel the wrist drag on the sheet, forearm lifeless from lack of blood. *How did that happen?* Now she was waking up, groggy and confused. Nicole had passed out with her head on her arm, pinching off the blood flow. Her head was on fire, a splitting hangover from drinking herself into an oblivion last night in order to dull the experience forced on her by the chimera. Chilled hotel room air brushed her nude flanks. Her ribs were the only thing covered by a corner of the sheet and she'd been trying to move her arm to cover herself when she bubbled up toward consciousness. Now the needles of feeling from returning blood flow

brought her fully awake, the memories of the night before rushing at her before she could stop them.

The alcohol had only put a thick barrier between her and what was happening, but couldn't block
it completely. Unwanted pictures of last night intruded, repugnant and shameful. The coarse flirting
with men at the bar, their hands on her, their fingers
jammed under her dress even as she sat on the stool,
and a stop in the alley behind the building to satisfy
an insistent stranger before heading back to her hotel
with him...with them. Three of them. She remembered
the disgusting smell of them, astringent aftershave and
sweat, remembered them manipulating her limbs,
spreading her open. The horrid feeling of them pounding into her, sometimes two at a time, sandwiching her
between their weight. Bile rose in her throat and she
tried to push off the pictures of it. Tears threatened. I
hate them! *Oh, God, I hate myself...*

She heard someone start to snore – a grating,
irritating, honking sound. Opening stiff eyelids she
looked off the bed at the carpet below. Yes, her clothes
were there along with others, wadded piles dropped to
the floor. Yes, they were still with her, in her room, in
her bed, violating it just by being there. Soiling it. She
didn't feel the chimera close by. *Are you sated for the
moment, you putrid bastards?* I'm getting rid of these
guys, she thought. I'm not waiting for another go-
around to feed someone else's gluttony.

She moved her head slowly to look over her
shoulder. Someone's arm was lying across her leg, and

another, different leg was flopped over the arm. She really didn't want to see them again. Fleetingly, she thought of using magic to transport them naked to some public location to wake up in embarrassment or possibly arrest. She actually smiled considering it but decided it wouldn't be quite satisfying enough. She needed a release, something she could do with her own two hands.

Using magic to flash herself off the bed and into clothing all at once she stood over them as they slept, splayed out in wanton poses, hairy and muscular. She squeezed her eyes shut, gritting her teeth to chase off the sight before she kicked the bed hard, following suit with the three men on the rumpled covers. She jabbed her heel hard into a shoulder, jostling him and finishing with a vicious push. They started to stir, half-asleep and groaning. One sat up to stare at her through groggy eyes. Not fast enough, she thought. Not anywhere near fast enough. She grabbed one, pulling him off the bed easily with supernatural strength and kicked at the others to rouse them.

"Get up. Get out. Time to go." She gestured briefly, conjuring a spell to throw their clothing at them. Hard. The button fly from a pair of jeans left a mark on a stubbled face.

"Hey!" He got up from the carpet, holding his pants, angry at Nicole. "What's your problem?"

"Fun's over. Get out."

"So what's changed?" His smile was smug. "You were pretty accommodating last night."

That infuriated her further. She grabbed his arm, hard, and propelled him toward the door. He barked in pain, amazed at her strength and stunned to realize he couldn't stop her from tossing him physically through the air and out the door. His clothing followed.

She looked back at the other two and fixed narrowed eyes on them. "Get out."

The two left were immobile, absorbing what had just happened. They slowly picked up shirt, pants, whatever was nearest to them and started to dress. *I can't stomach looking at you for another second,* thought Nicole. *I want you gone immediately.*

"Get out. GetOut, GetOut GETOUT!" Her scream was strident, almost hysterical, and she added some magical menace to her tone, which shook the two out of their surprised stupor. Then she started toward them with clenched fists. This time they didn't delay, stumbling as they tried to dress without stopping, one of them falling to the floor and crawling the remaining few feet to the door, fists clenching his shirt and shoes. Nicole resisted her urge to throw a damaging spell at them, something to break bones. She didn't need the karmic blowback in addition to her other problems. She threw the door to her suite closed with a reverberating bang and then looking around, vaporizing what little clothing they had left behind. Satisfying enough, she thought darkly.

An echoing, rumbling chuckle filled the room. "Very enjoyable." They were back, watching, coming closer when they felt her emotions peak, relishing the entertainment.

Nicole didn't react. Trying to twist an emotional response from her was a worn but favorite tactic of theirs to feed their addiction and her defense was to stay as neutral as she could. She tried to feel empty as she went into the bathroom, concentrating on how the carpet felt on her bare feet instead of anything else. She deeply needed a bath, something hot and fragrant, preferably with bubbles so she wouldn't have to look at herself. In the past she'd had to repair bruises, bite marks, sometimes cigarette burns. She could do that later but for right now, she wanted to be scalding clean, to put some distance between last night and this morning.

As she let the tub fill she changed into the fresh terry robe hanging on the back of the bathroom door. The hotel staff brought a new one and fresh towels every day at Nicole's insistence. They were always crisp and laundered, the smell clean and fresh. They were soothing, pristine even. She nestled farther into the robe as she sat beside the tub, waiting for it to fill.

While she ran fingers through the thick layer of bubbles rising higher in the porcelain basin, the chimera started their cadence again, whispering close to her ear. They wanted Taylor. Now they were trying a different tone: warm, cajoling, almost reasonable sounding.

"Wouldn't it be nice to have a friend to do this with? You could talk about it after, even make fun of them together if you wanted to." They were clumsy in their knowledge of people, knowing what they saw but not always why people did what they did. Nicole couldn't resist the chance to belittle them for a change.

"Are you stupid?" Her lip curled with her disdain of them. "Why would we want to talk about it together?"

"We see others do it. They have sex and then discuss it together later."

Nicole was sneering in her response. "You know nothing. Those are adventures people have of their own choice. They have experiences and share, or they reminisce to relive the memory. Why would I ever reminisce about what you make me do? It's humiliating. Slavery. I would never tell anyone about this."

They were quiet for several moments, not grasping the concept, she could tell. Then they changed and tried old tactics, stirring up feelings she used to ask for, caresses and sensations which used to be so pleasurable but now made her gag. When she didn't respond they changed again, trying to convince her that if she could get Taylor to allow them in, she would enjoy it, too. She steeled her mind against them. *No way will I ask her to accept one of you as her familiar.* She tried to pretend they weren't there, rejecting their advances and refusing to answer. She dropped the robe and stepped into the tub, the water as hot and painful as she could possibly stand it, to burn away the mortification of the night before. The sensation overrode the chimeras' artificial caresses, and they dulled into the background as she lay back in the tub.

But the respite was far too short. They changed course, bringing pain, describing a slow, agonizing fatality they claimed they would inflict. As pain flamed through her Nicole gritted her teeth, refusing to moan and give them any satisfaction. After a while the jabs dissipated when they brought no response, but the familiars continued to threaten a painful death.

"Go ahead." Her voice was expressionless. "You won't kill me and you know it." She had asked them let her die several times before, begged them for death. She had tried it herself, cutting her wrists and letting the blood flow into the beige carpet of a hotel room in Hong Kong, creating a huge red blossom around her that spread as she watched it in dull fascination, uncaring, the blood loss making her lightheaded. Then they stopped it, repairing the gashes and reversing the damage before she could die. Later on she'd tried it again, in different ways to the same effect, the chimera letting her go to the edge of death then bringing her back, until eventually she gave up. They let her sob and scream when she was alone, though. They glutted on her wretchedness and she hated them for it, and hated herself for being too weak not to cry.

There was, however, something left to her – token rebellion. She used it now. "I can't do this to someone else. I won't do this to Taylor."

The chimera were silent, brooding. Their smoky, coal-like fog coalesced over the bathroom floor and crept up the side of the tub to spill into it, cooling the water Nicole was submerged in and casting a sooty hue over the mounds of bubbles. The voices were close, dripping in her ear, and she could feel the delicate brush of something kissing her cheek.

"There are two of us and one of you...how long do you think you can last?"

Her lips went bloodless. It was no idle threat. She stared at the wall, focusing on the beadboard there while trying to steady herself. She wanted no outward clue to her tormenters that they had affected her so she closed her eyes and feigned calm, relaxing her head against the slanted back of the soaking tub. Finally they stopped, the water cleared, and lacy iridescence returned again to the foam on its surface. Nicole submerged herself into the once-again hot water, stretching her legs in the warmth. She'd won a moment of peace for herself. For the next hour she pulled up any soothing vision she could flood her mind with and kept the bath searingly hot.

She was considering getting out and drying herself when her cell rang. Lifting her hand she shook the droplets off before commanding her phone to appear in her palm. It was Taylor, of course.

"Hi, what are you doing?" Taylor's voice was a welcome sound.

"In the bath. How was brunch with the others?" She wished she'd been there with her, to say the least. She wasn't looking forward to Taylor leaving this week and was really anticipating their holiday visit – at least she hoped *they* would let her visit. Sometimes they ruined her plans on purpose, just because.

"It was okay. I mean it was good. I learned some new things about magic that Olivia hadn't taught me yet." Taylor resisted telling Nicole too much, she didn't want to call out that Nicole hadn't been invited. "Let's get together this afternoon. What time is good for you?"

Nicole really needed to sleep. Between the almost constant use by the chimera and the daily outings since she had arrived in Houston, she was nearly exhausted. But she wasn't going to tell Taylor she needed a nap. That was lame. She did some quick calculating.

"How about early evening? I have some things to take care of this afternoon."

"What time? You pick since you know when you'll be done."

"Seven, like last night? It's two now." Nicole knew if she overslept, magic would have her ready in a heartbeat. "Where do you want to meet? Here or your place?"

"I can go either way."

"Come over here then, in case things take longer than I think they will. Just let me know ahead of time so I can make sure I'm here."

"Where do you want to go?" Taylor hadn't the faintest idea where to start.

"I don't care – anywhere."

Olivia was sleeping finally, a blissful blackness that turned into dreams. She was looking across a meadow as she sat on a blanket with her friends; the sun was starting to slant its rays toward dusk. Everyone was there, picnicking under a tree and laughing at each other's stories. But why was Alejo wearing armor and holding a cluster of grapes? He was feeding grapes off the bunch to JaneAnn. Then he wasn't wearing armor; he turned into a statue of Perseus holding Medusa's head as ants invaded their picnic and started biting her. Fire ants – they burned her legs and arms as they stung her, settling into a huge nest under her shoulder blade. The pain was intense and...familiar. She studied Perseus holding Medusa's dripping head. Odd. It wasn't just sculpted to look dripping. It actually was blood that dripped onto the floor in red spatters. The pain was so intense now it woke her up to find Dantin there, just like the statue, only it was JaneAnn's head he held by the hair, her neck weeping red.

Dantin thrust JaneAnn's head at her. "You set this twit on me as a spy?" He was seething.

Olivia couldn't speak. JaneAnn...it was JaneAnn dead in his hand, and it was her fault. She'd asked JaneAnn to follow Beth. Oh, God, and now she was dead. She felt instant sobs come and didn't try to stop them.

"Why?" Her voice was scratched, rough through her tears. "Why? She was only following Beth!" She couldn't figure out how he could have gotten to a witch as skilled as JaneAnn. She wasn't cursed, weak like Olivia, when he was around. And then she remembered. What was Dantin's interest in Beth?

Dantin threw the head bouncing into the corner. Olivia was horrified. That was JaneAnn he tossed away like garbage. He didn't know her – how amazing she was, everything wonderful she was, now gone...

Dantin started to laugh. "Oh, the look on your face is priceless! How could you fall for that?" Confused, Olivia looked at him, then back at JaneAnn's head as it vanished. It was a glamour, the kind they had shown Taylor that day. A trick.

She could feel her sobs turn to a growl in her throat. She glared at Dantin, hating him intensely. "You fuck – God, I hate you!" A fresh stab under her shoulder contorted her. She panted through her pain. "She's alive, I assume?"

"For now. But you have a much bigger problem. You saw me with Beth. You had JaneAnn follow Beth to check on me. But who's checking on Jane-Ann?"

It took Olivia a moment. *Who's checking on JaneAnn?* Why would she need to check on JaneAnn? If Dantin hadn't killed her, then... She couldn't think through the stabbing in her shoulder.

He stepped over to her and kneeled on the bed where she lay. The thought that she was on her back, lying there exposed to him spurred her to flash away, but she made it only as far as the floor.

"Ohhh, you shouldn't be down there. Come back to bed." He patted the sheet and now she was back and he was sitting on top of her, looking down at her. He reached down and cupped her breasts through the shirt, groaning at their softness.

Revulsion eclipsed the blaze in her shoulder and she punched him in the throat with everything she could summon.

He was openly shocked, his eyes wide as he grasped his throat, coughing. Then he slapped her, a backhand that numbed her entire face and sent her to the edge of a void. She felt him vaguely as he shifted his weight to put her arms under his knees so she couldn't move. Then she was back, looking at his face through blurred vision she couldn't seem to blink away.

"You don't ever do anything like that again! You are *mine* to control!" With a huge effort he pulled himself back into his smooth demeanor. He was still raspy when he spoke again. "You foolish bitch. You have no idea what is going on." He sat on her, holding still a few more moments. Then he continued calmly, sounding like his usual unctuous self.

"Poor Silver-Tint, your kind are too nice, too stupid to comprehend. Doesn't have the power of a Blue/Black. You'll always be behind in the game.

Here's a hint: is it Beth or JaneAnn that needs to be watched? But then, what if it's not them at all? Who can you really trust?"

Olivia lay still, mostly to refuse him the satisfaction of watching her try to escape, but also trying to track his words. Not trust Beth or JaneAnn? Or maybe he was drawing her attention to them because he was onto her plan with Alejo? Alejo had already given the glaive to Schmidt. What if they couldn't trust Schmidt? How did Dantin find out?

He was looking down at her again, smiling, reading her face as she tried to work it out. He wished he could read her mind.

Later that night Nicole and Taylor appeared suddenly in the middle of Nicole's suite at the Icon, laughing so hard they were bent over double.

"I can't believe you were so mean to that guy!" Taylor was wiping away tears.

"Yeah, but I made up for it right away." Nicole was laughing as hard as Taylor.

They had been in a string of clubs that night ranging from the posh to a dive, flirting with and then discarding men in every one. At one point Nicole seemed interested in one very handsome guy, and he with her until she turned wicked on him. Commenting on his attire, she had asked if it were new. He had replied yes it was, and she had eyed him appreciatively, asking where he had gotten it. Hoping she was attracted to him, he had been willing to discuss whatever she wanted. But when he had answered her question, she snapped back, "Well, it's pretty weird looking. Doesn't do a thing for you." She could hardly get the last word out through her own chortling laughter. Taylor had been shocked at the cruelty of it, and after a second Nicole looked that way, too. After that she was kind to him, apologizing. "Look, I'm sorry; I don't know why I said that." She offered to buy him a drink, but of course he left. It had been horrible at the time, but somehow the more they drank the funnier it became.

Now they were reliving their adventures of the night, where they sometimes had decided they were in so far over their heads they had escaped into the ladies room instead of going back to their table, disappearing from there and transporting themselves outside the club in a flash. Taylor was glad she was from out of town; she'd hate to run into anyone they had spent time with tonight. What surprised her was that it had been so much fun. Nicole was so different from being with Olivia. Olivia was always so solicitous with people and Nicole seemed to cut loose. It was like she would dare anything, and Taylor was enthralled watching her.

Nicole went into the bedroom and climbed up on the bed, kneeling and facing Taylor as she entered the room. "Let's do some hits." She smiled at Taylor enticingly, ready for fun but Taylor shook her head.

"Oooh, that's a great idea, but I'm too buzzed. I don't know what would come out of my head."

"But isn't that half the fun? Could be something twice as awesome. I've done it."

Taylor stood wobbling for a moment, then nodded loosely. "That could be pretty choice." She thought of her embarrassment the other night. What would it be like if she let herself go and took it all in?

"Hey, Nicole, have you ever said, 'What the hell – I'm all in'? I mean, what's the big deal about it after all? It's just a game."

Nicole looked at her closely, apprehension clear on her face. This sounded like a different proposal Taylor was talking about, not just some surface fooling around with a few sensations.

"No, that's not all it is. In the game you don't open yourself all the way. It's only that one little piece of fantasy you're letting them touch for a second."

Taylor stood looking at Nicole with thick eyes, obviously not thinking clearly. Nicole decided to take command. "Here, sit down." She pulled Taylor onto the bed.

"Yeah, you're right. I'm done for tonight." Her stomach lurched. "I think I might throw up."

Nicole saw the extent of Taylor's condition and immediately felt for her. "Did you let all that alcohol affect you? Here, lie down. I know some magic to keep from getting drunk, but I don't know how to take it away after you're already there."

She pulled back the comforter and took Taylor's shoes off for her. "Here, just relax and I'll take care of you." She helped Taylor onto the bed. "I'm sorry – I didn't know you were getting so wasted."

Now that she was lying down and not distracted by laughing, Taylor felt really vile. The room spun a lot and it was equally bad whether she closed her eyes or had them open. She felt the cool wet washcloth Nicole had put on her forehead. A little better.

"Maybe my familiar can take it away." Nicole sounded hopeful.

"No, that usually magnifies everything and I am on the edge of puking right now." She groaned and turned her head to the side. "I think you were right. I don't want it to go through me."

"What do you want me to do for you?"

"I just need to hold still for a little while." She pulled the washcloth down over her eyes and tried to stop reeling. Nicole lay down next to her, keeping her company and holding her fingertips, trying not to disturb her with too much movement. After a few minutes, the soft moaning that came with Taylor's bedspins stopped. Nicole hoped she was drowsing or passed out. Being that drunk was really the worst.

She slid off the bed, careful not to make it jiggle and went into the sitting room. The voices were there again, slithering around her and lisping. "Do it now. She'll only be half-awake and you can talk her into it. She's right there... Right there." They were layered again, the voices, sing-songing in different cadences.

"I told you no." Trying to stand steadfast.

"She's helpless. She can't resist." The words infuriated Nicole.

"You make me sick! I hate you!" Her shouted whisper was clipped, bringing a little spittle drop that hung off her lower lip, which she chose to ignore. "You can't take someone unless they let you in, anyway. You know that."

"You could persuade her..." The voices coursed through her, trying to influence her. Just go in there, try – she could feel them pushing her to do it. But for all their power Nicole knew well they couldn't force her mind, only her actions. They didn't know the nuances it would take to convince another person, to read their responses and play off of them.

"And you can't make her let you in, either." That was also true. They couldn't possess a witch who didn't invite them in first. But once welcomed, there they could stay, malignant and growing. For the moment, she could feel them receding. But they would be back, oh, she knew they would. Always lurking and ready.

She sat on the couch, looking into the living room shadows without seeing. She didn't go back and lie down next to Taylor. She didn't want to disturb the bed while her companion was in her precarious state, but it wasn't just because of the alcohol; she didn't want her hideous chimera anywhere near her budding friendship with Taylor. She would sleep on the couch. She curled up on the sofa, tucking the pillow under her neck. Picturing the softest, downiest comforter she could think of, she willed it to appear and drape over her. Sleep was one of her few escapes, even nightmares had ceased to bother her years ago, and she was unconscious and breathing rhythmically in a few minutes.

Two hours later she woke to a pale breeze in the room and felt mischief in the air. She squirmed and tried to pull herself toward wakefulness and gain her bearings, looking around when she could finally open her eyes. The doors and windows were all closed. She felt the air settle and stop moving altogether. Occasionally she'd seen witches disturb the air like that if something was wrong. They didn't mean to, it was a side effect of magic coupling with their emotions and acting out on their surroundings. It could be the chimera or it could be Taylor, or rather some problem with Taylor.

Nicole crossed to the bedroom quickly and peeked in at her friend, but nothing appeared wrong. Taylor lay there asleep, half-curled on her side with her hair spread across the pillow. She was breathing heavily through her mouth, her soft lips barely open and rosy. She was still in the clothes they had gone out in and then passed out in on the bed. She looked pinched in the skinny jeans and Nicole thought about how uncomfortable they would be when Taylor woke up. She wouldn't want those stiff, tight things around her. Passing a hand over the sleeping girl she exchanged the day clothes for pajamas, light flannel ones with loose legs and top that she could move around in as she slept. Much better.

Nicole was filled with overwhelming loneliness as she stood looking at Taylor. It was so nice to have a real friend, someone to do things with. She wondered how long she could keep her secret from Taylor. What would happen if Taylor found out? Would she be disgusted and run away? Frightened... and run away? Or would she try and help? That suddenly brought up a real concern for Nicole: Would they let her help or would they try to stop her? They could keep Nicole from asking for help. They couldn't control Taylor, but what would they do to her if Taylor knew and tried to tell someone?

The slithery voices came again, and the tiny current of air, wafting across her forehead, brushing her bangs aside.

"What do you think we would do, Nicole?"

Taylor fidgeted in her sleep, moving her head to one side and curling up tighter. A tiny whine sounded deep in her throat and Nicole could see the beginnings of gooseflesh on her arm. She should leave the room before they woke Taylor, but she couldn't seem to stop looking at her, couldn't pull her eyes away from her unconscious form on the bed.

"Yes – look at her. Don't you want to be with her? Do things together and be friends? She would like us..."

Disgusting. She hated them.

"You're disgusting. Get off of me," she whispered and swatted at them, backhanding the air as if to brush them away. It had no effect and they moved around her still, one on each side, each saying something different.

"And what if she does find out? What if she doesn't want to see you anymore? We can't let her tell anyone. And we're not letting you go." The rasping whisper continued on, the last phrase repeating like an echo, "...not letting you go."

After a pause they continued, wicked intent in the voices. "Or we will find a more... robust companion for you. Someone who enjoys our company and will make you take a more active role." That thought frightened her more than anything else.

Nicole stood by the bed, looking at her sleeping friend who was naïve to all of this going on around her. She kept her face an emotionless mask while the chimera continued their threats. All the choices they gave her were appalling.

Abruptly she turned and left the room, taking quick steps across the carpet, leaving the suite. She began to run, transporting herself to the street below as she tried to leave the situation behind, down the broad sidewalk that passed in front of the hotel, past the closed boutique shops and empty parking spaces on the street. The park was to the left and she ran into it, past its scattered trees, moving toward the foliage until finally she stopped and crouched down under the branches of a bush, hidden from the open stretch of grass.

The chimera could do what they threatened. The thought of being forced to have a companion that enjoyed their vulgarity, had nothing in common with her, was too much to bear. At least when she and Taylor were together they had fun. Nicole sat in the bushes alone, reviewing her last days with Taylor. They were friends, they liked the same things, had the same sense of humor. They even had the same style. It had been years since Nicole had had a real friend. *No! I will not do it! I can't do that to Taylor.* She clenched her fists, digging the nails into her palms in painful self-punishment for even thinking it.

Better to let Taylor return to Seattle. She wouldn't visit for Christmas. She would disappear and never talk to her again. She wouldn't even tell her why. She sat in silence for over an hour, until the damp earth found its way through her clothes, making her skin cold and prickly. Feeling defeated she got up, emerging from under the bush to go back to the hotel. Then she stopped abruptly.

There was a man in front of her. Had he come from behind or from the other side of the bushes? It didn't matter; he was holding a gun, coming closer. She backed up and he pointed the weapon at her chest and told her "Stop – don't move. And don't scream or I'll kill you." He looked her over.

"Empty your pockets," he said. Then when Nicole complied: "Give me your money. And that bracelet." The bracelet was rhinestone, but he didn't know it. She held the items out toward him, her eyes unafraid, and he was surprised at her directness, she could tell. Then an entirely different look filled his face. He looked surprised, then uncomfortable. She watched it flit across his face as he winced, drawing his shoulders up and his mouth opened in a noiseless grimace, his fingers spread and contorted. The gun dropped to the ground with a quiet 'thud' that Nicole heard as if from a distance as she watched, full of dread. The man was choking, apparently, unable to make more than gagging, skitching sounds. The flesh around his neck pinched tighter, and the same happened to his head. Horrible things were happening, the flesh deforming as if someone were squeezing clay in their palm that extruded between their fingers. He tried to flail away from the invisible hands, but he was immobilized, held there to die, his eyes frantically dancing.

They were doing it through her, against her will, using her powers on this mortal. Nicole was trapped inside herself, watching it all happen. She was pushed back, forced down, and submersed in her own body. She could only watch, screaming silently.

"No! Stop it!" But no sound could come out. Her lips didn't even move. From inside her own eyes she watched her hands throwing the magic that powered the killing crush, unable to interfere. She felt them exult at her anguish and delight at their feeling of power over the man as he died, reveling in their own fascination at the butchery unfolding in front of them.

Blood and tissue were places they weren't supposed to be, coming through rips in the skin. His eyes bulged and then dimmed, the mercy of death making him limp. She could feel the familiars dredging up more emotions in her now, pulling feelings from her just to feel them while she was in this heightened state, wrong feelings. Suddenly she was laughing, wild, uncontrolled. Disgusted with herself for letting it happen. One of them wanted more... *Do it again.* With no second victim nearby it dropped control of Nicole. The other remained, stroking her after she folded on the ground like a rapist fondling his victim, enjoying her revulsion as she lay in the grass. Then they withdrew, leaving her terribly alone in the park.

Her despair was intense. She curled herself tight on the ground and dug her fingers into the dirt and grass as if she could transfer some of the pain to the soil, shredding bits of lawn and roots and trying to dissipate her anguish like the tiny green blades she tore out and set free. While she sobbed she crawled toward what used to be a man, now misshapen and grotesque, bloody gelatin where his head and neck once had been. She lay next to him in pitiful human companionship with his mortality.

"I'm sorry, so sorry... sorry." She didn't know what else to say, only managing that through the sobbing. She thought of lying there, waiting for the police to find him eventually and take her with them, but she knew her captors would not allow her to be seen. She knew they would make her invisible so that anyone walking by would not see the girl curled up on the grass next to the corpse. But there was no one walking by this late. No one to see...

Was it an hour? two? before she got up and stood there, looking at him sadly. Then she assessed the park around her – where to hide him? She saw a Japanese maple adjoining the hedge, small and close to the ground, its red leaves making a dome over a round expanse of grass. It would hide any disturbed soil and so she buried him there, sorcery making quick work of the job. She wandered back to the hotel, walking numbly on bare feet and hardly feeling her shoes in her hand. No one was in the lobby as she crossed except the college student reading her textbook behind the reception desk. After exiting the elevator she didn't bother to open the door to her suite but simply walked through it, crossing into her room, expressionless as she studied Taylor in the darkened bed.

I'm not strong enough to resist the two of them, she thought. *I can't bear the thought of an eternity alone, trapped with these two chimera. No escape for me, their little puppet isolated on its strings.*

She was afraid to whisper aloud what she was thinking. *Maybe if I take one, and Taylor takes the other.* She mouthed the words just to make them real, to infuse herself with the nerve to do it. "Maybe I could have more control if there's only one of them possessing me. Maybe I could get away finally...and if I could get away then Taylor can, too; she's so much stronger than I am, and she's been taught more about magic." She frightened herself.

Dantin was still sitting on Olivia, looking into her face. "God, you are *so* slow." He put his fingers on her chest, searing her shirt and burning her where they touched her. She screamed, but no sound came out, he'd spelled her to silence so no one could hear.

"No sense bothering the neighbors," he'd said.

Now he was drawing his initials on her with his finger, the meaty smell of burning flesh following his ornate tracings. "I'm branding you," he said amusedly. Then he thought for a second and brightened. "Oh! Does that make you part of my stable?" He laughed at his own stupid joke as if everyone should think it was funny.

Olivia was beyond debilitated. They'd been like this for hours. She lapsed into unconsciousness again and he wakened her. Again.

"Honey, you are the worst date." He looked around the room lethargically, musing. "Still, I would like to take you home with me, for my very own..."

Olivia couldn't fix on his face. *Something...something about trust, or...someone... I don't know.* All she could feel was that her face was puffy and loose-jawed.

"God, you are boring. I'm bored." He looked at the window. "The sun's coming up soon anyway. I need some sleep, don't you need some sleep?"

Olivia's head lolled to the side. *What is he talking about? I've been trying to get some sleep.*

Dantin perused her. "I suppose that softie Alejo will come and take away my artwork." He traced his designs again tenderly, loving his own handiwork. "No matter, I'll make more sometime."

He got up off the bed and stood looking down at Olivia. "We always have such a wonderful time...well, I do," he said modestly. "I think you should come and live with me, don't you?" He looked at Olivia earnestly. Then he touched her forehead with his palm.

"Yes...you do need sleep. Lots of it." He watched Olivia slide under his somnambula spell. "Can't have you awake and running around, spoiling my plans." He paused and perused her face thoughtfully, delicately moving a stray wisp of hair off her face.

"Why can't you be this nice to me when you're awake? Wouldn't it be better if we could just be like this?" He bent over to her, his face close, just centimeters away. She didn't respond. "We could have been historic together." He let his lips touch hers gently, the barest whisper of pressure, staying a few moments to draw out the experience. Then he pulled back and was gone.

Hours flowed by while the sun crept upward. It wasn't until eleven a.m. that Olivia awoke to the phone ringing. It was Alejo and when she answered he was absurdly ordinary, she thought.

"Good morning. So brunch wasn't as bad as you thought it would be, right?"

She didn't answer right away, still groggy from the spell and wondering something about...she tried to think...something about who she could trust. Was it Alejo? He was talking to her.

"Livy? Are you there?"

"Yes..."

"Did I wake you?"

"Yes. I just woke up." She wished she could remember details from last night. The last thing she remembered was that Alejo...something, or was it Schmidt or JaneAnn?

"Should I hang up? I can call later."

"No, come over, please. Wait – give me half an hour; I'm still in bed." She needed to think, just in case.

When he arrived Olivia had decided to approach him very directly. "I think Dantin knows what we're doing."

"How?"

"I can't exactly say. He was here last night."

Alarmed, he looked her over and saw the blisters Dantin had left. "Oh, my God. Livy!" His face darkened. "*Dar muerte a Dantin!* I'm going to kill him – right now. I'm going to find him and just do it."

Olivia grabbed his wrist. "No! Let's fix this the right way."

He jerked his hand from hers. "He's getting worse, Olivia! I'm not going to wait and see what he does next!" He postured, ready to disappear. Olivia grabbed his arm again, trying to reason with him.

"You can't do a revenge murder! You're a Silver-Tint!"

"I really don't care, Livy! How could things possibly be worse than what he's putting you through now?"

"You know it could – we've both seen the punishment the logos can mete out." That made him think, she could see that and tailed onto it.

"That might be exactly what Dantin wants – you don't know what he's crafted here." She caught his face in her hands and looked into his eyes. "Don't. Please don't leave me. I don't want to lose you, too."

He stood still, deciding, clenching his teeth and resisting his instinct to pound everything he could reach into splinters. Instead he gathered up Olivia in his arms and strode to the couch, where he gently set her and opened her collar.

"Let me fix those..." Olivia watched his hands as he worked, mending the skin until it was smooth again, fresh and almost satiny under his touch.

"Thank you."

He was calmer now. "What happened?"

"He came and taunted me, dropping hints that I can't trust anyone."

"What do you mean?"

"You know how he is; he thinks he's so god-damned smart we can't figure it out. But he's never been this obvious before. He must really be sure of himself, which tells me he's gotten one of us to side with him, or trust him, or do something they don't even know about."

"You can spell me if you want to make sure."

"Not sure enough. I need to see for myself."

He hesitated. Would she be able to tell? He saw suspicion flit across her face and realized he had no choice.

"All right, Livy, whatever you want." Then he held up a finger. "Except about women, of course. My feelings there are private."

That made her hesitate, but then she nodded. Of course his intimacies were none of her business, she thought, and Dantin wouldn't be there, anyway. Putting her hand on his cheek she slipped her thoughts into his and felt him give way, letting her into his consciousness. All his memories blossomed into view, many of them shared already between the two of them. Hundreds of years of friendship between her and him, the others, and Tristan, too. He had loved him like a brother. Good memories, warm feelings, trusting feelings. And there were their plans with the glaive. He'd given it to Schmidt exactly as promised. She stayed a moment longer to make sure, any layers or subterfuge? She didn't detect any. That was good enough and she stopped before intruding too far.

He looked into her eyes. "Okay?"

She nearly cried from relief. "Yes."

"So, Beth and JaneAnn next?"

"Yes, but first we need Marcus and Julia. I want a protection spell around Taylor so *he* can't get near her and no one does them better than those two. It will take all four of us to throw a strong enough one and it will only last a few days, but that should be enough. I'll call them to see if they're home."

She went to the bedroom and found she had a voicemail on her phone. It was Taylor, saying she was going to spend the day with Nicole if that was all right. She thanked Olivia for bringing her to Houston, which made her smile. Perfect. Taylor sounded fine – no problems there, and she would probably be all day with Nicole. That gave her and Alejo the time they needed. Whatever Dantin had planned, he wouldn't be able to get anywhere near Taylor – but she needed to find out what kind of mischief he was working toward JaneAnn and Beth.

Light didn't usually hit Nicole's hotel room until almost noon. Sunlight bleaching the side of the building softened as it entered through the beige sheers, warming Taylor's face and waking her gradually. She opened her eyes, her face feeling slack and puffy from carousing the night before and her mouth felt like someone had rubbed the inside with gravel. She needed water, and preferably cold, to cool off her stomach. She sat up and dangled her legs over the edge of the bed while her head cleared.

She'd had dreams...someone watching her...whispering like she'd become used to in the magical realm, but it was tinged with something twisted and she couldn't remember details. She knew she had spent the night in Nicole's suite and was relieved she hadn't encountered that distorted presence again. Maybe Nicole had been right – it had been something that had passed through. Or maybe she was extra sensitive to some things. Olivia had told her that people had different magical strengths. For whatever reason she was glad it was gone. The dream had faded, leaving her with a vaguely unsettled feeling.

Nicole came into the bedroom. "I thought I heard you. How're you doing?"

Taylor couldn't look up at her. "I feel kind of sick." She felt if she breathed too deeply she would throw up, but at least she wasn't spinning anymore. Now she was just ill. Apparently this was a hangover.

"You were really drunk last night. Next time we go anywhere I'll show you how to avoid getting plowed."

"If I ever pick up a drink again. Right now I'm leaning away from it." She groaned and held out her hand. "I need water." She called up a tall glass of the clear fluid and raised it to her mouth, taking long cooling sips until she was finally able to raise her head.

"Thanks for taking care of me last night."

"Oh, of course – I just felt so bad for you. I wish I had known how to make it go away." Nicole stacked up the pillows behind her. "Here – lie back on these for a while until you feel better, and then you can take a shower." She really didn't want Taylor to leave her.

"I need to call Olivia. I never told her where I am."

"Okay...where's your phone?" Nicole was looking under Taylor's jacket in the chair, then on the side table. "Where's your purse? Oh, I found it." She brought the clutch to Taylor. "I know you're leaving tomorrow but I hope we don't have to say goodbye just yet. Maybe we can all do something together..."

Taylor scratched around in her handbag until she found her phone, then scrolled to Liv's name and thumbed the "send" button. After four rings her voicemail answered.

"Hi, Olivia. It's Taylor. Hey, I spent the night at Nicole's and we're going to do something together this afternoon since it's my last day here. Hope that's okay with you." She hesitated, not really sure what to say next as she was Olivia's guest on this trip. She was surprised by sudden affection for her. "And thank you so much for bringing me to Houston and for everything...Okay, bye." That sounded stupid, she thought. But she meant it.

Nicole was looking at her. "Voicemail?"

"Yeah. We'll see if she calls. If not, what do you want to do?"

"Something low-key. I've had enough of clubs and drinking. First I need coffee, though. Want some?" She picked up the cup that appeared on the dresser next to her.

"Ugh. No – my stomach is still foul from last night."

"Here." Nicole produced a different cup and offered it to Taylor. "Try mint tea, it's supposed to soothe stuff like that and it works for me."

Taylor took a sip. The warmth was comforting and it was fresh and sweet tasting. "That is good."

"Why don't I call the concierge to see if they know something to do. Inside or outside?"

Taylor swallowed another sip. "Outside. And I want to go somewhere we haven't been yet."

Nicole sat on the edge of the bed and dialed the hotel desk. Taylor listened to Nicole's half of the discussion with closed eyes. The tea was working; her stomach felt better. She wondered if mint tea had some sort of numbing properties because right away she was less nauseated.

Suddenly Nicole was interested in one of the ideas the concierge presented. She turned to Taylor. "Hey, apparently there's an old neighborhood called Houston Heights just a couple miles from downtown. It's one of the first neighborhoods outside of Houston city limits and it has some old Victorian homes in a really nice neighborhood, and a retro downtown area with buildings from the thirties and forties. He says people have refurbished it and put in art galleries, vintage clothing and antique stores. They can put together a packet of details and a map for us. What do you think?"

Taylor thought it sounded like heaven. "So, we can just walk around slow and look at stuff and talk...yeah."

"It's a beautiful day, too." They both looked toward the window; outside it was a cloudless October day. This time of year the temperature stayed in the low eighties – perfect for an outdoor excursion.

"Let's do it. I'm starting to recover but still don't want to move very fast." *A plain piece of bagel might stay down if I ate it,* thought Taylor.

"No problem. I'm in no hurry. Let me know when you're ready to go." Nicole piled a couple of pillows behind her against the headboard and lounged next to Taylor, fishing the television remote from its hiding place under the nightstand.

While Nicole surfed the channels Taylor refilled her teacup and conjured up a plain bagel, tearing off bits to eat and sipping her tea. Thirty minutes later she felt nearly normal and got up, telling Nicole she was going to shower and get ready.

"I want a real shower, but then I'll just cast something for my hair and clothes." Looking at Nicole's cropped pants and the leather huaraches on her feet she decided on casual, too. After all, they were going to be walking. "I'll probably wear a sundress and flats. I'll be ready in about twenty-five minutes."

"Sounds perfect." Nicole lifted the phone by the bed. "I'll tell the concierge."

Thirty-five minutes later they stepped off the elevator into the lobby. Their maps and brochures were in a folder, waiting for them as promised. The hotel had even included two lightweight canvas shopping bags for them in case they picked up trinkets on their day trip.

"How do you want to get there? I don't really feel like using magic." Nicole looked a little tired, Taylor thought. "We could do this the normal way and ask the hotel van to drop us, take a bus, or a taxi."

"Oh – the bus, definitely!" Nicole said but then reconsidered. "Well, it depends on the bus. Who knows how many creeps might be on it." They both laughed to think that, witches or not, no one liked a public bus ride if there might be riffraff involved. They asked the receptionist at the front desk, who assured them that plenty of tourists and commuters took the route to the Heights nowadays and the likelihood of "creeps" would be low, and they hopped on the bus when it came, feeling like two little kids on an adventure.

Getting off the bus in the Heights was a wonder. The main boulevard was a magnificent lacy tunnel of massive trees on either side of the broad thoroughfare, huge trunks erupting from broad sidewalks and sprouting into a crisscross of branches and green foliage as far as they could see. Sunlight easily filtered through the canopy of branches, casting giraffe-type patterns on the street. On either side were Victorian and Craftsman homes, many behind ornate wrought iron fences. The delicate designs in the iron complemented the dark tree limbs as if purposely designed that way.

Neither could help the soft "Wow" that came out. A moment of stillness, almost respect quickly deteriorated into an urge to dive into the street and look around. They strolled down the sidewalk, occasionally peering through a fence or crossing the pavement to get a closer look at the beautiful homes with their round turrets, sharply peaked roofs, and gingerbread spandrels. These were homes people had poured their hearts into so many decades ago, and new owners continued the thought with their careful upkeep. The subtropical climate of Houston allowed for lush greenery, broad-leafed canna lilies with their fiery blossoms and crape myrtles were in profusion everywhere. Taylor had seen Victorian row houses in San Francisco, but those were stark and austere in their landscape of concrete, abutted against one another. These homes were spaced yards apart, green lawns and plantings softening their glory and making them look alive. In some places the sidewalk had been re-poured to curve around a huge tree trunk, in others it was starting to lift due to roots underneath but still trimmed with delicate flowers. Taylor half expected to see children on Schwinns riding up the street. A very old neighborhood.

"What a great day." Taylor was definitely feeling less hung over. She looked up through the long arms of the trees that crisscrossed over the avenue to the soothing triangles of blue sky between. Nicole stood beside her and did the same, feeling a warm patch of sun across one cheek. Close by one of the houses had a park bench built into the fence, its curlicues of black iron matching the artwork of the fence wall. They sat on it, soaking up the ambience of the neighborhood around them.

"This is perfect," said Taylor. "Good pick, Nicole."

"Thanks." Nicole looked around, also happy with her choice as they sat together, quietly appreciating each other's company.

For the next two hours the neighborhood was theirs. They walked and talked, Nicole describing her first forays into magic and how she had met her familiar. Taylor shared with her the details of her first encounter with Olivia and what had made her decide to accept Liv's offer of magic. She even told her about sleeping under the bench in Olivia's courtyard. As she had hoped, Nicole took it all in as if it were the most ordinary information in the world, not commenting on her circumstances or asking judgmental questions. She just listened, accepting Taylor as she was. Nicole's life seemed to be more exotic, but though she listed dozens of cities she'd been in and the array of things she'd done, she didn't mention friends anywhere, past or current. Taylor thought they were similar – her mom was gone and she didn't have anyone she kept in touch with except Karen, and now they seemed to be drifting because of her involvement with magic. She didn't dare befriend any mortals with her life the way it was.

"Hey, what's that over there?" Nicole was pointing at a little shop off the Boulevard. It was a dinky turquoise building with huge storefront windows. Poster-sized photographs of hands were placed behind the glass.

"Do you think it could be a palm reader? The concierge said we could find all kinds of kitschy stuff in the Heights..."

"I don't know..." Taylor was looking hard at it, trying to discern more.

"Wouldn't it be fun to get our palms read? I wonder if they could really see anything in it about us being witch." Nicole turned to Taylor with wide eyes and a huge smile. "Come on!" She headed straight for the shop in brisk stride. Taylor jumped up, too, and in a few steps she was caught up with Nicole and soon they were looking through the window at the posters.

"Look, it's not palm reading...it's henna."

The designs on the hands in the window were not like any henna painting they had ever seen with their simple swirls and curlicues in plain brick-red. These were works of art in shades deepening from light coral to almost black. Delicate paisley and swirls were interspersed with birds and butterflies, flowers and little scallops, fleur-de-leis, dots and fans. The designs were mesmerizing.

"Let's go in." Nicole turned toward the door, but Taylor was already ahead. She entered the shop first, where they found a casual, fabric-draped interior and a soft-spoken, brown-haired woman who was the owner. She showed them around, describing a few different items and explaining the henna designs. It was called *mehndi*, she said, traditionally a decoration in India for a woman's hands and feet on special occasions, like an engagement or a wedding.

"But anyone can have it. It's a beautiful piece of art and I have people who ask for special designs. Some people want it on their shoulders, or their back, or their leg." The other visitors in the shop had gathered, listening.

"How long does it last?" Taylor pictured a day, maybe two.

"Oh, it wears off in about three weeks. I have parents who bring their teenagers in to do this before deciding on a permanent tattoo."

"Should we do it?" Taylor hoped Nicole would say yes. She turned to the shop owner. "Do we need an appointment? This is our last day in town."

"I can fit you in. I have a couple of people ahead of you, but they'll be done within a half hour."

Taylor turned back to Nicole who was nodding, smiling. Perfect! They perched on nearby chairs to watch the artistry, astounded at the simplicity of her tools and how fast she worked. A little pointed bag full of henna with a hole in the tip that allowed a thin tracing line and a brush were all she used. The brush was used to feather a few places and create shadows or translucent patches around the darker, mounded lines.

The woman she was working on was hugely pregnant and she was getting her belly hennaed for her baby shower. The tight skin made a magnificent canvas for the swirls, leaves, and birds that flowed like living things from the artist's skilled hands. Over a square foot of intricate design was done in ten minutes, making the pregnant woman look like some fantastical fertile creature.

The artist looked satisfied and spoke to her client. "Just lie there for a few more minutes to let it dry and don't get it wet until this evening." Then turning to Taylor and Nicole: "Are you two ready?"

"I think we've decided. We want something on the back of our hand that flows up the wrist." Nicole traced her fingers from the index finger to the outside of her wrist. "Kind of diagonal."

"Do you want them the same or different?" She'd had experience with friends getting henna at the same time. She could never tell whether they wanted to match or not.

Taylor and Nicole looked at each other, a little hesitant. "What do you think? The same but not the same?"

"Yeah... Like the same basic pattern but different details. Like a long vine with leaves, and I'd like a tiny bird." Taylor was sure about the bird; she loved birds, especially ones with the most aerobatic abilities.

Nicole nodded. "I like the vine and leaves, too, but can I have that instead of a bird?" She pointed at one of the photos. "And maybe a couple of thorns on the vines?"

"Of course." They waited while the owner refreshed her supplies and the spot where she worked, next sitting down to beckon one of them to the chair. "Who's first?"

They decided Taylor would be first. She sat and stretched out her right arm, palm flat on the table. As she watched the patterns emerge on to her hand she was amazed at the life and artistry that seemed to flow organically from the other's hands, as if she were magical in her own way. She stared at her creation when it was done, turning her forearm left and right in order to take in every detail.

After hers was done Nicole sat where she had with her left hand stretched out for a mask of vines and patterns. They were a reverse match, in some places identical and very intricate. The shop owner had even extended the design to spiral around both of their index fingers, making the image even more three-dimensional.

They stood next to each other in front of the mirror and marveled silently at the markings that now seemed to bind them together. The owner had made their *mehndi* a mirror of each other, curling inward around the index fingers and crossing outward over the back of their hands so that the lacy diagonal pattern moved up and outward as they looked at their reflections.

"It's perfect," whispered Nicole.

Taylor turned to the artist who had created their treasure. "She's right. It is perfect... thank you so much."

They paid her, tipping her an insanely large amount that she tried to refuse, but they wouldn't let her and walked out before she could give any part of it back. Once outside Taylor opened the canvas bag the concierge had given them and dove into it with her un-hennaed hand, pulling out the map they'd been given. They pored over it together for a moment.

"Here." Nicole touched the map. "This says if we keep going up the street about six blocks we'll get into some antique shops. There're a couple of restaurants there, too, if we get hungry. We've got a whole list of things to do here and we're barely through Heights Boulevard!"

Taylor looked over at Nicole. "What do you want to do next?"

"There's Marmion Park a few blocks ahead. And if we go that way there's a bunch of art galleries." She pointed to the right. "Or we could just stand here and look at our arm decorations. I love this stuff." She held her left arm straight out next to Taylor's right arm and they compared the two again. Taylor laughed, throwing her head back, delighted with how the day was evolving.

"Let's keep going up the Boulevard and see where we end up. I'm not hungry yet, so I'm in no hurry."

"Sounds good to me." Nicole turned up the street with Taylor beside her and they ambled along, occasionally looking at their new *mehndis*.

They detoured into a few galleries they stumbled on, Nicole making up her usual silly stories about the paintings or sculpture and keeping Taylor amused. With her quick wit she couldn't help making up the little snippets and it was one of the things Taylor liked best about her. They loved drinking in what the Heights had to offer. They paused at Marmion Park as they continued up the street but decided to catch it on the way out. First they wanted to find the shopping district the hotel staff had raved about. They kept walking until finally they emerged from the canopy of trees off the Boulevard onto 19th Street where dozens of little businesses were clustered.

"Look at this – it's like a Main Street from back in the Forties!" Nicole was delighted. "The guy at the hotel said it was artsy and the storefronts were refurbished so I thought there would be some new construction, but you can't tell. This is cool, vintage."

Narrow old storefronts squashed close together lined either side of the street, the painted stucco in faded old pastels making their age apparent. A retro theater marquee halfway up the main thoroughfare proclaimed "HEIGHTS" in old paint and neon, and canvas awnings covered the walkways in front of open entrances, just like in old films. They half-expected to see classic Studebakers and Packards parked in the street.

The concierge was right about the artsy, kitschy shops and storefronts. Nearly every old building was chockablock full of vintage clothing or antiques, or little variety stores stuffed with every possible item you'd ever need – and many you didn't as well. They went into every establishment at least once and back to some twice, collecting a few souvenirs and purchasing cardigans together from an artist's shop of handmade clothing. There were boutiques that mixed high end with retro, and coffee shops and an old-fashioned deli and a couple of boutique restaurants where food was an obvious religion. They stopped at a funky little trailer parked off the main street to try one of their soft *dulce de leche* snowballs in a cup and then sat in the little city park to eat it, looking out at the storefronts from their perch on the grass.

"This is like a frozen custard cloud. Where do they come up with this stuff?" Taylor was scooping tiny bits of the flavored snow from the mound and eating them a morsel at a time.

"I don't know; it's good though." Nicole took another bite, savoring, then pointed her spoon at Taylor's wrist. "Hey, it looks like your henna has turned darker."

Taylor turned her wrist to look, almost dumping her dessert on the grass. "Oh, you're right. In these two spots it's dark maroon." She looked at Nicole's designs. "Yours, too, where she did the cross-hatch pattern. I wonder what it will look like when the clay comes off?" They weren't supposed to wash off the henna until later that night.

"I can't wait to find out. I'd always thought these were just one color." They inspected each other's arms, appreciating the complexity and delicacy of the designs for perhaps the fifth time that day. Even now they saw something new every time although they had watched each line as it was being drawn.

"Nicole, why did you get thorns with yours?" Taylor was looking at the sharp edges protruding from the vine with its leaves.

"It's a little edgier. Anything that's soft always has its flip side."

"I get that." Taylor mused on the idea. "I like them both...and I like that we match and they'll last for weeks." They both sat, holding their forearms next to each other and comparing patterns, tracing the raised henna with their fingers.

Abruptly Nicole turned to face Taylor, looking at her intently. Taylor could see multiple thoughts cross her face but fleeting, barely discernable. They looked at each other a moment and Taylor realized that Nicole's blue eyes were dark, nearly the color of sapphire. Then Nicole's expression smoothed and re-laxed.

"What is it?" Taylor was concerned.

"I'll just miss you so much." Nicole said. She looked past Taylor, at the little park they were in, at the little bench behind her and the snowball trailer where they'd bought their treats. She brought her eyes back to Taylor's. "You're the first person I feel like I'm friends with. It's been really hard without another witch to talk to. I mean, I knew a couple a little bit, but they were so far ahead of me, we didn't have anything to talk about. We never really..."

Taylor felt her heart melt. She had such a kinship with this blond girl she barely knew! She answered immediately. "I know exactly, I feel the same way. I was really lost at the party the other night until you came along. I didn't know anyone except Olivia, and I didn't have another person I could talk to."

"Me, too. I wish you weren't leaving..." Nicole trailed off and looked out into the street. *I wish you weren't leaving and I'm glad you are. Get away – get away from me before something happens to you. And I'll make sure nothing does happen. I'll never see you again.* Her internal sadness was immense. Even worse, the sun was low in the sky, the day would end soon, and Taylor was leaving tomorrow.

"But you'll be in Seattle pretty soon." Taylor tried to lighten Nicole's somber moment. She followed her gaze out into the street where they'd spent the afternoon, at all the shops and storefronts with their long shadows, also suddenly aware the day was nearly gone.

Nicole changed the subject. "This is a pretty cool old place." She was imagining the 1930's there, men in fedoras on the sidewalks and ladies in flowered dresses, as if from an old movie.

Taylor had the same impression. "Yeah. You know, it reminds me of the old Fremont neighborhood in Seattle."

"What's Fremont?" Nicole had never been to Seattle.

"It's a neighborhood of old buildings. It's kind of like these but not as many of them, just a few on a five-cornered intersection. There used to be some cool vintage clothing shops, and a little cake shop, and some restaurants there, but then some big businesses came in and built a bunch of new condos and a huge office building and just ruined it." She looked wistful and disgusted at the same time.

Nicole looked around. "I hope they have the sense to leave this the way it is. I wish someone could buy it all and freeze it like this, or put a time warp on it or something..." She set down her empty cup and wiped her sticky fingers on the grass. "Just do that and live here."

"Yeah." Taylor looked at the street in front of them. It was a time capsule of small-town Americana. It would be a shame to lose it.

Nicole was still staring down the main street. "You know what else is interesting about this place? There's some strong magic here." She looked up at the sky. "There's lots of energy, and it's powerful." Abruptly she was uneasy with the intensity she felt surrounding them. That didn't make sense, she thought, the day had been bright and beautiful and every person they'd seen was perfectly happy. She said so to Taylor.

"Oh, I know...I get the same feeling about Pioneer Square in Seattle. Like tense or something?" Taylor asked. Nicole was fascinated. She didn't seem fazed by it at all. They both could feel it, sitting there.

"Yeah, tense maybe, that's it." Nicole wanted to know more. "I've been a few places where it's like this, but why?"

"Olivia said there are just some places where that happens. It could be because they're old and they accumulate power over time, or something intense occurred there. The more things happen in a place, the bigger the pool gets. Maybe it gives off tension because there's so much of it, I don't know... But Pioneer Square feels the same way and I love it there."

Taylor was glad to have an answer for Nicole, who looked more at ease now. They looked around, reaching out into the energy and breathing it in. They could feel the power, smell it almost, like a deer sampling the breeze to see what was nearby. Taylor finished her snow, which was melted now, licking her spoon clean and then tapping it on the edge of her cup as she looked down the street. "I know we're kind of done with everything here, but I don't want to go back to the hotel yet, do you?"

"No, not really. And I don't feel like being around a bunch of people, either." Nicole held out her hand for Taylor's cup and spoon and walked them over to a nearby trash can. When she returned she picked up her canvas bag and slouched it over her shoulder. "Why don't we just walk back along Heights Boulevard? We can decide on the way what we want to do."

"Sure." Taylor stood and they started back down the concrete walkway, sauntering slowly and perusing the neighborhood in the fading afternoon. Soon they were back on the Boulevard where the trees were burnished with gold from the slanting rays of the sun. The west side was vibrant, lit up, but the east was mostly in shadow, casting a lopsided look to the tunnel of trees along the thoroughfare. They walked along this same street they had come up earlier that afternoon, not talking, each with their own similar thoughts. They came to a stone building, obviously a church with its gothic rosette window and block towers on each side, and stopped to look. Neither was in a hurry to get back to the hotel.

"How did we miss this?" Nicole looked across the street, remembering they had come this way earlier.

"We were on the other side of the street. Remember we passed by Marmion Park on the way in? We were going to go through it on the way home." Taylor pointed to the park, just across the street and down a block.

They came closer to the little church to read the large sign on the front lawn. It wasn't a church anymore, but a community center and apparently home to a local theater. It looked fairly old, maybe from the

1920's but was in good repair. Obviously the neighbors had a strong sense of community. Taylor thought about what Olivia had taught her, of her life in Seattle, so involved in all the philanthropy there.

"Wouldn't it be great to live here, buy one of these houses, and donate money to refurbish places like this?"

Nicole was taken by a wash of homesickness. "I would love that. I would really like to have a nice, boring life in a cute little neighborhood like this." She looked utterly dejected.

Taylor assumed it was because she was going back to Seattle. "What will you do after I leave tomorrow?"

"I don't know. I had planned to go somewhere warm for the winter." The truth was that Nicole wanted intensely to stay in one place. She wished she could. She wanted a home and friends, some roots. She brushed it away, rambling on just to fill the moment.

"...but I'm supposed to visit you next month, so I might stay awhile, then come to Seattle. I'll decide what to do after that, but I do like the idea of living here." *But would they let her? Probably not. Nicole, just enjoy the time you have left.* With an effort she wiped her thoughts away and changed the subject. She pointed up the street.

"Hey, don't forget about the park. Let's go before it gets too dark." The six-sided gazebo there was visible in the expanse of lawn, past the magnolia trees, but the colors were duller now, sapped of their vibrancy by the declining light.

"Okay, then after the park I'll flash us home." The bus would be a somber ride in the dark and Taylor didn't want the day to end like that.

"Oh, that's a great idea. And maybe coffee or a movie in the room would be nice." Nicole wanted to stretch out the time as long as possible.

Once they crossed the street and entered Marmion their mood lifted. Even in the gathering dusk the park was beautiful. There were a few old-fashioned streetlamps and under their light the grass shone in pools of emerald. The broad, waxy magnolia leaves were dark green, shiny and reflective wherever a piece of lamplight touched them. With the magical tension hanging ripe around them it suddenly seemed the perfect place to be, and to be witches in.

"Ahhhh…" Taylor spread her arms, welcoming the feeling and taking it in. She looked at Nicole. "Do you feel it?"

"Yeah, definitely." Nicole took a seat on the gazebo steps and pulled her knees up, looping her arms around them and tipping her head back. A few tiny points of light were starting to show high above them. Beautiful, she thought.

Taylor sat beside her on the steps. "Hey, remember I told you about Pioneer Square? Olivia showed me how to pull in magic from a place like this." She wanted to share her experience with her kindred friend.

Nicole turned toward her. Taylor's intensity was palpable. She was close, inches away, dark hair hanging over her cheek between them. "What do you mean?"

"Back when I was just learning, maybe a month or two at the most, she took me to the Columbia Tower, the tallest building downtown. It overlooks the Square."

Nodding, Nicole acknowledged and waited for her to go on.

"It felt the same way, just full of magic like this. Olivia showed me how to pull power off the Square and it enhanced everything about me, filled me up. If I compare it to the hits of magic you and I've been doing, they're light. This was something completely different. It was solid, deep."

"What do you mean? What happened?"

"It's hard to explain. It was like... it was as if I had ten times the strength. I could do anything in that moment, and like I'd been doing magic for a hundred years. And Nicole, the feeling was incredible."

"And it's the same way every time? Does it drain away or stay with you?"

"I don't know. I haven't had a chance to try it again. People are always around whenever I've been down there. But I want to do it again. It feels like we could right here." A thought occurred to her. "Nicole, what does your familiar know about places like this? Could it help us?"

Nicole turned a hard stare on her. "I don't know that you'd really want to do that. What if you got a level of power beyond your ability to control?"

Taylor's expression was innocent, an open question. "Nicole, I don't know what my abilities are. At brunch with all the others they said I was capable of a lot more. They told me not to hold back, that I should learn from them, too, or from Beth and her familiar. They said it was time Olivia pushed me harder."

She kept going, leaning in toward Nicole. "Maybe you have more power than you know, Nicole. You haven't had a mentor before, who knows what they could show you? Why don't you ask Julia to teach you?"

Nicole looked away from her friend, down at a crack in the sidewalk at her feet. There were little pointed mounds of dirt along the crack where insects had burrowed into it, throwing up the sand in-between the gray slabs. She ran the tip of her shoe over the points, flattening them. She wanted to do what Taylor was suggesting, was desperate to in fact, but she was trapped. She couldn't fathom how she could possibly get out of her situation and sure she would fail if she tried. Her hated chimera kept her afraid. When she didn't comply they muffled her and spoke for her, hiding her like an abductee inside her own skin. *Hidden right in plain sight.*

Taylor was unaware of Nicole's conflict, continuing with her idea to pull Nicole into her newly met circle of witches. "Come on, Julia already offered to show you! You could live with her at first, learn from her. I'll come here in the spring and we could learn to-gether, practice, do all kinds of things together..."

Nicole listened to Taylor blithely making plans. As if there weren't a care in the world, she thought. She wanted to tell Taylor everything, to warn her and explain why they couldn't be friends – or even better, to ask her for help – but nothing came out. She forced herself to nod until she finally found her voice.

"That's a great idea. I'll call Julia after you leave and let you know what we decide. But either way I'll be in Seattle in a month." She knew it was all a lie. The thought of losing her only friend had her close to tears. *I have got to get a grip on myself or I am going to lose it completely.* Clenching her jaws, she fought to compose herself.

Taylor was elated with her friend's answer. She was sure they would both end up as partners, the two new apprentices in Olivia's group of friends. This was all working out perfectly.

As dejected as she was, Nicole couldn't stifle her curiosity. "What do you think she'll teach me? What did they say was possible with more training?"

"They said a talented witch could do almost anything – speak different languages, live any dream, meet other magical creatures, transfix objects with magic to carry out a command for you, transform into almost anything for a short time... all kinds of things."

"I've never transformed before. I've done a few simple glamours, but that's about it." Nicole had hoped to learn something she could use, but instead the answer was making her miserable. She would need instruction to accomplish the magic Taylor was describing. Here was the life she would miss out on. Taylor would learn from the others and develop her powers, leaving Nicole behind in her wretched state, living the same horrors over and over. It was like being held just under water with the air a half inch away, drowning so viciously close to the surface. Here she was, doing things with Taylor and saying things that looked perfectly normal when she wanted to tell her the truth.

Suddenly she wanted to scream, to pull at her hair and throw things. She felt so helpless – and she was terrified the chimera really would find someone repugnant to pair her with instead of Taylor. *I cannot take this anymore! Bound for eternity to my horrible captors...* Abruptly her thoughts of the previous night came back on their own. *If there's only one for each of us we could control them. The two of us, combined, could break free.*

That thought she'd shoved far away, stuffed in a crevice in the back of her mind, now became her hope for freedom, everything suddenly hinging on gaining Taylor's strength to help her. *She's trained with a powerful witch. She's potent even on her own. But for me to escape we have to split them up. One with me and the other one with her. God, Taylor, I am so sorry for what I am about to do, but I have to.*

Nicole leaned toward Taylor, trembling at taking action on her idea. "Can you imagine what we could do if we trade? If I learn from you and Olivia, and you learn from my familiar?"

"Do you think it would teach me?"

Nicole shrugged. "Sure. I don't see why not."

"What can it do, Nicole?"

"Everything, almost. It has far more power than I have, of course. When my chimera combines with me it adds to my abilities. And they can control anything in the mortal world through a witch, even the elements."

"Are you serious? Like wind and lightning? I've heard of that but..."

"Yes. Watch."

Nicole looked around at the magnolias and oaks, outlined in shadow now against the night sky. Concentrating and narrowing her eyes she took a deep breath, expanding her chest, holding that posture a moment before letting it out with the magic flowing through her. Around them a breeze came up, ruffling the leaves in the trees and lifting the branches, causing them to sway. Taylor watched it travel around the park like a wave, swirling bits of litter and leaves and grass clippings into a wind devil that slid toward them, stopping just in front of them to show off its power and tug at their clothing and hair. The little cyclone made a whispering, hollow sound as it undulated in front of them and the leaves and twigs within scraped and scratched against each other in the vortex.

"What do you think?" Nicole was watching Taylor as she studied it, apparently impressed by its obedience. With a gesture Nicole sent it off toward a little playground in the park where it tangled in the swings and died.

"That's amazing."

"Try it."

"How – do I move the air or ask your familiar to help me?"

"I don't know – I just picture what I want and it does it for me."

Taylor was at a loss where to start but then thought of her ability to manipulate fire. She could do that on her own, why would this be any different? It would be a limited section of air that she was control-ling, like a limited piece of fire. She selected a column of air in the park and concentrated on moving it. She could feel it start, overcoming inertia and beginning to budge, as if it were a huge roulette wheel she was pushing that started to glide. As it passed the magno-lia trees their leaves stirred and flapped on their stems. Taylor pictured it turning tighter, twisting it like wringing a washcloth, and a weak twister was the re-sult. Then Taylor ceased her focus on it and it dissi-pated.

Nicole was impressed. "See? They can help you do anything."

"But I didn't need a chimera to do that. I just picked a section of air and moved it, like manipulating a flame. Bringing in clouds or lightning would be a bigger test."

Nicole was shocked at Taylor's ability. "Do you think you could do that on your own?"

"I don't know. I'm going to try it." Taylor looked up at the clear sky above them, picturing a cloud forming there. She continued for long seconds, concentrating, but nothing happened. She tried it again, pulling in some of the magic that lay heavily in the atmosphere around them, but even with the extra power no clouds emerged above. She realized she didn't know what the connection was between the sky and the magic to form what she wanted. She wished Olivia had practiced manipulating things using True Name and casting spells with her, there was only so far she could go simply wishing for something. Not knowing how the magic worked was limiting her. She turned to Nicole.

"I don't know where to start. Have you casted clouds before?"

"Yes, but only with the chimera. I don't know how to do it on my own." Nicole dared herself to say the next sentence. "You could ask it to help you, too."

"I don't know. Alejo doesn't have a chimera and he can do all kinds of things. Do you remember he was telling us about playing polo on magical horses? With the sky as their playing field? You'd have to fly to do that or make the mounts fly – and he does that."

Nicole thought fast. "But Alejo has been around hundreds of years. Our power grows with age and we're still novices. We need help." The lie came so easily it nauseated Nicole. *If there's a hell I'm going there for this.*

Taylor looked uncertain. She hadn't tried anything like this before, had always waited for Olivia to show her in one of their sessions. But to do something so powerful – and actually partner with a chimera! In the last few days she had seen magic she didn't realize existed and the temptation to try it was strong.

Nicole pushed herself to keep going. She took Taylor's hands in hers and pulled her off the steps. "If you don't like it just tell it to stop…" She hated herself.

Taylor considered Beth and Ethan, Eidolon and Olivia. *Both Julia and Alejo had said I should be doing more - and Olivia hadn't argued with them, had she?* She made her decision.

"I'm going to try it." Taylor's eyes glinted with the anticipation of such advancement. "What do I do?"

"You have to let it flow through you, welcome it inside of you."

"Okay…" Taylor stood on the sidewalk and waited, palms open and out. She closed her eyes and tried to feel the way Nicole said, waiting for something to come into her mind. Would it be like doing hits? Like a flash and then everything was magnified? She could tell she needed help – the air around her was easy to couple with, but she was going for something more. She tried asking the familiar for help with clouds and lightning, but couldn't tell if she was connecting to anything... She felt the breeze start, but it took massive effort. She dropped her arms.

"How do I get your familiar to help me? I tried but couldn't feel anything."

"What did you try? What were you thinking of?"

"I imagined being open, like you told me to, while I was concentrating on the air around me. And I asked it for help."

"Maybe you're trying too hard. Maybe you can't make it happen. Try letting it flow through you."

"Okay." This was like her early lessons with Olivia. Not so scary. Relax, she told herself, let it in, but it was hard to do since she was so used to protecting herself. She felt the air thicken around her, pressing in on her, and heard the rustling of the trees again. *Maybe if I pull in some of the energy here I can push through it.* She spread her arms wider and tapped into the magic around her, feeling it rush into her chest, expansive and strong. The air around her seemed to be affected and pressed in on her harder, squeezing her. Opening her eyes she saw the tree branches were all bowing toward her as if drawn to her in the little park. The effect spread farther now, up the Boulevard. Nicole's eyes were wide with expectation as she looked around – everything looked as if it would implode in on them.

Then they heard a branch crack and fall, followed by a crash and the sound of a car alarm going off. Taylor stopped and immediately everything returned to normal. As both she and Nicole looked toward the sound to see what damage had been done, a nearby porch light came on and someone stepped outside.

"Oh, shit... I'll fix it." Taylor saw the branch next to a mid-size red car parked on the street, a deep crease in the hood where the heavy limb had struck it. She shot a dose of magic over to it, removing the furrow and making it pristine by the time the owner got there. The wind had died down and everything was still again, but at this point several neighbors had come out to see what was going on. They were all on their porches now, looking around. Nicole and Taylor stayed still, hoping no one would notice them in the darkened park, as if people could tell just by looking it was they who had brought in the freak windstorm. But after a couple minutes the residents went back inside, bored with the false alarm and the absence of gusts outside.

"Well, we didn't think that through very well." Taylor laughed.

Nicole sat back down on the gazebo step. "Yeah, we have to think of something else. We need something powerful but quiet." She could tell the chimera hadn't taken Taylor. They had tried, pressing in on her but couldn't get through.

"Do you want to try transforming?" she asked Taylor. "Do you know if that's very difficult?"

"I don't want to do that – what if I don't know how to become myself again?"

Nicole forged ahead, ignoring her conscience. What else would work? She spied the bird in Taylor's henna.

"What about flight? Alejo said he does it all the time. A chimera could help you, and your transportation skills are excellent. If there's a problem you could flash yourself to a safe place."

Taylor thought about the Gulfstream with its huge windows. Almost like flying, she had thought at the time. Could she really do it? *My God, that would be incredible.* She felt a buzz of excitement.

"Yes! Let's do it." But a question still remained. "I still don't know how to combine with your familiar. You said drop my guard, but it's so difficult…"

Nicole considered a moment, then thought of a mortal explanation. "It's like resisting a seduction. You feel the urge, desire calling and pressing in on you."

Taylor was starting to track with Nicole. "I felt that but I thought it was the air getting thick, pressing in on me."

"That's only part of it. That's because…" Nicole tried to think. "…part of it's you refusing to give in to the craving for it. It's strong and you want it, but then you don't, or you should know better for whatever reason so you make yourself stop and go no further."

Taylor was listening, watching her intently and completely absorbed in what Nicole was saying.

"What you need to do is give in. Say 'I want it' and let go of your resistance. Like that moment with sex when you decide to stop fighting, remove all your clothing, and feel their skin against yours. Welcome it, revel in it. You take it all in – all of it."

Taylor said nothing. She was looking at Nicole transfixed, her lips parted slightly as she imagined doing what Nicole was saying. But then she winced, hardly discernible but unsure, eyes narrowing the tiniest bit.

Suddenly Nicole wanted out of this. "Look, I don't want you to do anything you're unsure of." A wave of guilt slammed into her chest. "Let's not do this at all. I can tell you're uncomfortable. Let's just stop this and go home."

She was able to spit out the words before the chimera could stop her, but it had an unintended effect. Instead of putting Taylor off it reassured her and she changed her mind.

"Okay, I'll do it. After all, it's your familiar and you've been doing it."

Oh, God... Nicole didn't like the idea after all, but it was too late. If she didn't finish this the chimera would since Taylor was agreeing to let them in now. At least she should be with her for this. She took Taylor's hands in hers again, swallowing through a stiff throat.

"Are you sure?" She felt sick to her stomach. Taylor nodded.

"Okay. If you still want to do this, then think about asking it to give you what you want. First you want it to enter you – imagine what I just said about surrendering – give in and let it take control of you. Then ask it for your wish." She used a reassuring tone.

"Okay." Taylor looked into her friend's face and nodded, thinking the air around them felt electric and strange, but wrote that off to what she was trying to do. It was beyond anything she'd tried before. She let out her breath and dropped her guard completely.

Almost immediately she felt the chimera rush in. The sensation was dizzying – she felt potent, invincible, a sensual explosion. The force of it dashed her, a pressure wave, moving up through her legs, her core, and then her chest and beyond, out through her fingertips and into the park around her, almost lifting her off the ground. Yes! She felt Nicole's familiar filling her, lighting up every awareness, reading her, knowing her intimately. No wonder Beth described it the way she had.

She looked at her hands in front of her. In her eyes they glowed with another presence, assuring her, caressing her, bringing every delightful feeling she had ever known. And power. This was the very essence of it, like tapping into the magical logos itself without any boundaries. She couldn't help sighing a long contented groan – and then laughing victoriously. This was sheer adrenaline.

She stretched out her arms and faced the sky. The chimera in her urged her on – do it! She shook off

Nicole's remaining hand. There was absolutely no doubt she could do this. The adrenaline coursing through her was so powerful it was nearly nauseating and for a sweeping millisecond, Olivia's words came to her: Go slow, practice, resist the power until you can control it. *Well, obviously I'm ready... Olivia said I was strong and could be a formidable witch. Now I know what it's all about.* She wanted to try everything, starting with a rush through the air. She opened herself wider, asking the chimera to give her every bit of power it could, and gathered herself to take control of the sky. She rose up on her toes and felt the earth disappear below her, not too high, just a dozen feet or so, and she laughed aloud from the joy of it.

Then suddenly the chimera closed in on her, restraining her, burying her in their essence and muffling her elation in a league of sensations. She was engulfed, then gagged and unable to control the rush of emotions being dredged up in her. A choking feeling started and Taylor was terrified almost beyond reason. She knew what this was, most definitely, and flailed about, struggling to free herself from the magical grip.

"Nicole!" She screamed to her friend, searching the lawn below her. Nicole was crouched on the ground almost under the gazebo platform, wide-eyed and terrified against the steps. Taylor was confused. Why didn't she help?

"Nicole!" She screamed again and then felt her mouth silenced. Nicole covered her ears now, then her whole head with her arms as if to protect herself...or make something go away.

Taylor was thrashing, trying to get a purchase on anything solid and get away, but there was nothing in the half-magical world she was suspended in. She was frantic and losing ground. *Too much for me. I can't get free...* She gathered herself together, pulling on any reserves of strength she could dredge. *"Olivia!"* She screamed it out, one word only, not daring to waste any of her energy on anything more. She was on the edge of being sucked down into torpid blackness. But how could Olivia hear? She was across town, not here with them.

Olivia was sitting in the zebra chair, facing the window and ruminating on her work that afternoon. All their protections were in place, but they'd still discovered nothing new on Dantin's motives. Taylor's magical block against him was cast; Julia, Dan, Alejo and she had crafted it with every spell, True Name, and piece of power they knew. No way Dantin could pierce it. Daphne and Chloe had been sent for; they would be in Seattle already when they got home tomorrow, prepared to protect Taylor. Then Olivia had linked minds with the other four, searching for any hint of the Blue/Black witch and watched as they did the same with each other to make sure no one was deceiving the rest. None of them seemed to be compromised. To create confusion for Dantin, they had all gone in different directions on false errands. After all, he couldn't keep an eye on all of them at once, or at least they hoped not. They'd sent Marcus to spy on Schmidt without looking like he was spying on him, just in case Dantin was watching, to make sure Schmidt wasn't the weak link.

Finally, Olivia had told Beth about Dantin and was grateful for her calm response. She'd been wrong on several levels not to tell her, she realized. Although Beth was hurt that Olivia hadn't confided in her before she also brought up a point that was uncomfortably accurate – because she had never known about Dantin she wouldn't recognize him, spell or otherwise. A mind read on her could read only her memories, not whether it was him in disguise. She suggested that Alejo or JaneAnn keep an eye on her until they could discover and stop Dantin's plans.

Now Olivia was going over everything again to see what they had missed. In no way was she calm, but at least she felt better, sure of her friends and reasonably sure her plans for the glaive were undetected.

Now from a source she didn't expect she felt the vibration of magic come on, something small but distinct touching her hand, and she raised her palm to grasp it. The Barrowman's Guild coin from Taylor's watch appeared there, hot to the touch. *Oh*, she thought, *this was not good.* The coin was a talisman she had put a spell on and given to Taylor – set up so that if she was ever in trouble it would return to Olivia like a warning, a cry for help. Closing her fist around it, Olivia was shocked by what came off of it. It was primal, a howling, instinctual feeling. She could feel Taylor's terror, and the sense that she was tightly bound in something murky. There was evil and anger there, too, far more dangerous in its composition than the blend of euphoria and excitement that magic usually brought.

Fear. She felt the blood drain from her lips. Now what? Fleetingly she thought: *Dantin.* But that wasn't possible – she had just re-checked the rebuff spell they had all conjured around Nicole and Taylor. He couldn't get near either of them.

She forced herself to stay calm, to be objective so she wouldn't interfere with the charm and then concentrated, connecting with Taylor through the talisman and letting Taylor's surroundings flow through her so she could pull her location from the coin.

Instantly the visions flooded her, glimpses of the afternoon, what Taylor had seen that day. *Cut to the chase.* Olivia stopped that urge immediately, best to slow down. She knew if she rushed it, forced it, her own thoughts would intrude and taint what she saw. She would waste vital seconds going to the wrong place and have to search for them again. She emptied her mind and let it flow into her….Houston Heights. Of course – she'd felt it all week; it would pull on Taylor and Nicole, too. A park… the park – Marmion Park. All in one motion she stood up and flashed to the park, looking around.

She saw Taylor immediately, suspended in the air a few feet above the grass, her legs dangling and head thrown back, lifeless. No one else was there. *Nicole – where was Nicole?* Swiftly she turned her head, scanning the park until she spied Nicole limp and lying in the flowers next to the gazebo steps.

In three strides she was on her, lifting her up by her shoulders to divine any information that she could by touch. By the way Taylor was suspended Olivia could tell something had her in its grip. Nicole should be an easier read. But Nicole was unresponsive, a blank void behind her wide open eyes. Olivia could barely feel her out in the logos, past the mortal world. She had no thoughts, almost as if she didn't exist. Something had ahold of them both, she was sure.

Two novices at once under this kind of attack was hardly heard of. *What could be this powerful?* It felt like a chimera, but it seemed to be everywhere around her. She laid Nicole back on the ground and went to where Taylor hung, placing a hand against her cheek and focusing hard to try and contact the unconscious girl. An entity was there, as she suspected, blocking her way, binding and muffling her apprentice. Olivia was strong, but it was intensely difficult to push past whatever it was and get through. She could hardly feel Taylor's personality from within the grip, just a mortal in a semi-catatonic seizure, unable to break free or do any better than just hold her ground against possession. Even directing her own energy into the two girls was useless – the wall around Taylor was deep and Nicole was too weak, fear making her even more so. Olivia would have to go to them.

She prepared quickly. No time to take anything except what she knew. Talismans and charms wouldn't work there anyway. She raised her arms over her head, pressing her fists together and pulled in every bit of magic she could lay her mind on from the Heights. She could feel it drive toward her as she crouched down, a circumference of ripples pulling inward, growing in stature and warping the very ground in concentric circles around her. She closed her fist tightly around the Barrowman's coin and then disappeared.

Where she materialized the sound was deafening, like being next to a freight train. Everything was amorphous, no up or down, no spatial reference. The very atmosphere stung, like vicious sand in wind, cutting into her from every direction. She had to rethink her stance. Mortal rules would not apply here. Ignoring the stinging grains she looked around.

There it was, a monstrously huge figure, charred-looking and sticklike, sweeping around to face her. A chimera. It was dense, rough, more solid in appearance than the vaporous form a familiar usually took. Very rarely had she seen them like this. Olivia knew how it appeared was just a representation out in this plane, an intermediate setting between human and magical worlds, but it was deadly nonetheless since they were all here in the same state. She could see Nicole off to the side, a nearly transparent figure underneath another chimera that crouched over her. *Two of*

them! No wonder... The other had Taylor in its grasp.
She appeared unconscious, head down, movements
fluid and boneless.

Olivia was filled with fury at the sight of her
apprentice like this, a helpless toy flopping about in a
bully's hands. Deep, dark rage came up through her
from somewhere primordial and she could hardly hold
it in through clenched teeth. "That is not yours..." she
grated at the chimera, "and you are going to give it
back."

There was no reaction from the entity. It
simply perused her mildly and retained its grip on the
witchling. Olivia suppressed the urge to address it further. What was she thinking – that she could just ask
and it would give up its new plaything? She stepped
toward it, gathering up her powers and launching a
pulse of magic at it, hoping to unbalance it, make it
loosen its grip on Taylor so she could pull her away. It
left an arc in its wake, igniting the grains in the air
like a tracer round. Her aim was point-blank, entering
the bulk of the creature and leaving a spreading hole
that crinkled in crimson embers.

"Taylor!" She reached into the maelstrom tele-
pathically, searching for Taylor until she finally connected. The girl was half-obscured. "Taylor!" She tried
to rouse her, but the hole in the creature was closing
and it was becoming defined again, weakening her link
with Taylor. She needed to keep it occupied longer or
find a way to reduce it to a manageable size so her
novice could break free. But what about the other one?

She decided to handle one problem at a time, if they let her.

She assessed her current opponent and then swept two powerful arcs toward it, one immediately after the other, the ignited grains slicing through it at different angles and burning into it. As soon as they struck she immediately called to Taylor again. Without the chimera blocking her Olivia could connect but just barely. She used all the energy she could spare to pull Taylor back to consciousness.

"Taylor, it's Olivia!" Urgency filled her tone and Taylor roused from her stupor just enough to recognize her. She needed an infusion or she would lose herself to the chimera.

"I'm going to give you some magic. Take it!" Olivia sent a stream toward her, watching as Taylor's shape became more defined. She also saw the chimera re-form in her peripheral vision and knew she had only a few seconds. She spoke quickly.

"Taylor! I need you to try and get away while I divert it."

Taylor was coming back to consciousness now, looking over at Olivia and then at the turbulence surrounding them. Confusion flooded her face a moment until she realized her situation, then desperation replaced it. She tried to grab at the beast holding her as if to pry open its fingers, but her hands only swept through the form. She struggled, twisting this way and that, hoping to find an exit somehow.

Olivia sent her a shock, a quick stab of electricity to get her attention. "Listen!" she told her. "Don't waste your energy. You can't fight it physically. Stay still and think it through. Feel for a weak point – then we'll attack it together."

She only had time to get that out of her mouth when she was knocked back, a brutal smash that numbed her and sent her reeling. She felt herself sliding, frictionless, and couldn't stop. She had to wait until the magic dissipated and she came to a halt, far from where the chimera still held Taylor. She couldn't do this on her own, she knew. She didn't reside in this dimension and didn't know all the rules or how to use them to her advantage. There was an abundance of magic here she could draw on but how? Worse, as a mortal it took magic to exist on this plane, so the balance was slightly negative. Eventually it would drain them both.

"Eidolon...!" She remained sitting and composed herself, searching for him in this netherworld they were in.

"Eidolon, Taylor and I need your help." She sent her message into the void and left it at that. He would get her communiqué and perceive where they were. The problem was that time wasn't consistent here – it could be seconds or days before Eidolon came, but the distress call was out there at least. In the meantime she would have to engage – she couldn't let that thing have Taylor.

She got to her feet, brushing imaginary dust off her trousers, more from habit than anything. Then she looked up, toward Taylor and the chimera.

"Okay, you hideous bastard...let's you and I dance."

She willed herself to them and was there in an instant. She could hear Taylor in her head and was relieved she was strong enough to connect with her – and was making sense.

"I can't find a weakness, Olivia. It's strong everywhere." At least she wasn't hysterical. She was trying to do what Liv had asked.

"No – that's good. That gives me an idea." Would size matter? If she could separate that piece holding Taylor would she be able to free herself? She told Taylor what she was planning and what her apprentice should do.

"All right." Taylor answered and readied herself. Both witches hoped the chimera wasn't reading their connection or it could defend itself easily.

Olivia pressed her palms together, willing the logos to compress and strengthen between them, crafting a curse and adding to it until the force spread her palms so far apart she couldn't hold it anymore. Concentrating hard, she spoke quickly, a few unintelligible sounds that called on True Name to add a "slippery" effect, intending to delay the thing from reintegrating quickly, then projected it with as much velocity as she could muster.

By now the thing had gotten wise to her actions and avoided Olivia's weapon, dodging upward
and taking Taylor with it.

"My god, no...please." Olivia's heart was in her
throat. Taylor was being pulled toward her spell; if it
touched her she would not survive. Olivia could only
stand and watch, unable call it back. The chimera saw
it, too, and hesitated, not wanting to lose its prize in
the fight. It dropped sideways, away from the curse
but not fast enough and Olivia succeeded, severing the
piece that was wrapped around Taylor.

Now Olivia saw what she had hoped for, Taylor
holding still and concentrating, creating a magical
layer between herself and the chimera, repelling its
grasp. She could see the shimmer between the two as
they separated, like something emerging from a cocoon,
but it wasn't enough. Although Taylor pulled magic
from her surroundings, only an inch of shimmer maintained its place around the novice. It should be growing. Why wasn't it working? Maybe, thought Olivia,
magic was connecting everything to some extent.
Damn! She wished she'd had more practice out here in
the *logos.*

"Here – I'll help if I can." She concentrated another orb of logos between her palms and willed protection into it. Then she flashed it onto Taylor, hoping
it would create a sphere to isolate her from the rest of
the chimera's power.

"Try to expand that around you and get free."
As Taylor worked on that Olivia used the connection

between them to pull Taylor toward her. But the effort was quickly tiring her, and the fiend was trying to re-form again. Fleetingly, she wondered how they could possibly get out of this if Eidolon didn't arrive.

It seemed like eons until Taylor was close enough to capture. Reaching through the glowing orb she grabbed Taylor's sweater, yanking her free of the chimera's sooty grasp. Disgust filled her as she touched the chimera. She hadn't felt something that vile in a long time. She kept it contained in the shell, murmuring a spell she hoped would keep it trapped there, and locked an arm around Taylor's waist. She didn't intend to lose her again.

"Are you okay?"

Taylor was shaking but lucid. She nodded vigorously and looked around, searching for something. "Olivia, did you see Nicole?" She had to shout above the howling noise. "Do you know where she is?"

Olivia put a hand up to block the stinging wind racing between their faces. "Yes, but I can't protect you both by myself. We need Eidolon. I called him, but I don't know when he could arrive."

Taylor looked distraught. "Nicole can't wait! I need to help her."

"Are you kidding me?" Olivia was dumbfounded. "That chimera is almost whole again and even cut up, it's formidable. It will take both our magic to get back. Even now we have to pull from the logos just to protect ourselves!"

"Olivia, please!" Taylor could be stubborn about some things, Olivia knew. Maybe she needed more information about their situation. She drew closer to Taylor and gripped her wrists hard, shouting through the noise.

"This is not practice! This is the real deal at its worst, nothing like you ever experienced in training!"

Taylor didn't shy away. "I know. Are you forgetting I was just trapped there like Nicole? Olivia, I felt what her life was like while we were all linked together. I can't leave her here with them!" When Olivia didn't answer she pressed.

"I know you called Eidolon and he might not get here right away, but he could at any moment, too." Adrenaline bubbled up in her, giving her confidence. She leaned in close to Liv's ear. "I'm not afraid, Olivia. Mostly now I'm really pissed off."

Olivia stared at her apprentice a second, stupefied. Then Alejo's words insinuated themselves: *Don't protect her too much or she won't learn.* She narrowed her eyes at Taylor, deciding.

"Olivia, I'm doing it." Taylor was staring back at her, daring her to say no.

Olivia dropped Taylor's wrists and pressed her lips together in a grim smirk.

"Okay then, let's get Nicole, but it will be a much harder fight – and no guarantees." She wanted to make sure Taylor understood. "We are way out of our element here. Those chimera are connected to everything around us. We have to keep a barrier between them and us so keep that in mind if we get separated."

Taylor nodded and Olivia added a piece of wisdom. "It will use less magic if we encircle ourselves instead of trying to contain them."

"Okay." Taylor began to move toward Nicole. Instantly Olivia grabbed her arm to stop her, seeing the area in front of them warping like a funhouse mirror, and she flashed the two of them away. Taylor was shaken to realize she would have walked right into the chimera that was materializing there if Olivia hadn't yanked her away.

Olivia's voice was like a slap. "Now you know what I mean... So if we can get to Nicole – *that's if* – we need to surround her with a protection spell. She wasn't being held when I saw her, just guarded so we won't need to pry her out of that chimera's clutch. She can't help us, either, because she's too frightened. When I picked her up in the park she hardly existed."

She could see Taylor absorb that, now serious and deliberate. "If we can grab her, what do we do next? Wait for Eidolon? Can't those things come out after us if we don't do something about them?"

"I'm not sure but if we get her, I'm not waiting – we get the hell out of here with her." Liv could hardly believe they were doing this at all. "And if they enclose her before we can...I don't know what we do. We can last only a little while here." *I hope I don't kill us all*, she thought to herself.

"Okay." Taylor exhaled hard to calm herself. Good, Olivia thought, she's thinking at least, not just running headlong.

They flashed closer to Nicole. From their spot she looked peaceful, as if a baby in sleep – except that they knew the truth. Taylor focused hard on Nicole, trying not to alert the thing standing guard while Olivia shielded them both and pulled in magic to sustain them. Carefully, slowly, she concentrated on creating an orb around her friend without disturbing the surroundings. A pale shimmering started, at first looking like pixilation that blurred Nicole's form, then cleared to a viridescent glow. Taylor began to pull her toward them.

Excellent, Olivia thought as she watched, now flash her back to the park... but the other chimera was there suddenly, blocking them. The second turned to see and followed suit immediately, striking out at Olivia and Taylor. Liv had to bolster their protection, putting one palm out to feed the protection orb around them and the other into the turmoil outside to anchor their position.

Then she saw they were concentrating on her and Taylor and not attending to Nicole at the moment, but so far the chimera couldn't touch them through the orb.

"You hold onto her tight and try to flash us all to one place," Olivia said, "but be crisp about it because I can't hold us like this for long."

Taylor concentrated but nothing happened. Olivia became impatient. "What is going on?"

"I'm afraid to flash us out of here – it feels like I'm barely hanging on to her and any action will shake her loose!"

"No, Taylor, those two chimera can make you think that, but it doesn't mean it's true...well, maybe it could be. Look, you'll have to tell by feel but do something, don't waste time thinking about it!" *Oh, that was brilliant, Olivia*, she thought. She knew it was confusing; nothing here followed the rules they were used to.

Then they quit talking, no energy to spare for it. Olivia shielded them and Nicole came closer in Taylor's grasp, but they were drawn nearly empty by the effort. The larger chimera enveloped their shell, obscuring them and Olivia could feel it closing in, pressing hard on them. *We really need to get out of here right now.*

She turned to face Taylor and saw her novice looking back at her in anguish. Olivia saw the chimera had pierced her protective orb. Was it taking her apprentice? *Oh, no, no, NO!* She hadn't the stamina to keep the protection going and fight them at the same time.

Taylor was still with her, though. "I can't feel her anymore!"

"What!?" Olivia sucked back an involuntary sob, wildly relieved it hadn't possessed Taylor again.

"I lost Nicole – I can't feel her anymore." Taylor was urgent. "We need to look for her."

"*No!*" Olivia was brooking no argument this time. "That was it. We leave now – if we still can."

Taylor glanced around and wavered. Olivia was quick.

"We flash out of here together. Neither one of us has enough left to get out alone. And we have to do it at exactly the same time." They were fading, exhausted.

Taylor nodded and gathered herself for the jump. Then they were gone. They reappeared but still in the howling mess, both dizzy with the effort and nearly spent as they tried to keep the two chimera at bay. Now Olivia was really frightened. She tried to rally Taylor without admitting the dire circumstances.

"We'll keep trying until we get out. We can't help Nicole if we're in this maelstrom." But Taylor was dazed and didn't respond. Olivia jerked on her arm.

"Come *on,* Taylor. We have to *go!* Look at yourself!" Taylor was becoming translucent from weakness and when Olivia looked at her own hands she saw the same thing.

They were trying to gather enough focus to make the jump and almost beyond the effort when a flood of sensations gripped them. The chimera...Taylor was nearly insane at the thought. "*No!*" She tried to fight, impotently squirming to avoid the grasp.

This time, Olivia saw, it did have a hold on Taylor. Her throat plummeted. *Oh, please, no...please!*

She just learned her powers. She's barely twenty – hasn't even started to live yet. Olivia tried to pull Taylor away from it but remembered; they had nowhere to go.

Her thoughts turned desperate. *I cannot let this happen again… I will NOT let this happen again.* Steeling herself, Olivia plunged her hand into the chimera's essence.

"Take me."

She could feel it hesitate, its attention switching from Taylor to her. "I've got more power, more stamina." The figure eyed her, considering. She added a sweetener. "And more experience, I've done things you would love to feel." She dredged up a few sordid memories for it. *Take me instead, you bastard.* She opened herself to it, ready to take it in, and resigned herself to whatever came next.

Abruptly she felt the chimera pull back. She could hear it in her head, too experienced, too disciplined, too strong. You don't have enough fear and you'd never be controllable…and Dantin doesn't want you that way. It dismissed her and focused again on Taylor.

Dantin doesn't want you that way. For a second she was confused. What did Dantin have to do with this? Then the pieces fell in line. Oh, that sonofabitch! This was his plan – get to Taylor by setting his chimera on her through Nicole! No wonder JaneAnn's charm hadn't worked. Dantin didn't need to be anywhere around to get what he wanted. All he had to do was keep us chasing our tails and looking for him everywhere except with Nicole and Taylor. And he'd succeeded.

Wildly, Olivia cast about for another idea. None came – they were out of options. There was nothing else to tempt it with, and it was too strong. End of game. She was damned if she was going to let them have Taylor, though. She'd kill her first. She couldn't believe how painful the very thought was. She resisted the memories that flooded her from their months together. She had to make herself do it. Life as a chimera's slave or death at Dantin's hands; both were a hundred times more cruel than what she was about to do. It burned that she wouldn't get to explain or say goodbye, but at least it would be quick. Just a light touch, pull her spirit and release it into the logos before she lost all her powers.

Taylor was still fighting, resisting the chimera when Olivia touched her. She looked surprised, then frightened as she lost consciousness. Olivia steeled herself to finish it.

"I'm so sorry honey..." She said goodbye, sick at heart.

Then she was shocked to find something coming back through her touch – vibrant energy coming from Taylor to her. Something was bolstering her – and the protection spell.

"Eidolon!" She burst into tears. "Oh, my God, I thought this was it." He was soothing, an influx of energy and magic. "I don't have anything left."

She was on the edge of consciousness and could only hold Taylor as her familiar protected them both. He'd brought other chimera with him and she watched vaguely as they combined with Nicole's two tormenters, wrapping them, or... diluting them, it looked like. They disintegrated from their corporeal form and became mist again. She couldn't comprehend the rules out here, but it didn't matter. They surrounded the two, enclosing them, and then were gone.

Taylor began to stir in Olivia's arms, trying to open her eyes, but it was too hard. There was a chimera with her – but it was warm and soothing, not like the frenetic emotions of the others. Eidolon, she recognized drowsily. He was comforting, like smelling freshly-baked cookies, she thought ridiculously. Oh, and Olivia's here, too. They were still out in the logos but the anxiety and roar of it was muffled. She lapsed again, waking to find herself and Olivia back in the park with Alejo. He had been waiting for them and rushed to catch them in his arms, lowering them to the ground and kneeling over them to check for any mortal injuries or occult damage.

"I'll get Nicole and bring her." Eidolon's voice was low and heathery, layered in cadence and reassuring. Then he was gone but back in moments, bringing a half-conscious Nicole to them. He'd retrieved her transparent self as well and combined them as she lay in the flower bed, returning her to mortal life before setting her gently in front of Olivia and Taylor.

Both witches were spent. It was all they could do to sit up and pull Nicole to them. She began to wake but slowly, the sapphire eyes becoming visible a bit at a time under sluggish eyelids.

"Hey." Taylor pulled Nicole closer. "Nicole, it's Taylor... is it just you? Are they gone?"

The faintest smile. "Ooohh. Yes. So good..." She looked almost beatific.

"I think no more excitement for a while, okay?" Taylor was submerged in relief.

"'kay." Nicole closed her eyes again.

Eidolon was still enrobing them all and Alejo spoke to him: "Eidolon, could you please tell the others? We'll need everyone's help to get them somewhere we can take care of them." The mist darkened and thickened a moment and then vanished.

Olivia surveyed Nicole, a deep sadness in her expression. "She's really damaged, Taylor," she said softly.

Taylor cradled her friend in her lap, stroking her hair and looking at the cherubic cheeks, thinking of the first time she'd seen them at JaneAnn's party. Was that barely five days ago? The henna clay on Nicole's arm was partially gone, revealing the matching designs they'd gotten together that afternoon. She looked at her own, smiling. The clay dust on Nicole seemed to have gotten everywhere, she thought. But this was different; Nicole's skin was ashy and grey now. Probably from what they'd just been through. She looked at Olivia, who was tired looking, with dark circles around her eyes and maybe a little drawn, but her skin still had color. Not the same with Nicole.

Looking at her she saw a bigger difference – the ashen countenance was now crisscrossed with tiny lines everywhere, like little crazes in the glaze of old pottery. Taylor looked at Olivia, who was staring at Nicole silently, also inspecting her. As they both watched, the crazes spread, barely at first, then began to deepen. Liv put her hand on Nicole's thigh, pressing as much life-giving magic into her as she could spare.

Taylor didn't understand at all. "Olivia, what's happening?"

Carefully, Olivia touched Nicole's shoulder to rouse her. "Nicole, how long did they have control of you?"

Nicole tried to look at her, but the effort to raise her lids was insurmountable. "I don't know."

Olivia empathized. "Just keep your eyes closed. It will be easier. Can you remember anything from when you met them? Can you remember the year?"

Nicole's voice was drowsy. "I don't know, seventy... nineteen-seventy. Eighteen-seventy?" The effort was too much and she lapsed into silence again.

Taylor was shocked. "Do something Olivia!" She felt completely helpless.

Olivia turned a compassionate smile on Taylor, her voice low and patient. "I don't think we can. That's just so long for her to be possessed. They've bled her dry, like a spider does a moth. Now there's only a shell left."

"But…" She looked Nicole up and down, at her flesh becoming more desiccated every second, the crazes widening into cracks. "Can't I give some of my power?" She was only able to trickle the tiniest bit to Nicole, no more than that.

Olivia shook her head, carefully trying to break the news to Taylor that her friend would die. She hated to squelch Taylor's desire to rescue her but had to for Nicole's sake.

"Taylor, even if we could repair her mortal body she's more susceptible now, easier than before to possess – if not by the same chimera, others will try. They'll smell her weakness… hunt her."

Taylor was horrified at that thought, even more than seeing her friend disintegrate in her lap. A deepening ash had begun to appear in place of flesh. "There's nothing we can do?"

Nicole's voice came to them, almost inaudible, like a tiny mewling kitten: "I don't care…" The effort it took was obvious, but there was finality in her plea. "Let me go."

Taylor could hardly stand the bitterness she felt. She tried to hold the grayed hand, but it crumbled away, the bits sifting through her fingers. Carefully, she put her hand to Nicole's face, which had been so plump and creamy when they met, now shrunken and decomposing. Gingerly, she touched her cheek and forehead and tried to tell her how much she loved her, their friendship, all the memories they had made in so short a time. But Nicole didn't answer.

Taylor's chest was tight with misery for her friend – all that had happened, all they would never do. She held back the sobs jerking her chest, afraid any movement would hurt the dying witch. That was a revelation to her – realizing prolonging Nicole's life was the worst torment. She turned to face Olivia.

"I'm letting go..." Her intent was clear Olivia should do the same.

Olivia agreed, withdrawing her magic as Taylor did and saying goodbye to the tortured girl. The crevices opened wider, dismantling the form. Taylor watched the last bits of their exquisite matching hennas turn to grey ash on Nicole, then disappear as it slid from her bones. The bones crumbled too, falling into the emerald grass where they knelt.

Their vigil was silent as they watched. Eidolon reappeared and he and Alejo remained quiet as well, watching with respect this transition from life to death.

"I don't want her to just disappear like that." Taylor stared into the ashes, the last remnants of her companion. Olivia said nothing, no words could help. As she reached for her apprentice's hand they saw something pearlescent flowing from what was left of Nicole. It coalesced and took shape before them, human but featureless, possibly feminine from the delicacy of the frame. It wafted in front of them, beautiful, shimmering and soft like moonlight.

"It feels like Nicole..." Taylor didn't recognize the form but felt her friend distinctly in the apparition before them. She reached out to it and a celestial hand mirrored her own movements, their fingertips almost touching. Slowly, like a drop from a leaf, a glowing orb on a dainty thread grew and suspended from Nicole's hand.

Olivia's lips parted in shock. "My God..." she whispered, then touched Taylor's arm. "Take it! She can't stay long."

"What is it?"

"A gift," said Olivia. "Quickly – she hasn't much time." Her tone was urgent.

Taylor plucked the drop from Nicole's fading form. Olivia whispered to her:

"Just hold it.... let it absorb into you." Taylor did and was elated to find it was Nicole's essence, her powers, her memories. Then the luminous form disintegrated, dissipating into nothingness and leaving everyone subdued under the twinkling stars.

The park around them was quiet and Taylor noticed for the first time the rippling folds in the turf, the damage done from Olivia's preparations to rescue her, but she hadn't the strength to ask. The exhaustion of their efforts overwhelmed her, then Olivia as well, and blackness overtook them.

They slumped back against Alejo and he cradled them protectively, an arm around each. "What do you think, Eidolon? Marcus and Julia's?"

The chimera concurred. "That's the best place to protect them until they regain their strength. Tell everyone to stay close, and don't underestimate Dantin, especially now."

Olivia's familiar took the two away and left Alejo alone in the park looking at the remnants of Nicole's mortal crust in the grass. Standing up, he cupped his hands together and called her remains to him. They complied, flowing upward into his palms and from there became fine, silky talcum that easily swirled into the air. Raising his palms upward he allowed her to dissipate back into the logos, lifting into the night and disappearing with finality.

Standing on broken sidewalk, he looked around to survey the evening's damage. There was the folded ground, the trees bent inward and cracked from the wave of magic Olivia had pulled into her, the gazebo that was damaged and leaning. He had to admit, her power was one of the things he found captivating about her. He was proud of her ability to bring these results and he smiled thinking about her as he took it all in.

"Jesus, Olivia, you can really leave a mess."

When he had arrived at the park earlier he'd thrown a massive protection spell over the area to prevent prying eyes. He left that in effect now as he cleaned up the aftermath, tapping into the same energy Olivia had but not as strongly. Sweeping his arms down and outward he put everything right in reverse order. After a quick look around and a few tweaks, he removed the thick magic dome and disappeared just as the air rushed in to replace it, leaving a crack of thunder that set off car alarms and caused neighbors to come out a second time that night to see what had happened.

Olivia awoke in Julia's guest room and it took a moment to orient herself. *Marcus and Julia's house.* The revelation was soothing. She needn't worry about anything; they would take care of it. Where was Taylor?

"She's right next to you." Marcus materialized at her side and pointed to Taylor sleeping in the huge bed next to her. "Easier to watch over you both."

The precautions were necessary, while a witch was so weak any number of things could happen, not the least of which was possession by another entity. Olivia peered at her apprentice.

"How long?" She felt like someone had cracked a board against her head.

"Two days. She'll need at least one more before she can stand."

"We missed our jet."

"So rent another. You're not going anywhere by magic for a few more days." Julia had come in and was looking at her keenly. "Also, I think Taylor will need time to adjust. She's been through a lot already and it wouldn't be good to just flash her home."

Olivia nodded agreement. Julia was pretty savvy. They both would need time to absorb what had happened. She scooted out from under the covers. It was strange being vertical, like she'd had the flu for a week and could finally get out of bed. Suddenly she felt woozy and quickly Alejo was next to her, supporting her.

"Where did you come from?"

Marcus watched Alejo take her to the big chair in the corner. "Are you kidding? He hasn't been out of this room since you got here."

"Thanks – I'm still a little foggy, I think."

"I can understand that. Maybe you're hungry?"

She realized she was famished and tried to cast for something but couldn't. Her powers were still very weak and she'd better not push it.

"I could use something. Do you mind?" It was a weird feeling not being able to conjure on her own.

"Of course, Livy. What do you want?"

"Surprise me."

He conjured a chicken sandwich and Olivia ate while they talked. God, food tasted good. Marcus and Julia went downstairs, leaving just her and Alejo.

"Livy, why did you go after Taylor alone? You almost killed yourself." His concerned look pained her. *Well, no wonder,* she thought. He was right about nearly getting killed – and she'd almost taken Taylor with her. She tried to explain.

"There wasn't time – you should have felt what came off that charm. I'd show you but my power's not back yet."

"No, there's no need for that. I'm sure you had to, and you did call for Eidolon. I just wish you wouldn't take chances, Livy. I..." *Should I tell her?* he thought. He wanted to but paused, deciding.

"You what?" Olivia was waiting for him to finish his sentence.

"...I don't want to lose any more friends."

"Oh, Handy..." She reached for his hand. "I take chances but not stupid ones, you know. And if you're worried about Dantin, he's never wanted me dead – he wants to keep tormenting me as long as he can."

"That does not make me feel better, Olivia. And what about your plans for dealing with him? They're not dangerous?"

"Do you see another way? What then, just let him go on playing with me like he does?"

Alejo shook his head. "No, of course not." The moment had passed. He was relieved and kicking himself at the same time. Damn it.

Julia came in and sat down, putting her feet up on the chaise. "So Eidolon told us what happened out there, but I still don't trust that Blue/Black bastard Dantin."

"And you know he's going to be pissed as hell about his plans being ruined." Olivia looked at her unconscious apprentice. "Julia, do you mind if we stay here this week? I don't want to take Taylor out until we're almost a hundred percent again."

"Sure – stay as long as you need." She pointed at Alejandro. "You, too, if you can."

"I'll stay as long as you need me." He looked at Olivia. "I'll fly back with you."

"That would be great, thanks. A week here, and then we should get Taylor home."

Daphne and Chloe burst into the room. "We knew one of you was awake. How are you doing?" They came close to inspect Olivia and then drifted to Taylor, hovering above her.

Olivia answered. "Well, I'm vertical but that's about it right now."

Daphne touched Taylor's forehead. "She's not ready yet. I think two days."

Chloe shook her head. "I disagree. She's tougher than you think."

"Well, we'll see... In the meantime," Daphne turned to the others, "we'll keep watching the house and the layers around it." She was referring the different dimensions in the logos. "We can take care of anything that comes through."

"Thank you – I really owe you."

"That's okay, Olivia," they said in unison and disappeared again.

"Are you really okay?" Alejo looked her over. "Do you need anything?"

"No, I'm fine for now. I feel really tired, but I'm sick of sleeping. Maybe I'll look out the window or read. I know I can't do anything else yet."

"Okay. I have an errand to do." He headed for the door.

"Were you able to get what we needed?"

"Yes," said Alejo. Olivia looked at him questioningly and he nodded. "So far it looks like our plans are unknown."

She watched him as he walked out, hoping he was correct, but right now she didn't know what to believe or how many layers Dantin had put into his subterfuge. And she didn't know how to tell, either.

Olivia made sure she was there when Taylor came out of her recuperative coma, sitting on the bed with her while she asked dazed questions about what had happened.

"I want to call my sister."

"Of course." Olivia gave her some privacy while she made the call. While Taylor was on the phone Olivia realized what it must be like for her, not being able to tell the only family you had left what had happened or your wonderful, horrible secrets.

She came back in the bedroom after Taylor hung up. "How is she?"

"Great. She's getting good grades and is really busy. Sounds like she has a lot of new friends, too."

"You might be able to tell her someday – you never know."

Taylor nodded, looking down at the comforter. "I miss Nicole."

Olivia put her arm around her. "I know."

"I miss Doobie and Bailey, too."

"Do you want JaneAnn to go get them for us?" To tell the truth, she'd be happy to have them here, too. Julia also loved them, she'd be fine with them in her home. Taylor said yes and two hours later Jane-Ann arrived with the dogs. They spent the evening chasing each other through the house, making everyone laugh, and then hogged the whole bed when Olivia let them sleep with her and Taylor. They were the perfect balm.

The next afternoon unexpected rain depressed everyone. The clouds were darker and heavier than any they'd seen here in Houston, rain drummed hard on the roof and the windows, pelting the garden with huge drops. Taylor found herself in their room with the greys, a sad and wistful pall pressing down on her as she remembered Nicole. She couldn't stop thinking about her, remembering her expressions, her crazy jokes, her sense of adventure. Then she couldn't stop crying, dropping tears like little crystals on Doobie's velvety neck, kissing her soft little head and staring into her brown eyes. Bailey got up from his spot at the end of the bed and dropped down beside her, pressing against her leg to sandwich her between them. *How do they know just what to do? The perfect quiet companions, they match your mood, try to give silent comfort.* Taylor decided dogs must be magical creatures.

Olivia knocked on the door and slowly opened it. "What's going on?" She saw the miserable look on Taylor's face and sat on the bed with them.

"Nicole..." Taylor said simply.

"Oh, honey, I'm so sorry." She put her arm around her, "I'll miss Nicole, too." She had developed a soft spot for her. The poor girl – it hadn't been her fault.

"I don't know whether having her essence makes it better or worse. All those memories of hers, so horrible..." Taylor put her head on Olivia's breast, crying anew. Hard, racking sobs tugged her and she gave in until she felt calmer again.

"Taylor, I need to tell you something."

"What?" Taylor asked as she wiped tears off her cheeks.

Olivia took a deep breath. "I'm sorry I didn't treat...I'm sorry I wasn't kinder to you. I'm not sorry I pushed you so hard, but I could have been friendlier."

Taylor was silent, listening.

"I was afraid of..." She couldn't think how to finish.

"I know. JaneAnn showed me. You couldn't risk him thinking we were close like you and Celeste."

"Yes, but that's only part of it. Losing her was so painful, everything about it just horrible...I didn't want to go through that again. But it was selfish to treat you that way because I didn't have the nerve to get hurt." She leaned back to look into Taylor's face. "I know you miss your sister. I know I haven't made you feel welcome, but you are. We're your family, too, if you want us and I want you to stay with me until you feel comfortable going out on your own. You're one of us and you always will be – no matter what."

To her surprise Taylor started to cry again. "What's the matter?"

"Nothing – I mean, that's just such a relief."

"Oh, sweetie. I'm sorry." She hugged her closer. It was a relief for Olivia, too, releasing the fears she'd been holding onto as she embraced her witchling. If only Dantin wasn't still out there.

A week later they packed to go home, JaneAnn helping Taylor and acting like a protective aunt, which amused Olivia as she watched JaneAnn give gifts and advice with a liberal hand. The two had been thick as thieves, even going out to lunch and shopping one day. But Taylor always wanted to sleep in Olivia's room at night.

Now Olivia was sitting at the kitchen table with Alejo, watching the two add Taylor's suitcases to the luggage by the stairs.

"I don't know what I was thinking," she told him, "treating her like that. I told myself I was trying to protect her, but I know that's not the biggest reason."

"What was?" Alejo already knew the answer.

"You're going to make me say it, aren't you?"

"Yep."

"I was afraid of getting attached and getting hurt, which was stupid. The only person I hurt is Taylor."

"Yep. It was stupid and mean." He startled Olivia with his honesty. Well, no wonder, she thought. He was right and she'd been an ass about the whole thing. She shook her head sheepishly.

"I've been such an ass."

"Yes, you have."

"Oh...thanks a lot, Handy."

Alejo smiled at her. "Next time, listen to your friends. Here..." He pulled a folded cloth from his pocket. "Schmidt charmed this for you."

He laid the tiny bundle on the table and opened it. Inside was a silver chain with something hanging from it, an inch-long shard of metal. Alejo picked it up by the chain and suspended it between them.

Olivia looked it over. The workmanship was sophisticated. The shard gleamed within a cocoon of spells. A mortal eye would have to look hard to see them, but they were plain to a witch, the translucent symbols and True Name syllables that encircled the metal without touching it, sliding over it like a gavotte. She could tell it was a piece of the glaive. The chain was slim, its silver links smooth and sleek, but the shard didn't touch them. It hung suspended a millimeter away from the chain, floating by itself.

She looked at Alejo. "Tell me."

"As long as you wear it the curse is blocked – you won't have the retching or the pain. You won't feel it. And you'll be able to move."

"And magic?"

"Schmidt assured me you'll be able to cast."

"I didn't think it was possible."

"He said he didn't know of anyone who's ever been successful. But you haven't used it yet. And you still have to get to the Columbia Tower."

"I know. You might have to get Taylor out of the house. I don't want her in the middle of this, even by mistake."

"Her Will-O-Wisps will be with her. I want to be near you in case something goes wrong."

"And if it does, then she'll need you to protect her from him. Alejo, if it goes that way will you take on her apprenticeship? JaneAnn will help you."

He had a sick feeling. "Yes...but let's assume that it won't. That offer is still open for both of you to come to Europe with me."

Olivia looked at him, thinking she would like that very much. "Plan for the worst and hope for the best? Let me ask Taylor if she would like to come, but I would love to." She picked up her teacup but it was empty. "Damn."

Alejo reached over and covered her teacup with his palm. When he removed it the bowl was full again.

"Thanks." She took a sip of the chai, the sweet and spicy aroma filling her nose. "I'm sure Taylor will want to come with us. We'll get settled back in Seattle and I'll ask her."

"Whatever you want." He took the charm and came around behind her to clasp the chain around her neck. From above he watched her smooth the chain and arrange the shard to lay against her skin.

JaneAnn and Taylor came in just then. "We're all ready. Oooh – is that chai?" Taylor was sniffing the air and looking at Liv's cup.

"Yeah, here...you can have the rest." Olivia still didn't want Taylor to cast for herself and they both hated asking others to do it for them. It was like asking someone to turn on the light switch when you were right next to it.

"Thanks." Taylor finished it, pulling it dry in a few big sips, and put the cup down as Julia announced they were ready to leave.

Marcus and Julia drove them to the private terminal for the flight home. When they arrived the staff took everyone's bags except for Alejo's two, a leather messenger and a long case.

"I'll carry those with me up front – no sense in taking up room in the cargo bin." He set them briefly at his feet to shake hands with Marcus while Julia exchanged hugs with everyone, saying goodbye to Taylor last in her oh-so-faint Texas drawl.

"Sweetie, you are just a joy to have around. Come back and visit us."

"I will," Taylor said, giving Julia an extra squeeze before following the others.

Julia and Marcus stood hand in hand as they watched their friends pass through the lobby and out of sight. Julia sighed.

"If that woman can't tell how in love he is with her than she's a damned fool."

Marcus pulled her closer to him. "Julia, you keep your nose out of it. They've got to figure it out for themselves." He kissed the top of her head and they turned away to go to their car.

The staff ushered the other three directly through the lounge and onto the private jet, a Citation this time. This one was different, Taylor saw as they entered. Olivia had chosen well. It was an interior world all in white, from the leather upholstery to the curved cabin walls and frosted glass separating the aft section ... snowy white and oddly pristine and pure after their hideous experience in the netherworld. The flight attendant on this trip was also a special request by Olivia, one of two whom she trusted completely and who went about her business discreetly, efficiently, and stayed aft after takeoff to give them privacy.

Once they were aloft, Alejo swiveled his seat to face Olivia. Taylor was against the opposite wall looking out the window but turned to listen when he spoke.

"I think you two will be pretty strong by tomorrow." He could feel their effect returning, the subtle vibration of magic emanating off them, giving him a touch of gooseflesh. It was the same effect Olivia had gathered from Taylor the first time she had encountered her in the market. "How do you feel? Can you tell how much you've gotten back?"

Taylor was unsure. "I kind of feel like myself again, but I don't know how to tell."

"I know what you mean. When we get to Olivia's, I'll teach you a spell that shows your level of strength."

"Okay. Thanks." She pulled out her iPod and untangled her earbuds. Olivia looked at her, thinking how far she'd come in the last two weeks, and then realized Alejo was leaning close to her, looking intently at her face. She pretended to ignore him until she finally had to know what in the world he was doing and turned toward him.

"What?" she said, irritated.

"You have a few more little wrinkles around your eyes now." He was smiling.

Liv shoved him away. "Get off me. They'll go away after my powers return, but they're the last thing I plan on repairing."

"I've never seen that many on you before – I like them. They have character instead of just smooth beauty."

Olivia looked at him suspiciously to see if he was teasing, but he wasn't. She scowled at him and looked away, shaking her head. "Whatever. I choose my look for me, not you."

He laughed aloud, throwing his head back. So confident. "I think I like that best about you."

Now Taylor removed her earbuds to see what was going on. "What?"

"Nothing," said Liv. "He's being a jackass. As if his opinion is everything."

Taylor loved that the two were teasing each other again instead of Alejo so solicitous and hovering constantly. Things were getting back to normal. She put her earbuds in again with a happy smile.

Walking in the front door at home was strange, though. Olivia and Taylor both looked around, thinking the same thing. Everything seemed changed. It was the same place, the same dining room on the left with its painted ceiling and walnut table from the plantation house, the same living room on the right with its familiar furnishings ... now all different somehow. They were glad Alejandro was with them.

Thankfully, Daphne and Chloe flared into the entryway as well, exclaiming "Welcome home!" in their familiar unison. They assured everyone the house was fine and then Daphne followed Taylor upstairs to her room. Chloe stayed behind at Olivia's request.

"Remember, Taylor doesn't know the chimera had anything to do with Dantin. I don't want her further stressed out in addition to what happened. I'll tell her later but not for a while."

"Right."

"Let him near me if he comes here but not near her."

Chloe's luminous gaze on Olivia was sharp. "I think you're out of your mind."

"Yeah," said Olivia, "me, too."

Chloe faded and Alejo flashed Olivia's luggage to her room for her before they went to the breakfast nook with its comfy velvet chairs. An hour later, Jane-Ann arrived with Doobie and Bailey and things felt a bit more normal. Still, Olivia and Taylor weren't quite a hundred percent and they spent the next few days at home with Alejo, padding around the house and occasionally ordering take-out. They were eating Thai food in the nook one evening when Taylor asked a question that had been smoldering, making her fearful.

"So, back in the park – Olivia told me those chimera would come after Nicole because she had already been possessed once, that they would hunt her. Will they come after me?"

Alejo was careful replying. "No, you weren't in as deep or under their control long enough. Plus you're much stronger than she ever was."

Taylor looked down at her curry bowl. "I don't feel like it."

Olivia stepped in. "You are – don't worry. You're here, aren't you?"

Taylor didn't reply. She was still afraid, Olivia could tell.

"Taylor, you'll be fine. Nothing is going to get to you. I promise you that."

Taylor was still silent. Alejo put down his phad thai.

"Okay – that's it." He stood. "We're getting you out of the house tonight. You have to get back to normal sometime. I don't care where we go or what we do, but you're going out somewhere."

Olivia jumped on the opportunity. "And you're going alone with Alejo. We can't spend every minute together from now on, the three of us. I'm staying home." She tried not to notice Alejo's expression and went on with her declaration.

"You know I'm right. Finish your food and go find a movie or something. The sooner the better." They both protested, but she stayed on them until they left, finally, with the invisible Will-O-Wisps in tow. Then she was alone in the house.

The realization she was expecting Dantin gave her chills. It was different than him suddenly appearing out of the blue, this knowing that he would come here and that she intended to confront him. She touched the amulet to bolster her confidence and went to the kitchen for a cup of hot tea. Taking the cup and a book she went into the living room to read.

Two hours later she was still in the same spot, pages turned but not read, the anticipation making her sick to her stomach. *Just show up, damn you...let's get this over with.* When the front door opened she snapped to look at it, startled he would use the door, but then she never could anticipate his appearances. When Taylor walked in with Alejo she let out a breath she hadn't realized she'd been holding.

The evening had been good for Taylor, apparently. She looked way more relaxed and Taylor confirmed it when Olivia greeted them.

"How was it?"

"You were right. Getting out was good." She was more like her old self, talking about the movie and what she liked about it, then about the fact she hadn't been to a movie in months. Finally she started to fade.

"I'm going to bed – thanks, Alejo. G'night, Olivia." She went upstairs.

Alejo waited until her door closed. "I know he didn't show up. I scryed you while we were out to keep an eye on you."

"Thanks. You know, you can't do that forever. You can't stay with us forever, either. He's probably waiting until you go home. He's never shown up before with you around."

"Well, at least we know we have a few more days of calm until I leave, then." Actually, they both were hoping that would goad him into coming sooner, but he wasn't easily predictable. They talked a while longer until Alejo said he was tired.

"It's after midnight, Livy. I'll see you in the morning." He kissed her cheek and they both went to bed, he on the couch in the media room and she in her suite upstairs.

At least, Olivia thought, her nerve-jangling evening had taken the edge off of waiting for Dantin. She almost felt normal as she brushed her teeth and changed into silk pajamas. The damned things were slippery to button, she thought as she walked from the bathroom and right into Dantin's arms.

She drew in a breath to scream, but he covered her mouth with his hand, holding her tight with his other arm around her waist. His face was within inches, his dark eyes holding hers. How had he surprised her? she wondered, and then remembered the charm around her neck. She wouldn't feel him, of course.

"I'll come to you any damned time I choose," he hissed. "Anytime I feel like it." He had her pressed so tightly against him she could feel him breathe between sentences.

"Saving Taylor was luck. If you hadn't been there she'd be mine right now. Just like you are mine. But no matter ... I'll have her eventually." He pressed his cheek to hers, his mouth at her ear. "I can play this game with you forever."

Olivia was disgusted at feeling him so intimately through the thin silk. She wanted to pull away, to remind him it was her spells and charmed coin that had caused him to fail but stayed silent. *Not here. Not yet.*

His fingers dug into her flesh as he squeezed her. "You are so going to pay for the loss of my chimera. I don't know where Eidolon took him, but he'll be back eventually. Of course I can always find another one if I have to, plenty of them are willing to be my accomplice for what I can give them. There's no more potent high for a chimera than me."

Then he noticed something missing. "What, no sarcasm this time? No grunting through your misery, my pet?" He uncovered her mouth, ready to silence her scream, but she didn't make one. Dantin grabbed her wrist tightly and pushed her away to get a better look at her. No pain, he saw, complete surprise washing across his face. Olivia relished the satisfaction it gave her to see that.

"What is going on here?" He jerked her around to capture her other wrist and inspected her closely, spying the chain under her collar.

"What is this?" He reached for it and she flashed away, next to the fireplace and out of his reach. She wanted to piss him off really well to make sure he followed her. He flashed and was next to her before she could react quickly enough, though. Just as she disappeared for the Columbia Tower he snagged the amulet in his palm and the chain snapped, leaving him holding it in her empty bedroom.

She reappeared downtown in her pajamas, looking around to see where she was. Westlake Plaza. Not far enough. She felt her throat. No amulet. Losing it in that last millisecond had obviously cut her powers and she ended up short – but he wasn't here now. She would have her abilities until he found her. She gathered herself to finish the trip and then twisted from a red-hot jolt as Dantin appeared on the Plaza twenty feet away.

"Oh, you little bitch!" He strode toward her, infuriated, as she sagged to the pavement. Olivia saw a few late party-goers crossing the Plaza and held up her arm to beckon them, not at all confident Dantin would check himself just because there were people around. He saw them, too, and flicked a spell at Olivia, replacing her silk with outdoor clothes before anyone got too close to tell.

Then he ran over to her with an exaggerated, "Honey, I told you not to have that last glass of champagne," and put his arm around her waist, hoisting her to her feet.

A concerned couple came over to help, but he waved them off smoothly, saying "Thank you so much, but we're okay. It's our anniversary and she's just had too much to drink. Celebrating, you know." He silenced her when she tried to talk. "We're going to the car now, Honey. It's a good thing I'm the designated driver tonight."

The couple nodded their understanding. "Do you need help taking her?"

"Oh, no thanks, she's light. Probably why three glasses of Chandon hit her so hard." The couple smiled; they'd seen plenty of inebriated people downtown this late at night. They kept going and so did Dantin as he held her close, walking her into an adjoining alley and hissing threats in her ear. He actually shook, he was so enraged.

"What is this? What the hell makes you think some trinket like this will help you?" He backed her up against the building and rattled the amulet in her face to make his point. He grabbed her cheeks with his hand, pinching her jaws with his fingers until her mouth opened and he shoved the amulet into it, stuffing it painfully back into her throat where it sat a moment until she swallowed reflexively. She could feel it stab its way down for a good six inches before the sensation disappeared into the burning waves already washing through her. Through her red mist she realized she'd never seen him like this. She didn't know what he might do.

"This time," he said, "I'm going to kill you. Something bloody. Maybe I'll dismember you like Celeste…" Olivia looked into his eyes and saw flat black in return.

Dantin stayed pressed against her, his breathing ragged. He looked from her eyes to her hair, then at her lips pouting out from where he still trapped her face with his hand. Was he deciding where to cut first? she wondered. He held her immobile, pinning her to the alley wall. When she closed her eyes she could actually hear him grinding his teeth together. She waited an eternity for him to speak again, afraid to look at him in case it angered him more.

With massive effort he regained some composure and then took a deep breath, letting it out slowly.

"Five hundred years… Olivia, do you realize, we've known each other five hundred years?" His voice was less ragged now. "That's a long time, five hundred years."

Why does he keep saying that, she wondered, and then noticed he didn't have the smarmy, evil tone he usually took. He sounded ... hurt.

"Why do you have to be this way, Olivia? Why can't you ever be nice to me, just once? I didn't start out hating you like this. I had so many plans for us." It was almost compassionate, the way he said it.

She opened her eyes to see him looking at her sadly, tenderly. He was silent as he looked into her face for an eternity of moments, his expression slowly changing until it was completely unreadable. Then he took on a settled look as he made a decision.

"Killing you would only deprive me," he said. "Instead I'll take you home with me to live. It's not exactly the way I wanted it; I'd rather you chose to love me, but either way I want you for my very own." Then his face shadowed. "Of course, at first you'll try to get away and I'll have to bring you back and punish you. I can't see any other way to break you of that. I wish I could make you promise not to leave me and you wouldn't. But I can't trust you, can I?"

He paused, but Olivia didn't answer and he continued. "No. I'll have to keep you penned up at first, won't I?"

Then he looked pained again. "Olivia, I don't want it to be this way. If you could see just once how much I love you..." He shook his head, intent on making her understand. "I never wanted to hurt you, but you really hurt me sometimes. I open myself to you and you reject me. I lose my temper and lash out only because I'm so hurt. But then you see only my bad side, not who I really am. If you give me a chance you'll see how wonderful we would be together."

He mused on that, talking to himself and making plans as she listened in disbelief. "Once you see who I really am – how much I love you – you'll decide on your own to love me back. I know you will."

He looked past Olivia, imagining it. "I have so many beautiful homes. All over the world. You can pick your favorite and if you don't like the décor you can change it – however you like. Whatever you want. I have an apartment in Paris – I know how you love Paris," he looked at her with a knowing smile.

Olivia was sure he had completely lost what was left of his sanity. He kept going, talking himself in a circle. How only he knew her, how much he loved her, how frustrated he was that she wouldn't see it. It was her fault that he lost his temper, yes. He looked into her eyes affectionately, paternally. From now on, none of this being hateful and snotty all the time, he said. He couldn't have that or he'd need to hurt her, train her to stop. In one breath he'd moved between torturing her every day to giving her gifts and then back again. She watched him, numb with horror and hardly feeling the red-hot burning that the glaive curse always sent through her.

That hit her like a slap. The pain had softened a little, not the searing bolts that usually twisted her inside out. She wasn't on the edge of retching, either. Tentatively she looked behind him at the opposite wall

– could she cast? A dumpster there moved slightly at her command. *Oh, hell, yes!* It had to be the amulet! Wear it or eat it, it was working, even if only a little bit. She pulled her attention back to Dantin.

"Yes, I like that idea," he was saying, "I'll take you home to live with me." He took her hand calmly. "Come on."

She looked up between the buildings, the Columbia Tower was there, just a few blocks away. She wasn't sure if she could get that far but took a breath and willed herself to the rooftop. She felt the rush of magic and then the breeze that was constant atop the Tower, saw the familiar rail around the edge with the scaffold attached to it. *Yes! But I'm on the wrong side,* she thought. *I need to get closer to Pioneer Square.*

She turned to go as Dantin caught up with her, appearing on the roof and looking around. The effect was immediate. Even if the pain was less it was still like slogging through molasses. Every move was a giant effort, weakening her, and she found herself on hands and knees as he came closer, almost catching up.

"It won't matter," he said, "even if you get to Pioneer Square and call to it, most of whatever you pull from there will pour out of that wound I gave you. You still won't be strong enough." He was strolling after her unhurried, confident, knowing the closer he got the weaker she would be.

Blinding light between them stopped them both. The Will-O-Wisps! Daphne and Chloe appeared, facing Dantin and ready for a fight. She could see his face in the white-hot light as he recognized them and then immediately looked up to Capitol Hill where Olivia's house stood. *Taylor.*

She saw Dantin smile at her. If he got to Taylor before they did she wasn't strong enough to keep him off her. "No!" She shouted at the flaming forms. "Go back to Taylor!"

Chloe turned to her uncertainly. Then Alejo appeared on the rooftop as well. "Go!" she repeated and the two disappeared.

She put up her hand at Alejo. "Stay away! I don't want you on the wrong end of this!" Alejo stood his ground but didn't move toward her. It was agonizing to be confined to a spectator role.

Olivia was at the edge, against the rail overlooking the Square, but Dantin had been right; any magic she pulled in was watery at best and hardly helped. She reached over her head, feeling along the rail and using it to pull herself away from Dantin, but he caught up with her.

He chuckled as he stood over her comfortably, possessively. "This is how it should be – me standing over you, and you helpless and submissive." He reached down easily and grabbed her arm. "Come on, let's go."

Alejo had had enough. Stepping in closer he cast a curse on Dantin to make him release her and was shocked to see him instantly put up an orb that rebuffed it. Dantin was strong, more powerful than Alejo had imagined. *Fine,* Alejo thought, *let's see you rebuff something mortal.* In two steps he was on the Blue/Black and punched him in the face with all the muscle he could put behind it, feeling a machismo satisfaction at the result when Dantin reeled back, falling to the rooftop. Then he grimaced and cradled his fist. He hadn't expected broken knuckles to hurt so much.

Before Dantin could get up Alejo dragged Olivia away from him, up the rail another five feet. He straightened to face Dantin again, but the witch wrapped an orb around him that prevented any more interference.

He thrust his jaw toward Alejo smugly. "You can watch me take her." Then he bent over Olivia, who was on her back, still against the rail.

Dantin gripped her throat, lifting her to her feet. She scratched at his fingers with her left hand, trying to pry them off her neck while her right hand reached under the rail where Alejo had placed her. Yes! It was there – the hilt of a sword. She grabbed it, pulling it from under the rail as he pulled her up to him. At the metallic scraping sound Dantin looked down to see the weapon in her hand come up to his ribs.

"That's weak," he said easily. "A sword? You know that can't kill me." He leaned in closer. "Go ahead," he said, unfazed.

Olivia looked into his eyes as she jammed in the blade. "Except one made from your glaive – with your blood in it. And mine and Tristan's as well. You have no escape from that." She pushed deeper, hearing it squeak against a rib inside and watched a fleet of emotions cross his face as the magical weapon killed him: surprise, betrayal, hurt, and then anger and hate won out. He turned it on her, angrily ripping at her to try and break her hold on the hilt and leaving damage wherever he could reach as he tried to fight.

If I don't finish this he's going to kill me first. She looked at Alejo to see if he could help, but he was still pinned in the orb, although it was weakening. Gritting her teeth, she drove the blade upward with all her strength, through Dantin's neck and into his jaw, finally cutting his throat from the inside out. As the blood drained from his face, his eyes were confused, tender on her. Then she watched the vibrancy leave his eyes, only inches from hers, as he died.

She felt a storm of magic coming from him suddenly, going through her and out into the logos, pulling them both upright. Essences, she realized, the other witches whose powers he had swallowed, escaping their prison. Hundreds of them lifted her and Dantin off the ground as they left him – and then they were gone. She was still standing with him pinioned on her sword when it finished and she pulled it out to let him slump to the ground in a pile. She was shaking, horribly, and she tossed the sword to her side, falling to her knees. Alejo was on her immediately, freed from the orb.

"Any serious damage?"

"I don't think so."

CATHLEEN DUNN

He wrapped her up in his arms. "My God, you really took a chance. I was flying blind taking that glaive to Schmidt after getting your plan – and through a spell, at that." He was referring to the time Olivia slipped him silent instructions through his hand at Palomino's. "I only had one chance to get it right."

"Yeah, but we couldn't risk him knowing." She glanced at Dantin. Then she took a longer look, suddenly feeling his humanity wash over her. All those conflicting emotions he had showed her in the alley, and then at the end, the misery he felt stirred in with the rage.

Alejo saw blood everywhere as he inspected her. "You are really cut up – here, let me help you." He pressed a hand to the first of several gashes to heal it, then looked at his palm. His look frightened her as he showed her. "Look at your blood."

Olivia looked down to see her blood in his hand, a reassuring red with a silver tint – nothing unusual there. "What?" she asked Alejo.

"You don't see it?" He held it closer. Along with her well-known Silver-Tint were streaks of Blue/Black. She looked at her other gashes; all of them had the same Blue/Black streaks.

"We fought – he was bleeding too. He must have left something behind?" But she knew that was false. They'd fought other times and their blood had touched, but hers had never looked as it did now.

"I've never heard of that." Alejo looked into her face and was instantly sorry he'd said it.

"Look," he said, "I'm sure it's nothing. We'll check you in a few weeks to be sure, but it will probably be gone."

Olivia looked at her arm, then nodded and remembered Dantin. "We should take care of him." She remembered what he'd said in the alley and felt sorry for him. "I don't know what a Blue/Black would want, but I want to show some respect. Something powerful."

Alejo didn't understand her reasoning but went along. "Maybe a fire?"

They set up a magical pyre there on the rooftop, setting his body ablaze in a brilliant copper flame that flared once and was gone, taking him with it. Then they headed for Olivia's house on Capitol Hill.

The next night they went to dinner, including JaneAnn, at Alejo's insistence: "Come on – I'm not going to visit Seattle without going out at least once." He asked Taylor where they should go and she didn't hesitate.

"Oh, Palomino's, definitely." It was Taylor's favorite with the open atrium and frosted glass and the pumpkin-colored ceiling lit up by the sparkling halogen lights. They were all ravenous, ordering sumptuously and eating heartily as they laughed and talked.

Olivia asked Taylor if she would like to go to Europe with her and Alejo and was not at all surprised by her exuberant, "yes!"

"First we'll show you where we grew up and tell you the stories. How about Christmas in Austria? It's beautiful in Salzburg, the Kristkindlmarkt and all the lights."

"That sounds awesome."

"Well, nothing too exciting – we'll just look at old churches, walk in the snow and look at decorations, maybe eat some decadent food," said Olivia.

Back home, Alejo showed Taylor the power spell he had promised to back on the flight and they talked late into the night, sitting on the velvet slipper chairs with the greys at their feet, thinking they hadn't a care in the world.

Image by Barbara Roser Photography

Cathleen Dunn writes urban fantasy in her real life while holding down a full-time job to pay bills. She lives in Seattle with her husband, rescuing greyhounds, attending the Opera and Symphony, and doing random volunteering. She's been onstage with the opera several times, has been known to paint faux finishes and murals inside homes for her friends, and occasionally goes hunting and fishing with her husband.

Cathleen is about to release her first full-length novel, *Chimera*, in December of 2013 and is working on her second novel, *Blue/Black*. She sets her stories in Seattle, where the dark and rain create the witches' stories in her head. She just writes them down.

Cathleen is a member of the Pacific Northwest Writers Association, established in 1956.

A note from Cathleen:

Thank you so much for purchasing my book! If you enjoyed it, please tell other people and I would greatly appreciate if you would share your favorable review on Amazon.com.

Chimera is Cathleen's debut novel. The second novel in *The Witches Trilogy* is titled *Blue/Black* and is scheduled for release in 2014.

For more information on Olivia, Taylor, Alejo, JaneAnn, the rest of the witches and the world they live in, visit us at www.CathleenDunn.com, Follow me on Twitter @cathleenDunn Like my author page on Facebook: Cathleen Dunn

THE WITCHES TRILOGY
CONTINUES WITH
BLUE/BLACK IN 2014

This time danger and betrayal comes from within. One of the Silver-Tints is turning Blue/Black. The others are helpless as they watch one of their family become distant, then violent, and they may have to say good-bye. But one exotic Blue/Black with a kind streak offers to help them and as much as Alejo loves Olivia, he finds this new woman irresistible, sensual, sexual as he's never known – and he is obsessed with her.

Meanwhile Taylor's power is astounding the witches. She can open a dimensional door by herself – a talent thought lost centuries ago. When secrets about the Blue/Blacks and Silver-Tints come through from the other side, the revelations stun everyone and change the way they live forever.